APR

2012

P9-CCP-008

A Wandering
Heart

A Wandering Heart

An Angel Island Novel

THOMAS KINKADE
& Katherine Spencer

BERKLEY BOOKS, NEW YORK

THE BERKLEY PUBLISHING GROUP
Published by the Penguin Group
Penguin Group (USA) Inc.
375 Hudson Street, New York, New York 10014, USA

Penguin Group (Canada), 90 Eglinton Avenue East, Suite 700, Toronto, Ontario M4P 2Y3, Canada
(a division of Pearson Penguin Canada Inc.) • Penguin Books Ltd., 80 Strand, London WC2R 0RL,
England • Penguin Group Ireland, 25 St. Stephen's Green, Dublin 2, Ireland (a division of Penguin
Books Ltd.) • Penguin Group (Australia), 250 Camberwell Road, Camberwell, Victoria 3124, Australia
(a division of Pearson Australia Group Pty. Ltd.) • Penguin Books India Pvt. Ltd., 11 Community
Centre, Panchsheel Park, New Delhi—110 017, India • Penguin Group (NZ), 67 Apollo Drive,
Rosedale, Auckland 0632, New Zealand (a division of Pearson New Zealand Ltd.) • Penguin Books
(South Africa) (Pty.) Ltd., 24 Sturdee Avenue, Rosebank, Johannesburg 2196, South Africa

Penguin Books Ltd., Registered Offices: 80 Strand, London WC2R 0RL, England

This book is an original publication of The Berkley Publishing Group.

PUBLISHER'S NOTE: The recipes contained in this book are to be followed exactly as written. The
publisher is not responsible for your specific health or allergy needs that may require medical supervision.
The publisher is not responsible for any adverse reactions to the recipes contained in this book.

This is a work of fiction. Names, characters, places, and incidents either are the product of the author's
imagination or are used fictitiously, and any resemblance to actual persons, living or dead, business
establishments, events, or locales is entirely coincidental. The publisher does not have any control over
and does not assume any responsibility for author or third-party websites or their content.

FIRST EDITION: April 2012

Library of Congress Cataloging-in-Publication Data

Kinkade, Thomas, (date)–
A wandering heart / Thomas Kinkade and Katherine Spencer.
p.   cm.
ISBN 978-0-425-24584-2
1. Cape Light (Imaginary place)—Fiction.   2. New England—Fiction.
I. Spencer, Katherine, (date–)   II. Title.
PS3561.I534W36 2012
813'.54—dc23
2011047722

PRINTED IN THE UNITED STATES OF AMERICA

10   9   8   7   6   5   4   3   2   1

Dear Friends,

Once again it is my pleasure to welcome you to the Inn at Angel Island. I am happy to hear from so many of you that you have enjoyed your previous visits to the homey inn on quiet and peaceful Angel Island. You may find the place a little changed this time.

Liza Martin, the innkeeper, is still here managing the lovely inn where she spent so many happy summers as a child. And of course Claire North is there, as always, serving up her nourishing cooking along with her nourishing wisdom. But yet the inn is different this time. The fact is . . . it has been hit by a force more powerful than a hurricane. No, I don't mean the invasion of the inn by a film crew and its glamorous stars . . . although that has certainly caused some excitement. But the force I am talking about is much stronger. That force is love.

A Wandering Heart shows us many kinds of love. Love for our wives and husbands, for our friends, our families, our pets, our homes, and of course, our love for God. Surely love is a blessing. Not only does love bring us happiness, but it also shines a light on our lives, reminding us that whether you are a famous movie star like Charlotte Miller, who is staying at the inn, or a self-sufficient fisherman like Colin Doyle . . . love will show you what is really important and meaningful in life.

A star like Charlotte Miller certainly has a life that many people envy, but she is carrying a secret that tears a hole in her heart. Audrey Gilroy, who, with her husband, runs the island's goat farm, has little in common with Charlotte's high-pressure lifestyle, but she, too, feels an emptiness that holds her back from truly appreciating the many blessings of her life. But here on Angel Island, where a glimpse of the cliffs that are shaped like angel wings can be as inspiring as the nave of the grandest cathedral, miracles are known to happen. On this island where help and hope are never farther than a few doors away, it is always possible to be in touch with our faith and the most important love of all—God's love for us, His children.

I hope you enjoy your stay at the Inn at Angel Island. We are always glad to have you back.

Share the Light,
Thomas Kinkade and Katherine Spencer

Chapter One

"There's a space, Liza. Look, that blue car is about to pull out." Claire North pointed to a dark blue compact parked in front of the Cape Light post office.

Liza Martin had noticed it, too. She hit the brakes and flipped on the turn signal, then waited to pull in.

"Finally," she said. "I thought we were going to have to turn around and go back to Angel Island. What in the world is going on around here?"

"Main Street does seem crowded for a Monday," Claire observed. "Maybe it's just summer people."

"I guess," Liza answered as she steered her SUV into the parking space.

The town of Cape Light and nearby Angel Island, where Liza ran an inn—with Claire's indispensable assistance—entertained their fair share of tourists. But this amount of traffic and lack of parking spaces seemed unusual, even for August. Though Liza and Claire usually came into Cape Light once a week to shop and pick up supplies for the inn, Liza had never seen the town so crowded.

Maybe the quiet, off-the-beaten-track town had been included on some New England bus tour route? Liza thought she wouldn't mind a few buses driving over the bridge and steering in her direction. Rainy weeks in July had washed away most of the inn's advance reservations.

"I wish a few summer people would drive out to the island and fill our driveway with cars. Plenty of parking spaces there. Maybe I should leave some brochures around."

"Couldn't hurt," Claire agreed. She picked up her shopping bags from the backseat and Liza put a few coins in the meter.

Claire was wearing one of her typical summer outfits—a sleeveless cotton blouse, very neatly ironed, and a long cotton skirt with a pattern of small flowers, loose fitting and falling below her knees. Her sandals, with thick rubber soles and crisscross straps around her feet, were neat and practical. The same went for her hair, which was pinned up in its usual style, parted in the middle and coiled in a bun at her nape, emphasizing her round face and pale blue eyes. Her long hair had once been blond but was now a shade of golden gray.

Claire had very smooth skin, almost wrinkle free, and Liza thought Claire was a pretty woman for her age, which she guessed to be in her late fifties or early sixties. She would never say. It was one of the many mysteries about Claire North. As honest and plainspoken as Claire was, she could also be quite elusive.

The two women headed down the street toward the harbor. The sky was low and hazy, the heavy air hinting at more rain in the forecast. Liza's cotton sundress stuck to her skin in an instant.

"First stop, hardware store?" Claire asked.

"I think so. Let's see . . . we need a doorknob for the upstairs bathroom, and I have to pick up the new window shutters."

Liza walked along, staring down at her list, and suddenly heard quick footsteps behind her. A distinct bump nearly knocked her off her feet but luckily Claire grabbed her arm before she lost her balance completely.

"Whoops, sorry, ladies. Didn't even see you there."

Before Liza could respond, the culprit sprinted by. But she easily recognized him. Charlie Bates, owner of the Clam Box Diner, still wearing his apron and a Red Sox baseball cap.

Liza and Claire stood side by side and watched him jog down the street. "What in the world has gotten into him?" Claire murmured.

"Maybe there's a big sale on clams going on at the dock," Liza joked. "Charlie must go through bushels every week."

Before Claire could answer, more people rushed out of the Clam Box. Liza recognized one of them as Sophie Potter, the woman who owned the orchard outside of town. She didn't recognize Sophie's companion, also a senior, her arm looped in Sophie's as they walked along rather briskly for their age. They were headed for the harbor and chatting excitedly every step of the way.

Liza and Claire stepped back to keep from being mowed down again.

"Kitchen fire?" Claire asked.

"No chance. Charlie would be in there, beating down the flames with his own apron. I don't think they're running from something in the diner," Liza speculated. "I think they're running toward something at the harbor."

"Yes, of course. That makes sense," Claire agreed.

Liza glanced across the street and noticed more people hurriedly leaving shops and offices, heading toward the harbor and village green.

They had walked down another block and stood in front of Harbor Hardware. Claire tried the door but it was locked. They both saw the note taped to the glass at the same time. Claire read it aloud, "'Be back in fifteen. Frank.'"

Claire looked up at Liza. "I guess Frank is jogging down to the harbor, too."

Liza knew she was talking about the shop owner, Frank Krueger. In a small town like Cape Light, you knew everyone. Of course, he might be out buying coffee or doing an errand. He wasn't necessarily chasing Charlie Bates down the street to see what was going on in the park. But for some reason, Liza felt he must be.

"Now I'm curious. Let's find out what's going on down there."

"I'm curious, too," Claire admitted. "I recall a morning like this years ago, when everyone in town was racing down to the dock. Turned out an amateur fisherman had reeled in a huge shark. It must have been twenty feet long and weighed five-hundred pounds. Its teeth as big as . . . as lemons. It was quite a sight." Claire nodded as they picked up speed.

Liza glanced at her friend but didn't answer. She guessed the shark had stretched a bit over the years, starting out as ten or even fifteen feet long. Though Claire rarely exaggerated, she had to be given some leeway for a bona fide shark story.

The women soon reached the green and could see the dock and harbor. An elated fisherman with a prize catch were nowhere in sight. But there was definitely something unusual happening. A large crowd had gathered and stood milling about around the harbor.

The parking lot on the harbor side was filled with several long white trailers and a few big-box trucks and vans. A good portion of the village green and dock were blocked by wooden barriers and yellow tape. Even the local police force had been dispatched to keep order in the crowd. Liza noticed Office Tucker Tulley strolling around, making sure that no one crossed the barrier. She also noticed a reporter from the *Cape Light Messenger* wandering through the crowd with her camera, interviewing the locals and jotting down replies on her notepad.

Whatever was going on was definitely newsworthy.

It was a movie set, Liza realized, with a large crew, big lights on metal tripods, miles of long black cables, and camera equipment on rolling machinery. People wearing headsets scurried in all directions. They looked stressed and distracted, Liza thought, as if the work they were doing was extremely important.

Claire stopped in her tracks as they stood across from the green. "For goodness' sake, it's a movie. I read about this in the newspaper a few weeks ago. But I didn't pay much attention to the details."

Liza was not surprised. Claire was not the kind of person to be awed by that sort of news. She was more likely to just turn the page and look for the gardening column.

"I read about it, too," Liza realized. "I think it's some sort of romance movie. Charlotte Miller is in it. And Nick Dempsey." She glanced around at the crowd again. "I get it now. I'd knock a few people over to get a good look at him."

"He is a good actor," Claire agreed. "And Charlotte Miller is very charming. I always enjoy her films. I wonder what she's like in person. She seems so sweet and down to earth in the roles she plays."

"Movie stars are probably very different in real life, don't you think?" Liza mused. "They have so many people rushing around to do their bidding. It would spoil anyone."

"I think it must be difficult to be famous. So much pressure and attention. I wouldn't like it at all."

"I'd try it for a few weeks, see how it goes. There must be a few perks," Liza said with a laugh. "The shopping sprees might be fun. And the travel. And the designer gowns."

But none of that was to Claire's taste, she knew. Liza often wondered if Claire had ever gone much farther ashore than Cape Light. She seemed so rooted to the area, as if she were as much a part of Angel Island as the windblown oaks beside the inn.

They stood at the back of the crowd, trying to see what was going on. Or spot a movie star. But the area set off for filming seemed empty and inactive, and there were no famous faces in sight. Liza did recognize Lucy Bates, Charlie's wife, standing nearby and tapped her shoulder.

"Hey, Liza, Claire." Lucy smiled at them then shook her head at all the activity. "A real Hollywood film crew, right here in Cape Light. Can you believe it?" Before Liza could answer, Lucy said, "I saw Charlotte Miller, just for a few seconds. She is so pretty. She came out of a limo and scurried right into her trailer. She had on big sunglasses and a baseball hat. But I knew it was her." Lucy sounded triumphant. "Charlie's over there. He's looking for the producer. He's going to try to persuade them to film a scene in the diner. Wouldn't that be something?"

"It would be," Claire agreed dryly.

Liza knew that Claire did not think much of the Clam Box, especially the cuisine served there, which was cooked by Charlie. Claire was an outstanding cook and baker. She was very modest about her talents but did have high standards.

"So all of these people are just standing around, waiting for something to happen?" Claire asked in her direct way.

Lucy nodded happily. "Isn't it exciting?"

Liza glanced at Claire. She could tell Claire's feelings were similar to her own. It was fun to have a movie crew in town, but they had a lot to do today. They couldn't wait around for celebrities to pop out of their hiding places for a moment or two, like very glamorous whack-a-moles.

Claire glanced at her watch. "Liza, I think we'd better get moving. We have a few stops to make."

"Yes, we do. You have fun, Lucy. I hope you get to see the movie stars."

"I'll let you know," Lucy promised. She waved as Liza and Claire walked away, heading back to the shops on Main Street.

They were walking against the tide now. The word had spread, and a parade of people were marching down to the park to watch the film crew, leaving stores and offices empty all over town. Liza even spotted the town's mayor, Emily Warwick, and Reverend Ben Lewis, the minister of the old stone church that stood on the other side of the green. Everyone in town was starstruck. Liza and Claire had to shoulder their way out of the crowd.

When they finally stood across the street, clear of the gathering, Claire seemed a little breathless. She pushed a few stray strands of hair back into her bun. "Well, that was an experience. If I'd known this was going on today, I would have postponed our shopping."

"Oh, I don't know. I think it's fun to be part of the excitement. Even for a few minutes. Even if we didn't get to see Nick Dempsey."

Liza and Claire found most of the stores they visited empty, which made it easy to fly through their list in nearly half the time. They carried everything to Liza's SUV and headed back to Angel Island.

It had been fun to see the movie set but Liza was relieved to get back to the island, to the open vistas and serenity. No milling crowds or humming movie machinery. The island was a step beyond the movie madness, and she was sure it would stay that way.

With the tide low, she didn't anticipate any problem crossing the long, thin land bridge that connected the mainland with the island. The road had been covered by water and was impassable several times over the summer, when heavy rains had combined with a high tide. It was one of the drawbacks of living on the island though, to her mind, there were so many wonderful aspects to living out there, she hardly noticed a washed-out road or two.

Liza reached the land bridge a short time later. The gate was up, signaling that it was safe to cross. The water on either side was dark blue, dotted with whitecaps. The sky was still hazy, promising more rain.

She steered her SUV onto the two-lane bridge, which had a rail and paved shoulder on each side, edged by large gray boulders. The road was newly paved but narrow, and she drove the black ribbon of highway carefully. From the middle of the bridge, she could see the coastline curving around to Cape Light's harbor and the low mass of buildings on Main Street.

From time to time, building a real bridge to the island was proposed. When Liza had first returned to Angel Island, five months earlier, she would have been all for that idea. But now that she was an official year-round resident, she valued the island's privacy and liked the idea that it was a bit challenging to reach.

The Inn at Angel Island was not far from the bridge, a short drive along one of the island's two main roads, the one that followed the western coastline.

Suddenly on the right side of the road, the inn came into view. Liza stopped for a moment as she often did before pulling up the drive. She liked to try to see the inn as if for the first time, as a stranger might see it. This was difficult, if not impossible, considering she had known the place since she was a little girl, coming here to spend summers with her aunt and uncle.

She had always loved this house, three stories high with matching bay windows on the first and second floors. The windows on the second floor were fronted by a balcony and there was even a turret on the right side of the building. When Liza was a little girl and had heard the extravagant Victorian referred to as Queen Anne style, she had instantly known the term was perfect for the house. It was definitely a place worthy of royalty, something right out of a fairy tale.

Set on a large piece of property that sloped toward the road, the house faced the bluffs and the expanse of ocean that stretched out below. The wraparound porch was filled with sitting chairs—Adirondack, wicker, and straight-back rockers—where guests sat and enjoyed the view, sipping glasses of homemade lemonade and iced tea. Just as it had been in her aunt's day.

Liza had made many repairs and improvements since she'd taken over the place last spring, but she tried hard to maintain the integrity of the place so that guests who had visited years ago would still feel comfortable and familiar with the place—the same, only better.

A walkway bordered by summer flowers led up to the porch. A sign swung from a post along the way: ANGEL INN—ALL ARE WELCOME. Her aunt Elizabeth had painted and hand-lettered that sign with a scroll of vines and flowers on the border. Liza had restored it herself to its former glory. Below that plaque hung another that now read, VACANCY.

There had been so much bad weather this past month. Liza tried to stay positive, believing the rooms would fill up again for the last few weeks of the summer season.

She turned up the drive and spotted Daniel Merritt's pickup truck parked near the back door, then saw him up on a ladder, leaning against the inn. He was working on one of the window shutters that had come down during the last storm.

Was he supposed to be working here today? She would have remembered. Liza took a quick glance at her reflection in the rearview mirror. Large blue eyes peered back at her. She looked pale and sticky, her long dark hair an outrageous mess of curls. And she really needed some lipstick.

"Oh, Daniel's here," Claire said happily. "I wonder if he's had any lunch."

"As if that has ever stopped him from eating your cooking, Claire."

"It has nothing to do with that. He has a healthy appetite. He works very hard," Claire quickly defended him, though she did seem pleased by Liza's compliment.

Daniel Merritt did work hard, and Liza was grateful to him. She had more or less inherited Daniel—a carpenter, painter, roofer, and all around fix-it man—with the property. She was sure that if not for his persistent care, the place would not be standing. She sometimes wondered if she would be herself, if not for his support and encouragement.

Liza was always happy to find Daniel here. She hadn't expected to see him until Wednesday night. They had planned to go up to Newburyport for dinner and a movie. They were officially a couple now; at least that's what everyone on the island said. Though their courtship had hit a few bumps along the way.

But Daniel's life was still unsettled, and Liza tried not to look too far into the future or make too many demands. She simply loved being around him, which was enough for now. Even if he made surprise visits when she looked like a complete mess.

Claire waved up at Daniel and carried her purchases to the inn, going in through the front door.

Liza walked back to the ladder. "Hey, up there. Want some lunch?"

He came down a few steps and kissed her hello. "Sounds good. I'll be done in a minute. Did you pick up the shutters at the hardware store?"

"I tried, but the store was closed."

"In the middle of a Monday? That's funny. I hope Frank isn't sick or anything."

"There was a note. It just said, 'Be Back in Fifteen Minutes.' We're pretty sure where he went. There's a movie crew in town filming at the harbor. Claire and I saw a huge crowd down there, mostly just waiting for something to happen. Or one of the movie stars to come out of a trailer."

"A movie crew? Why didn't you tell me sooner?" Daniel jumped down from the ladder and smoothed out his paint-spattered T-shirt. "I always wanted to be in a movie . . . you know, one of those guys you see walking in the background, looking very busy and in a rush to get somewhere?" He faked a serious expression and glanced at his watch.

With his tall, strong build, dark hair, and eyes to match, Daniel was just as attractive as any movie star Liza had ever seen. Including Nick Dempsey. She laughed and rested her hand on his broad shoulder. "I'm pretty sure they have enough candidates trying out to be one of 'those guys.' Besides, I think Claire is serving chowder for lunch today."

Daniel grinned at the mention of one of his favorite dishes. "Hollywood will have to wait. I'll have some lunch and think about it."

"I was hoping you would say that." Liza slipped her arm through his, and they walked around the house to the brick patio that was covered by a lattice filled with thick wisteria.

Claire had already put out three place settings on a blue-and-white-checkered cloth. There were tall glasses of iced tea and a basket of warm cornbread squares, covered by a cloth napkin. Liza went into the kitchen to see if Claire needed any help and Daniel followed, washing his hands at the kitchen sink.

Together they carried out the rest of the lunch: a bowl of salad made with fresh lettuce and tomatoes from Claire's garden, and half a peach and blueberry crumble left over from the weekend. Last but not least, Claire carried out the chowder pot and ladle.

As she filled the three bowls with the hot, fragrant soup, Daniel snapped open his napkin with a flourish. "You're right, Liza. The lure of fame and fortune pales in comparison to Claire's cooking. What was I thinking?"

Liza laughed. "I was never really worried."

Claire bowed her head a moment, offering silent thanks for her meal, and Liza and Daniel did the same. When Claire lifted her head she was smiling. "Start everyone. I know it's warm outside, but the soup will still cool down and taste pasty if you let it sit too long."

As they started on their chowder, Daniel said, "So you never said who was starring in this movie. Anyone famous?"

"Oh, yes." Liza quickly swallowed. "Very famous. Charlotte Miller and Nick Dempsey."

Daniel's expression looked blank for a moment. Liza could tell he didn't know who she was talking about. "You know, she was in that comedy about the two sisters and one of them becomes a female pirate? And the one about the secretary who becomes a country-western singer? She's been on all the magazine covers the last few months. Haven't you been in a supermarket lately?"

"Oh . . . right. I know who you mean." He smiled and nodded and started eating again. "She's pretty," he added.

"Yes, she is," Liza agreed. No question about that.

He met her eye and smiled. "Come to think of it, I'm lucky you didn't hang around there that long. Some producer would be signing you up to be an extra, too."

Liza rolled her eyes at his heavy-handed compliment, but appreciated it nonetheless. "Thanks, but I like my job. Maybe I'll go to Hollywood if the inn doesn't work out."

Daniel laughed. "I know who Nick Dempsey is. I'm not that far out of the loop. He's been in some suspense movies, playing police detectives or CIA agents. Those two truly are movie stars. I wonder how long they'll be around. This could bring a lot of publicity to Cape Light."

"Charlie Bates thinks so. He wants to persuade the producer to film a scene in the Clam Box. I guess he plans to be in the background, flipping burgers and shouting out orders."

"That sounds about right." Daniel laughed. "I hope he doesn't give the cast and crew heartburn with his hometown cuisine."

"Or worse," Claire chimed in with a serious expression. She suddenly stopped herself from saying more. She rarely said a negative word about anyone. Liza could see that she regretted even that small comment. "Just seems a shame that the Hollywood people might get the impression that the Clam Box is the only type of food we have to offer here. There's definitely more to New England cooking than fried clams and Charlie's pasty chowder."

"That would be a shame," Daniel agreed. He helped himself to another chunk of cornbread and slathered on a pat of melted butter. It just wasn't fair; he ate whatever he wanted. Liza didn't know where he put it. Wherever it landed, though, it looked just right on him.

Liza cleared away the soup bowls and chowder pot and brought them inside while Claire started to dish out their dessert. Behind the sound of the running water in the sink, Liza suddenly noticed someone knocking on the screen door at the front of the house.

She shut off the water, quickly dried her hands, and ran to answer it, trying to smooth out her hair with one hand as she ran.

As she drew closer, she saw a man and woman standing on the porch. The woman, who looked to be in her early thirties, nearly had her face pressed to the screen, trying to get a look inside.

Had her wish for an overflow of the town's tourists come true? Liza sure hoped so. With her brightest innkeeper smile in place, she sallied forth to answer the door.

"Sorry to keep you waiting," she greeted the couple. "I was back in the kitchen. I didn't hear you knock." She opened the door and welcomed them inside. "Are you looking for accommodations?"

"In a way, I guess you could say that," the woman replied.

Liza noticed she was carrying a large black notebook that looked very businesslike. The man, who seemed younger, had a 35mm digital camera slung around his neck. Two cameras actually, Liza realized. He was looking around, his head craning in all directions, from the molding to the floors and back again.

Professional, she guessed. Her brother was a photographer, and she could spot one a mile away.

"My name is Judy Kramer," the woman said, digging around in her big black nylon tote. "This is my assistant, Zach Engle."

Liza smiled and extended her hand. "Liza Martin. I run the inn."

"I guessed as much," Judy replied. "It's a lovely place. We were on the island a while back and passed by. It caught my eye, but we didn't have time to come in."

Liza nodded. She wasn't quite sure what this was all adding up to. She could tell they were not a vacationing couple, as she had first assumed. But she couldn't guess what they wanted and just hoped they weren't here to try to sell her something.

"You've probably noticed that there's a movie filming in town. I work for the production company, booking accommodations and catering, that sort of thing." The woman finally pulled out a business card and handed it to Liza.

Liza read it quickly. *Judy Kramer, Production Associate. Winding Hill Films.*

"We're going to film some scenes on the island over the next week or two. I wondered if we could speak to you about reserving the inn for the use of the cast and crew. We would probably need most of the space," she added, looking around. "That might be a problem. I mean, if you have a high occupancy now."

Liza stared at her and blinked. She felt like she might be going into shock. *Get a grip,* she scolded herself. *You just hit the jackpot. Say something smart or this woman is going to think you're a total flake.* "I think we can accommodate your group. It's not a problem at all. We have plenty of rooms available . . . Why don't we go into the parlor and discuss it?" Liza quickly turned to lead the way, using the break to take a few deep breaths and compose herself.

"Would you like some coffee or tea? A cold drink, maybe?" she offered. "There's some wonderful peach and blueberry crumble on hand. Homemade," she added.

Judy smiled politely but didn't look tempted. Zach seemed more interested, though. "My grandmother used to make crumble. That's the one with crumbs on top, without any crust, right?"

"That's the one." Liza nodded. "We do all the cooking and baking right here. All the ingredients are fresh, most of them locally grown. Many of the vegetables come out of our own garden."

As if on cue, Claire appeared. "Hello everyone," she said cordially.

"This is Claire North. She's our cook and housekeeper and . . . everything in between," Liza said. "Claire, would you bring some crumble for Judy and Zach? And some iced tea? They're with the film company that's in town. They want to talk about lodging the movie crew here."

"That would be very nice," Claire said in her usual even tone. "I'll be right back with that crumble and maybe some ice cream alongside. It goes perfectly."

Claire quickly headed back to the kitchen, and Liza took a notepad and pen from her small writing desk. "So, tell me what you need and I'll tell you what we can do."

"I like your spirit, Liza," Judy said, "but I think it's only fair to warn you, this is a big group that includes some prima donnas. It will be challenging."

"We can handle it. No worries," Liza replied, sounding far calmer than she actually felt.

Judy sat back, looking reassured. "Let me start at the beginning. When we came to the island the first time, we were scouting for outdoor scenes. We found the beach below this property. It's perfect. We'll definitely shoot down there."

"Really? That's exciting," Liza said, feeling the same goose bumps she had felt earlier that day, seeing all the cameras set up on the village dock. It was silly she knew, but she couldn't help it.

"We've heard that the road between the mainland and the island washes out pretty often. So we thought it would be more efficient if we housed the crew and some of the cast out here. Right now the crew is in a motel just outside of town. But it will cost tons of money if they can't get over to the island to work when we need them here."

"I see your problem. There has been a lot of rain this summer. How many rooms do you need?"

Judy told her the number. "Some of the guys can bunk together. They're used to that."

"I think we can accommodate that number of guests. No problem."

They would have a full house, packed to the rafters. But Liza was thrilled. She hadn't had that many people staying at one time since June, when the inn had hosted a wedding, and that was just for a long weekend.

"The big stars and the executive team will be staying in New-buryport. So we don't have to worry about them," Judy added.

Liza had been worried about entertaining the big stars and was honestly relieved to hear that they were taken care of. There were several far fancier hotels in the nearby town, some with spas and all the amenities. She could even guess where the stars might be staying.

"We sometimes have long breaks between shooting, especially outdoor scenes. The light and the weather . . . who knows what. Normally, the actors rest in their trailers, but it's hard to bring the trailers out here. There's no place to hook them up and other compli-cations. So we will need rooms for the stars just for pit stops. Nice rooms," Judy added, smiling a little too widely.

Liza guessed she was wondering if the rooms would be up to her standards. Liza was wondering the same thing. She had only taken over the inn in March, after her aunt died, but she had renovated almost every room.

"I can show you the rooms as soon as we're done here," Liza promised. "Almost every room has been freshly decorated."

"That sounds great. If it's anything like the downstairs, I'm sure it's lovely," Judy said quickly. "There is also the matter of feeding everyone while we're filming," she continued. "We normally do that with catering trucks but it's hard to get those out here and up and running as well."

"So you need the inn as home base while you're shooting, and some of the crew will stay a few nights. Is that it?"

Judy laughed. "Basically, yes. But you make it sound so easy."

"That's what we do here." Liza shrugged. "We give people a comfortable place to sleep and plenty of good food. And a little peace and quiet," she added.

Before Judy could reply, Claire appeared again, carrying a tray of dessert dishes. She served Judy, Zach, and Liza and poured the iced tea into tall glasses decorated with sprigs of fresh mint and thin lemon slices.

"Wow . . . this is . . . outrageous," Judy said between mouthfuls of crumble. She pointed at her dish. "I bet it has a million calories, but I can't resist. You really made this?" She stared up at Claire in disbelief.

Claire nodded. "And the ice cream. Though it got a tad frosty in the freezer. It's best right out of the churn."

"Tastes fine to me," Zach said. He looked over at Judy, and they seemed to silently agree on something.

Once the crumble was finished, which didn't take very long, Liza gave the pair a tour of the inn, downstairs, and then the upper floors. Judy seemed genuinely pleased by the size of the rooms and the decor. She made a lot of notes and Zach took photos. She even picked out rooms for Charlotte Miller and Nick Dempsey, mentioning a few items the stars liked to have handy: favorite brands of bottled water, organic dried apricots, ginger tea, and chocolate-coated Oreos, chilled in the refrigerator.

"I'll e-mail a complete list," she added. "Don't worry about that now."

Liza forced a smile. She did worry about it. They didn't exactly live on a desert island; there was a well-stocked general store, and stores in Cape Light and beyond were easily accessible. But it was hard to shop by such specific brands. She could only imagine one of the stars having a hissy fit because she'd bought the wrong brand of dried apricots.

But look at the upside, Liza, she coached herself. *A full house for several days, great publicity, and such excitement.* There were definitely more pluses than negatives to this situation.

Judy and Liza talked a bit more about the business end, the rates for the rooms and meals. Liza offered a group discount, and they agreed to confirm everything by e-mail once Judy got back to her boss, who was with the crew in Cape Light.

"This is going to be great," Judy said, shaking Liza's hand as she left. "I can't wait to come back . . . and get more of this crumble."

"I look forward to seeing you again. Claire will have more crumble ready and waiting," Liza promised. She watched as their white Land Rover drove off. Then she stood by the door a moment, feeling a bit stunned and wondering if she had just imagined the whole thing. Were the cast and crew of a real movie actually coming here? It was just too unbelievable.

"Are they gone?" Claire asked quietly.

Liza turned to see her standing by the stairway.

"Yes, they left. But they'll be back," she quickly added. "And we have a ton of work to do before they get here."

Claire's pale eyebrows rose a notch or two. "How long will that be?"

"Two days." Liza waited for her reaction. "That's their schedule right now. They're coming to the island to shoot some scenes on the beach in two days. So that's our deadline."

Saying it aloud, she honestly could not believe she'd agreed to this. But there it was.

Claire, in her usual way, seemed unfazed. "That is soon. How many will there be?"

"A full house. Some of the rooms will be doubled up, in fact."

"Yes, I'd imagine they would be," Claire said calmly. "We might need those cots in the attic. Maybe Daniel can help get them down. It will be nice to entertain a big group. Your aunt loved to see the inn filled to the brim. One of her favorite things was to put out the 'NO VACANCY' sign. I love to see a full table. That's what we're here for, don't you think?"

Liza nodded. "Absolutely."

Trust Claire to look on the bright side and not complain about the work. Liza was thankful to have her help, as always, and the blessing of her positive perspective.

"Having all those movie stars with us is a bit intimidating, though. I hope the inn is up to their standards."

Claire smiled calmly at her. "We don't have all the bells and whistles, that's for sure. But I think the inn offers something rare and special in its own way. We can't try to be something we're not, Liza. We can just try our best to entertain them in our unique style."

When Liza looked at it that way, she had to agree. Just let the inn be the welcoming, peaceful place it had always been. That was the best strategy, even for hosting Hollywood.

Chapter Two

THE Gilroy Farm stood just beyond the fence that bordered Liza's property. Heavy rain in the morning had tapered off to a steady drizzle. Liza considered driving but felt silly taking her car just to go next door. Dressed in her yellow slicker with the hood up, she walked through the trellised passage in the fence, now covered with blooming roses. Then she followed a path through the outlying meadow that led to the big barn and a smaller shed, which housed the farm's retail shop.

Her friend Audrey Gilroy would most likely be in the shed at this time of day, selling cheese, fudge, skin lotion, and soaps, all made with goat milk. Audrey and her husband, Rob, also grew lavender, which took up an entire field beside the barn, a wide purple wave of blossoms. Audrey had told her they were selling the blooms this summer as fast as they could grow and dry them.

The Gilroys had both quit jobs in Boston to move to the farm. The place had been vacant, the buildings run-down. But now, only a few years after they purchased it, the buildings were in perfect condition, and the fields and gardens flourishing with flowers and vegetables.

The herd of frolicking goats—who often escaped to Liza's property—were nowhere in sight. The goats must be hiding in the barn, Liza thought. They didn't like the rain very much and made a real racket in a thunderstorm.

Liza entered the shed that served as the farm's shop and found Audrey sitting at a side counter, making lavender wreaths. Her long red hair was neatly braided, a few strands hanging loose around her face. Dressed in a cotton T-shirt, baggy shorts, and high rubber boots, Audrey looked like she had been working hard this morning. Her tall, sturdy build seemed to fit the typical idea of a farm woman. But Audrey was also a registered nurse and kept up her practice, volunteering at the island's medical clinic.

But the farm was her true love and she had many creative ideas for the shop, including the lavender products. Today the air was filled with the wonderful scent, and Liza took a deep, calming breath before saying hello.

Audrey turned and smiled. "Hey, Liza. What a nice surprise. This isn't your usual shopping day."

"My usual day? When is that?" Liza asked curiously.

"Thursday. Or sometimes, Friday morning. Before your weekend guests check in. Didn't you ever notice?"

Liza laughed. "No, I didn't, but I think you're right. We're getting a big crowd in tomorrow, and I've got a huge order for you. I hope you can fill it."

Liza handed Audrey the list she and Claire had made of items they needed from the farm. She watched as Audrey's eyes widened. "Who are you expecting? Napoleon and his army?"

"Almost. You know that movie crew that's in town? They're shooting a few scenes on the island, on the beach just below the inn, and they're using the inn as a home base. We have to feed them, pamper them, house a lot of them overnight. The works," Liza concluded happily.

Audrey's mouth hung open a moment. "Get out . . . Really?"

"Really." Liza nodded quickly, feeling like a bobblehead doll.

"Even Charlotte Miller and Nick Dempsey?" Audrey's tone changed in pitch a bit, giving the hunky movie star's name special reverence.

"Even Charlotte and Nick," Liza quipped, feigning familiarity. "Though the big stars aren't staying overnight. They're just using rooms to rest and freshen up between takes and review their lines, that sort of thing."

Audrey gave her a look. "You're starting to sound like you're in the business, Liza. They haven't even arrived yet."

Liza shrugged. "What can I say? We're all bitten by the Hollywood bug. Except for Claire," she added with a grin.

"Claire has a built-in immunity to any bug like that."

Audrey glanced at Liza's list and began gathering the items, laying them out on the wooden countertop to be wrapped and packed. "When the Hollywood stars gasp with awe and delight over our goat cheese, please direct them this way. I'd love to see the farm mentioned in one of those celebrity interviews. Maybe I'll be sending packages to the West Coast in dry ice, special delivery."

"It's very possible. I can just see it—Gilroy Farm, Goat Cheese of the Stars."

"Very good. But you did have a former life in advertising."

"Can't deny it. Though I've tried to better myself since those dark days," she teased back. Liza picked up a grainy cracker from a plate and tasted the free sample Audrey had set out, which was a tasty herb-infused cheese. As she watched her friend move about the shop, Liza sensed something dragging at her spirits. "So, what's new with you guys? How's it going?" she asked. Liza didn't want to come right out and ask the obvious question. But it suddenly hung in the air.

Audrey and Rob had been trying to start a family for almost a year without much progress. Liza usually waited for Audrey to bring up the sensitive topic; she didn't want her friend to feel pressured. But she sensed from Audrey's expression there was some news on that front. And it wasn't good.

Audrey walked over to the wooden counter where Liza stood and set down an armload of tomatoes. "I thought I was pregnant, but it turned out to be another false alarm. I was just really late."

Audrey lowered her gaze and sighed. Liza's heart went out to her. She reached over and squeezed her hand. "I'm so sorry, Audrey. What a roller coaster. It must be so hard to get all excited and then, it doesn't work out."

Audrey nodded. "That's it, a real roller coaster. And it's not just me. Rob is riding it, too. We get so excited then . . . crash again." She took a long breath and squared her shoulders. "My doctor says we have time and shouldn't get discouraged. It just takes some couples longer, you know?"

Liza nodded. "Sure it does. I've heard of women who take a long time to have a first child, and then have several more, one right after the other."

"I've heard those stories, too," Audrey answered with a small smile. "We'll just take one for now. One healthy one. There's a lot that can be done these days. I think we're ready to figure out our next step. But we're not quite sure what that should be."

Audrey had been a nurse before coming out to the island to run the farm. She still practiced nursing, donating a great deal of time to the island's medical clinic, where Liza's friend Daniel also worked as an emergency medical technician.

"What does your doctor say?" Liza asked.

"He referred us to a specialist in Boston. He thinks that's the best place for me to go and get more information. More tests and an evaluation."

"I see." Liza nodded. "That sounds like a good plan. It could be something very simple."

"It could be," Audrey agreed, but sounded as if she really doubted it would be a quick fix. Liza hated to see her friend feeling sad and defeated. It just wasn't Audrey. The issue of having children was so momentous. Starting a family came so easily to some couples, Liza was sure they hardly appreciated the blessing. But when couples like Audrey and Rob struggled, it became clear that having a baby was truly a miracle and one of life's greatest gifts. Liza hoped that the problem would soon be solved for her friends. She knew they would make wonderful parents.

"I'll say a prayer for you," Liza said finally. "Let me know when you have to go to the city. I can come with you if Rob is busy here or you need company."

Rob was very supportive of Audrey, and the couple had a great marriage. But Liza knew that there were days when at least one person had to be on the farm, for the animals or the cheese-making and other responsibilities.

Audrey squeezed her hand. "Thank you, Liza. That's sweet. I'll keep you posted."

As Audrey tallied up the order, the conversation turned to other topics—the rainy days that were starting to seem endless, with more predicted for the rest of the week.

"Will they still film the movie in the rain?" Audrey asked as Liza prepared to go.

"I don't really know. They did say they take long breaks so we need to be prepared for a lot of downtime. It's hard to say. I think we're pretty well stocked if they stay in."

"I'd say you were. Can you even carry all that stuff home on your own?"

Liza looked at the pile of packages and considered the rain. "I'll be okay. I'll just grab what I can carry in my bags for now and come back later with the car."

"I can give you a lift back."

"No, don't do that. You need to stay at the store. You might miss customers," Liza insisted. "It's not far and I'm already wet."

"Yes, you are," Audrey agreed. "I have an even better idea. Why don't I bring the rest over tomorrow?" Audrey's grin was mischievous. "What time do you think they'll get there?"

"They told me eight sharp."

"Great. I'll be there at eight fifteen." Audrey fluffed her long red hair and batted her eyes, making Liza laugh. "I can hardly wait to meet Nick Dempsey."

Liza had a feeling that half the population of the island and Cape Light village felt the same. The female half. How could she deny her best friend this once-in-a-lifetime opportunity? "I'm sure he'll be excited to meet you, too. Especially when he tries the cheese."

The two women hugged, and Liza set off through the meadow, lugging her purchases in two large canvas tote bags. As she sloshed through the muddy field and felt the raindrops drip down her face, she recalled that she'd often heard the movie business was a lot of hard work and not half as glamorous as it seemed. She was starting to see that was true.

*   *   *

RAIN continued to fall through the day and into the night. Thunder boomed and a flash of lightning lit up Audrey's bedroom. She woke with a start, then sat up in bed, listening to an even louder rumble in the sky overhead and the goats braying out in the barn. Waves of windswept rain struck the house, and she jumped up to close the windows.

Out in the yard between the house and barn, she heard another sound. A dog barking, out there somewhere in the darkness. It stopped for a moment, then started again, frenzied and more insistent.

Audrey pulled the curtain back and looked out. She couldn't see much at all. She was about to go back to bed when a bolt of lightning lit up the yard and she could see it clearly. A large yellow dog, huddled against the barn, pacing back and forth. It was drenched and looked very frightened.

She turned to her husband, his long, lanky body outlined under the sheet. He lay on his back, his head sunk in a pillow. All she could see was his brown curly hair and full beard. But his loud snores told her he was fast asleep. Once Rob dropped off, he could sleep through a locomotive running through the room.

"Rob? There's a dog outside. It's driving the goats crazy."

"Hmm?" he seemed to respond for a moment, then turned on his side and fell back to sleep again.

No help there, Audrey thought. She was awake now. No sense in the both of them losing sleep. She pulled on a sweatshirt, pulled up the hood, and went downstairs. At the side door she found her high rubber boots and a flashlight. Moving quickly, she headed out toward the barn. The rain beat down, soaking her to the skin. Audrey felt a little nutty, out in the rain in her pajamas and boots but what else could she do?

She swung the light on the dog and it stared back at her, looking fearful. But its big tail wagged. Then a clap of thunder made it shiver and pace again. She almost thought it was going to run away. But instead, it ran toward her, then jumped up and put its big muddy paws on her chest.

Audrey stumbled backward and dropped the light. "Get down! Down, dog!" Audrey pushed the dog's paws off her sweatshirt, leaving long streaks of mud. The dog sat at her feet, staring up at her. Its tail beat the wet ground. Its eyes were wide with an eager expression, and it was panting a little.

She found herself giving in. "Okay, come with me. You must be lost. Do you have a collar?" She leaned over and checked the dog's neck. There was a collar, but no tags. She slipped her fingers between the collar and the dog's wet fur. Her first thought was the barn, of course. But she knew the goats would not like sharing the barn with a dog, and she didn't know how the dog would feel about it either.

The dog seemed to have a nice disposition, but how much could you tell from just leading an animal across a rainy barnyard?

They reached the house and Audrey decided the screened-in porch was the best choice. She opened the screen door and the dog quickly ran inside. Audrey flicked on a low light. The dog was eagerly sniffing around, especially under the wooden picnic table where Audrey and Rob often ate in the warm months.

"You must be hungry. That figures. I'll bet you need some water, too."

Audrey went into the kitchen, careful to close the door behind her. She got out two plastic bowls and filled one with water. It was harder to decide what to put in the other. But she remembered a leftover container of potatoes and some cold chicken in the fridge and mixed it all together. She had no doubt the dog would devour the tasty people food but hoped it wouldn't get an upset stomach. That was all she needed tonight.

When she came back out to the porch, the dog ran over to her, then quickly sat in an obedient position while she set the food and water down.

"Okay, go ahead. I guess you've had some training. Maybe that pounce outside was just a moment of desperation?"

She watched the dog inhale the chicken and potatoes, then lap up the entire bowl of water. The dog was a female, Audrey finally surmised, and much larger than it had looked from the window. She had a long wolfish muzzle and triangle ears, like a Labrador or a golden retriever. The dog's coat was long and shaggy, like a retriever. But it was bigger and bulkier than any golden Audrey had ever seen, more like a Bernese mountain dog. It was obviously a mixed breed. Maybe a little bit of bear in there, too, she thought.

When the dog was finished eating, she came over and stood right next to Audrey, leaning against Audrey's leg. The dog's big head came almost to Audrey's hip. Audrey absentmindedly petted her. The dog's fur was wet and muddy, but there was nothing to be done about that tonight. Audrey had already been down here for longer than she expected and had a full day of work tomorrow. "I have to go up to bed now. You go to sleep."

The dog looked up, listening and watching Audrey with her big brown eyes. But she didn't budge.

"Wait. I'll get you something to sleep on."

Audrey looked around the porch and spotted an old afghan slung over a rocking chair. She folded it twice, then piled it in a cozy corner of the room, away from the door and windows.

"Here you are. A nice bed. What do you think?" Audrey patted the spot with her hand, showing the dog the soft cushion she'd made.

The dog sniffed the afghan. Then she circled around a few times and lay down, curling her big tail close to her nose.

"Have a nice sleep. Tomorrow we'll check around for your owner. No offense, but I've always been more of a cat person. Better to be up front about these things from the start. I don't want you to get any needless expectations. Besides, someone must be looking for you, and I bet you want to go home. Wherever that is."

The dog stared back at her, then let out a long, rattling sigh. Audrey shut off the little lamp and headed back upstairs. She did seem like a nice dog. But they already had several felines roaming the barn and grounds, doing their cat job at the farm. She and Rob didn't need a dog, too.

The dog had a collar and must belong to someone. Audrey told herself she would check around tomorrow and try to find her owner. Or bring her to a shelter.

Audrey closed her eyes and pulled the comforter up over her shoulders. The storm had passed, and a gentle patter of drops on the roof quickly lulled her back to sleep. Even though she didn't care much for dogs, she fell asleep with a good feeling. At least she'd done a good deed today.

"I guess you could say we've been up since the crack of dawn, if the sun was out. But it's still like pea soup out there."

Liza turned to Claire. The housekeeper didn't answer, but smiled gently at her. Claire always took things in a much calmer manner, and she was endlessly patient. She just had a different sense of time, Liza decided.

They had finally finished getting ready for their unusual guests and were waiting on the front porch for the movie crew's arrival. It was just about eight a.m., and Liza hoped some extra coffee would give her a second wind. They had been up since six, taking care of those preparations that could only be done at the last minute, like the baking and putting fresh flowers in all the rooms.

She had hoped last night's storm would clear the way for blue skies, but there were only more low gray clouds in sight. Though it wasn't exactly raining, the fog was thick, especially down at the beach, and a light, damp wind blew off the sea, making it feel as if you were standing in the bow of a boat.

"Will they really shoot a movie in this weather?" Liza asked Claire. "Down on the beach, you probably can't even see your hand in front of your face."

"I was just wondering the same." Claire set her mug down on the wicker table and smoothed her apron. She'd been baking all morning and had just put on a fresh apron for the guests.

"They might be in the inn all day. At least I made a double recipe of the scones. Wonder how long those will last."

Liza glanced at her. Either Judy Kramer had been trying to scare her, or two double recipes wouldn't last very long with this group.

Finally, Liza saw the first van down the road. It steered into the parking lot, followed by a caravan of more vans and the big-box trucks, which parked on the opposite side of the road, next to the cliff over the beach.

"Here they come. It's showtime," Liza said.

"Indeed," Claire replied, rising to watch the parade from the porch railing. "How will they get all that heavy equipment down to the beach? They can't carry it down all those steps, can they?"

"They lower it with special winches or something. Judy explained it to me," Liza said without taking her eyes off the cars that were rolling up the circular drive.

The last time they had entertained this many guests at once, they'd held a wedding. Though the preparation had taken weeks and nearly driven Liza crazy, the event itself had only taken a few hours. But this group would be camped out for days, and there was no telling how long if the weather didn't break.

Well, you wanted the inn filled, Liza reminded herself. *Be careful what you wish for next time.* As the vehicles continued to arrive and empty out, Liza felt as if an army was invading.

Claire seemed to sense her trepidation and patted her hand. "We can do this, Liza. Never fear. Stay calm and carry on," she advised.

"I can do it with your help," Liza replied, casting an affectionate smile Claire's way.

"And I can do all things through God, who strengthens me," Claire answered quietly. "So together . . . we make quite an invincible team."

Though Liza was not as strong a believer as Claire, it was almost impossible to live on the island, immersed in the beauty of the sky and ocean and magnificent landscape, without humbly recognizing that there was something more at work in the universe. Something powerful and sacred. Liza felt touched by that power almost every day in this place. It was one of the many reasons she had chosen to live out here.

The sound of car doors slamming and people calling orders and instructions to one another snapped Liza into action. She spotted Judy walking toward the inn, along with two men who both looked like they were important players on this team.

Liza came down from the porch to greet them, and Judy quickly introduced her to Mike Herald, the film's producer, and Bradley

Scott, the director. Both men smiled politely and shook her hand, but Liza could tell they were engaged in a serious conversation and didn't have time for small talk. Especially with the innkeeper.

Liza didn't take it to heart. She was thankful for the business; she didn't need attention from the Hollywood moguls. Judy was nice enough, she thought, as she reviewed the room assignments and gave out keys to the crew members checking in.

"Will they really go down to the beach and shoot the film today?" Liza asked her.

"I don't know," Judy said quietly. "Mike and Bradley are trying to work that out."

She glanced over her shoulder at the two bigwigs, who now stood across the road, pacing back and forth in front of the steps to the beach.

"Where are Charlotte Miller and Nick Dempsey?" Liza asked, suddenly realizing that the mega stars were not among the crowd.

"Oh, they'll be here any minute now," Judy answered, putting her phone to her ear. She wore a black baseball cap with her long blond ponytail hanging out the back. Pale blue cursive writing across the peak of the cap read, *A Wandering Heart*, which was the name of the film. With her shiny black raincoat and wide belt, Judy looked very stylish for someone who was going to work on a wet beach all day.

Liza stared down at her own worn jeans, running shoes, and Cape Light sweatshirt, which had a big lobster printed on the back. With an amused shrug, she went back into the inn. Many of the crew members had already found the coffee station and were wandering about with cups of coffee or mugs of tea and Claire's fresh, fluffy blueberry scones.

"Is he here yet?" Liza turned at the urgent whisper.

Audrey stood by her side, wearing lipstick—for possibly the first, or maybe second time in her life—and an urgent, excited expression.

"Not yet. They should be here any minute. When did you get here? I didn't even see you come in."

"I came through the kitchen. I gave Claire the rest of your order. You can just call in tomorrow if you need a refill," Audrey added, gazing around at the milling crowd.

"Thanks. I might do that."

Mike and Bradley now stood on the porch, talking with Judy. Through the open doorway, Liza saw a long shiny black car cruise up to the inn.

Audrey gripped her arm, her fingers digging into Liza's skin. "He's here. He's in that car. I can't believe it." She headed for the door, and Liza followed her.

Liza didn't think it was a good idea to pounce on the stars as soon as they stuck a toe out of their limo. She looked down at her shabby outfit again. Why hadn't she changed her clothes after working this morning? In all the excitement, she hadn't thought about it.

Oh, well, she told herself. *This is an authentic New England look, that's for sure.*

While the movie executives rushed down the steps to meet the stars, Liza and Audrey hung back, watching.

The rear door of the car opened and Nick Dempsey came out first. Liza heard Audrey quietly gasp. "Oh, wow . . . I have to take a picture with my phone, Liza. Please?"

"Okay. But just one. Try to be subtle about it?"

Audrey had already slipped out the phone and clicked several shots.

"He's not as tall as he looks in the movies," Liza said.

Audrey laughed. "He's tall enough for me . . . Oh, look, there's Charlotte Miller. I need a picture of her, too."

Liza just shook her head. She watched Judy and the film producer, Mike, walk around the car to greet Charlotte while Bradley hung back, talking to Nick. A driver took several black duffel bags and rolling suitcases from the trunk of the car and then everyone headed back into the inn.

Liza suddenly felt frozen to the spot, though she knew she had to at least welcome them and introduce herself.

Audrey gave her a firm push. "Jump in there, Liza. Nothing to it. They're people just like you and me."

Liza turned and looked at her friend. Audrey hardly seemed to have that attitude a few minutes ago when she was snapping her souvenir photos.

Suddenly she had no choice. Judy stood at the top of the steps and smiled at her. "Liza, I'd like you to meet our stars, Nick Dempsey and Charlotte Miller. This is Liza Martin, our host," she added.

Liza extended her hand and forced a big smile, which she hoped was warm and welcoming, and not the expression of a deer caught in headlights.

She shook Nick Dempsey's hand first. "Welcome to the Inn at Angel Island. We're delighted to host your visit. If there's anything at all I can do to make your stay more comfortable, please let me know."

Nick Dempsey's smile was quick and practiced, his teeth incredibly white. He gave her hand a quick, strong shake. "Hello, Liza. Nice to meet you." He gazed around at the entrance to the inn. "Isn't this cozy? Wow, how did you ever find this place, Judy?" He began talking to the production associate as if Liza had suddenly disappeared.

Liza sensed that he would have been happier with a more modern, conventional hotel. But what could she do? He wasn't staying over, thank goodness. She and Claire would cater to him during his breaks. She hoped he wouldn't be too fussy.

She studied him more carefully. He was dressed in a denim jacket and jeans, with a black polo shirt underneath with the collar flipped up. Expensive sunglasses hung from a little rubber string around his neck. His clothes did not set him apart from mere mortals, yet he still looked like a celebrity somehow, practically glowing as he stood gazing around the foyer. His skin was very tan and smooth. His thick dark hair was combed back from his forehead, still wet from a shower.

In fact, he looked like he'd just woken up, Liza realized. "Would you like some coffee, Mr. Dempsey?" she said quickly.

"I'd absolutely love some. Lead me to it." His deep voice was very dramatic and echoed in the foyer, even in this small exchange. He was an actor 24/7, wasn't he?

"Audrey will get it for you." Liza turned to her friend, who hovered at her shoulder. "Would you get Mr. Dempsey some coffee?"

Audrey nodded quickly. She couldn't even speak. Her hands were actually trembling.

"That would be fantastic. A little skim milk. Half a pack of no-cal sweetener. And please, call me Nick."

Judy's assistant, Zach, came over and drew Nick into the front parlor. "Is Mike serious?" Liza heard Nick say to Zach. "We can't shoot outside in this fog. It will look like a slasher film."

So that's what was going on. The head honchos were debating about whether or not to work outside. The answer seemed obvious to her, but what did she know about making a movie?

Charlotte Miller's entrance drew her full attention. The star was finally coming inside, flanked by the producer, director, and Judy. The chauffeur followed with all the bags.

Charlotte was tall and willowy, even more so than she looked on screen. Her long golden-red hair was wound in a hasty bun with curly tendrils falling down perfectly around her beautiful face, which was bare of makeup. The term porcelain complexion didn't even come close to describing her smooth, fair skin. Her features were fine and delicate, her heart-shaped face nearly overwhelmed by her large blue-green eyes.

Like many other actresses, Charlotte Miller had begun her career as a model. *Hardly a surprise,* Liza thought. Her posture and even the way she walked was graceful, controlled, and assured. Liza could easily imagine her strolling down a designer's runway.

But on-screen, Charlotte didn't seem remote or plastic in the least. She was suddenly transformed into the down-home, girl-next-door, American sweetheart. At least, that's what they called her on this month's magazine covers.

Dressed down to start her workday, she wore faded but expensive-looking jeans and a slim-fitting black yoga jacket.

Liza walked over to introduce herself, feeling a bit less intimidated by this star for some reason. The director and producer were gone now, and Charlotte stood alone with Judy.

"I just wanted to welcome you to the Inn at Angel Island, Ms. Miller," Liza said, stepping forward. "If there's anything I can do to make your stay more comfortable, please let me know. We're really thrilled to have you visit with us."

Charlotte's smile was warm and genuine as she shook Liza's hand. "Thank you so much. This place is just beautiful. I'm so glad Judy found you."

"Me, too," Liza said sincerely, making them both laugh.

Bradley walked into the foyer and waved his hands. "Listen up everyone. We've just checked the beachfront, and Mike and I have decided it's too foggy to shoot. We're going to hang out here awhile and hope that in an hour or two, it clears."

There was a rumbling murmur from the crew, but Bradley ignored it. "You can all use the time to set up the equipment and settle into your rooms. Once the fog burns off, I want to be ready to go. No excuses."

Bradley stepped away to meet with Mike again. Liza heard a bit more murmuring while her guests put their coffee and tea aside and headed off in various directions.

Judy was called away by one of her coworkers, and Liza was suddenly left alone with Charlotte.

"May I show you to your room?" Liza asked.

"Lead the way. I'm right behind you." Charlotte took one of the many duffel bags piled nearby, and Liza took two others, one in each hand.

Charlotte paused and looked around. "I wonder what happened to Meredith. My assistant," she explained.

Before Liza could reply, a harried young woman with dark hair and glasses emerged from the parlor. She was carrying a big black binder.

"Sorry, Charlotte. I was trying to track down those scene changes for you. I put them in the script. You're ready to go." She handed Charlotte the binder and took the duffel bag.

"Thanks. At least I have a little time to go over them." She turned from Meredith to Liza. "How long do you think the fog will last?"

Liza was stumped. "I'm sorry, I really don't know. The forecast predicted showers on and off all day."

Charlotte sighed and then tucked the binder under her arm.

"Mike won't let us sit around here all day, that's for sure. But it sounds like I have a little time."

Liza was surprised at the movie star's tone. She sounded stressed. It even showed in her lovely features as they climbed the stairs.

Once they reached her room, Liza unlocked the door, holding it open for Charlotte to enter first. Charlotte just stood for a moment, glancing around at the canopied bed, the small wood writing desk and antique dresser, and the big bay window. Liza felt herself getting nervous when Charlotte didn't say anything. "I'm sure you're used to much more luxurious accommodations," Liza began.

Charlotte was standing at the window now, looking out at the ocean view—what she could see of it—veiled in the fog.

She quickly turned to face Liza. "This is beautiful. It's perfect. Really," she assured her. "It reminds me of my grandmother's house . . . except for the ocean view. I used to stay there a lot when I was growing up." She sat on the bed and smiled. "They're going to have a hard time getting me out on the set."

Meredith bustled in with more bags. "Do you want some ginger tea, Charlotte? Or mineral water?"

"Tea would be nice," she replied. "Thanks."

Meredith nodded, then turned to Liza. "Charlotte would like some ginger tea. That special brand she drinks? I'm sure Judy gave you the list."

"We have it covered." *Miraculously,* Liza wanted to add.

"You should find Claire, our cook, down in the kitchen. She'll make it for you. There are some fresh blueberry scones down there, too."

"Charlotte doesn't eat sweets," Meredith said, practically laughing at the suggestion.

"Fresh scones? I'll try one of those," Charlotte said.

Liza hoped Claire had set at least one aside.

"All right, I'll be right back." Meredith quickly headed out of the room.

"If there's anything else you need, please let me know," Liza said to Charlotte. "We want to make your stay as comfortable as possible."

"I will, Liza, thank you. But I'll try not to bother you too much. I'm sure you must feel as if this place was just invaded by aliens."

Liza had to laugh at the apt comparison but quickly denied it. "Not at all. It's all very exciting. Part of me still can't believe it's happening."

Charlotte smiled knowingly. "That's the movie business. It feels unreal somehow. I still pinch myself once in a while," she confided as she set the black binder on the desk.

Liza could see that she was eager to get to work and quickly left the room. She stood in the hallway a moment, thinking about the day's surprises.

So far, Charlotte Miller seemed the most genuine and down-to-earth person in the group. Really sweet and unspoiled. Was that just an act? *She'll be here long enough for me to find out,* Liza reflected. *This was going to be one unforgettable week at the inn. If only I had time to pull out the video camera, I could make my own movie about it.*

Chapter Three

THE wide canopied bed, with its flowery cover and inviting mound of pillows, was lovely but too tempting. Charlotte knew if she stretched out there to study her lines, she would be fast asleep in no time. She'd hardly slept at all the night before, memorizing the script and working on her character's accent.

She settled instead at the small writing desk and chair near a large bay window that framed a view of the beach across the road. The drifts of foggy clouds obscured the view but couldn't hide it completely. The fog was beautiful in its own way, she thought, smoky and mysterious. Behind the gray mist, she could still make out the rugged outline of the cliffs above the beach and the shifting dark blue sea.

Charlotte loved the ocean. Her house on the beach in Malibu was her special retreat. There, the sight of the Pacific calmed her and helped her feel in touch with something vast and greater than herself. It helped her put things in perspective.

Yes, this role was going to be a challenge for her. Bradley didn't really like her. She hadn't been his first choice for the role, though he hid it well. He wasn't her first choice for a director either, but she was determined to be professional. *All I have to do is knock him off his feet with an amazing performance and he'll like me fine,* she decided.

At least the film's location was beautiful. She'd loved the little town of Cape Light as soon as her car had pulled down Main Street. And this island was fascinating. She hoped there would be some downtime to explore it. She was happiest when she was near the ocean and beach. She could never get enough of it.

She sometimes joked that she had a landlocked childhood and was ocean deprived. But it was true. She had grown up in Ohio, and her family rarely took vacations. The closest she had ever been to a beach was the sand trucked in to the lakefronts. When she ran away to California, the first thing she did when she got off the bus was to go straight to a beach. Charlotte would never forget the first time she saw the ocean. She had picked up as many seashells as she could carry home in her knapsack. She still kept them in a jar by her bedside, a reminder of her first sight and scent of the blue Pacific. Sometimes she still couldn't believe she had wound up with a house in Malibu. She had always wanted to live with the ocean in sight, and now she did.

Her cell phone rang and she pulled it out to check the caller ID, hoping that she wasn't being summoned down to work already. It was her sister Lily and she quickly answered. "Hey, Lily. What's up?"

"Not too much. I just wanted to say hi. How's the movie going?"

"It's going. Slowly but surely. I'm on an island in New England. We're shooting outside today, on a beach. We're just waiting for some fog to clear. I wish you could see it here, Lily. It's a really beautiful place. Tell you what, I'll bring you back here sometime."

"Maybe . . ." Lily didn't seem to believe her promise. *Probably because I'm hardly ever able to keep them,* Charlotte thought with a pang.

Lily was so young, only sixteen. *She has no idea of what it's like for me. She'll get it someday. Someday we'll have more time together, too.*

"So how is everyone at home, Lil? How's Mom?" Charlotte tried to keep her tone even and natural, but Lily was smart. She knew how Charlotte worried.

"She's doing fine, keeping up with her meetings. When are you coming home for a visit? You said you would come this summer, Charlie. It's already August. I have to go back to school soon. I just got my new schedule."

"You did? Wow . . . I didn't realize." The summer was flying by. Charlotte had been meaning to go home for a visit since May. It would have to wait now until this film was done. But she didn't want to make any more promises she couldn't keep. She quickly changed the subject. "I can't believe you're a junior already."

"I know. It's a big year for me."

"All you have to do is study hard. You remember our plan, right?"

Lily was off-the-charts smart. Charlotte wasn't sure where all those brains had come from in their family, but the girl could be anything she wanted if she put her mind to it.

Their mother didn't really care where Lily went to school. She thought any building that had the word college on the sign would be good enough. But Lily deserved the very best, a place where her intelligence and talents could flourish. Charlotte could afford to send Lily to any school, even Harvard, without sweating scholarships or student loans. She wanted Lily to choose a school in California, like Stanford or Berkeley, so they could be closer. That was the plan. She hoped Lily would keep up her end of the bargain.

"Don't worry. That's all I'm thinking about. Graduating and getting out of this place."

"I know it's hard, honey. You're growing up. You want to be out on your own. The time will go quickly, believe me."

"Charlie, you always say that," Lily groaned.

"I know I do, but it's true," Charlotte promised.

It was true, but it still pained Charlotte to hear her sister talk that way. She wasn't sure if Lily was desperate to escape from high school and the small town, or if it was their family that Lily needed to escape from. Charlotte had felt the same way at that age. She couldn't wait to get out of that house. She had barely waited to graduate high school before she bolted for the West Coast, never mind college plans. But Charlotte had been lucky, blessed. She knew now that she'd been too young to be on her own in a strange city. It could have turned out very badly.

"As soon as I'm done with this film, I'll take the first flight out to Ohio, and we'll have a nice, long visit," she told her sister.

"Okay, that's cool. I hope it goes well for you, Charlie. I'm sure you'll be great."

"Thanks, honey. I'll do my best."

They said good-bye, and Charlotte put down her phone. She missed her little sister and loved talking to her. But their conversations always left her with a bittersweet feeling. Not exactly homesickness. Once she had stepped out that door, she never had the desire to go back. But she did feel lonely. Which was ironic, since she was surrounded by so many people so much of the time; she hardly had a moment's privacy. But even with everyone buzzing around her, she felt lonely for people like her sister, who really knew her, who knew the real Charlotte, not Charlotte Miller, the picture on the magazine cover, or the flickering shadow on a movie screen.

Charlotte let out a long breath. She couldn't figure it all out now. She had work to do and flipped open the script to the pages she'd marked with orange stickies. Meredith had brought the tea and scone just after the innkeeper left. Her assistant had wanted to stay and help, but Charlotte needed to be alone.

She stared down at the script and tried to focus. Bradley was not only hard to please but asked for rewrites every five minutes. The dialogue was always changing. Charlotte hated to flub her lines or miss her marks. She arrived on the set totally prepared and ready to work. At least she knew that Nick Dempsey had the same approach. He seemed like a cutup and a bit of an airhead at first, but Nick was a total pro and a great ally, especially when Bradley got in a mood.

There was definitely more going on behind the scenes on a movie set than she'd ever imagined in acting school. But even if she knew then what she knew now, she would never trade her life with anyone. She knew she was lucky to be where she was. The work was hard but she knew that people back home worked harder and never got the attention and comforts that her work brought her. But sometimes if Bradley was in one of his impossible-to-please moods, he could make her feel so small and pathetic. And it seemed the more he pushed her and asked for new takes, the more she tightened up. She got too self-conscious trying to please him. Which was the very antithesis of a good zone for acting.

Charlotte hoped the fog would clear soon. She was eager to get to work today. She was a good film actress, even if Bradley didn't agree. And she could be even better if she could take on more complex roles. She desperately wanted to break out of romantic comedies, but those were the roles coming her way and she couldn't risk being picky. That's what her agent warned. She was hot and sought after now, but the clock was ticking, and the next young new actress would soon arrive on the scene, and Charlotte's ride on the grand Ferris wheel of fame could end all too soon.

Everyone at home depended on her. Without the checks she sent, they would be back to square one—living in a trailer park, her younger sisters and brother with no chance to go to college or do anything worthwhile with their lives.

She knew her mother sometimes squandered the money, never realizing it might not last forever. Still, Charlotte had given them a new place to live and a real chance at a brighter future. Maybe she hadn't won any big awards yet, but that recognition would come. She was sure of it. She just had to keep at it and keep studying her craft.

Charlotte took a sip of tea and stared out at the sea. The fog had begun to melt away and the sky was brightening. It wouldn't be long now. Someone would be up to get her any minute. She looked over the script pages for the scene they would shoot next on the beach, and placed herself in the head and heart of her character, Alexa. It was almost like meditating, but not quite. It was a matter of opening herself to a well deep within, where the power and authenticity of a performance came from. Some actors were so adept at "getting there," their performances left her in awe. But she was getting there, too, and starting to live in Alexa's skin. Sometime soon, even Bradley would have to notice, she thought with a grin.

A short time later, she heard a sharp knock on the door. "Charlotte? It's Meredith. They want you in makeup. We're going out soon."

"Okay, I'll be right down." Charlotte grabbed the script and a few other essentials, ready to start her workday.

WHEN Judy Kramer told everyone to go down to the beach, Liza thought it looked like an army, breaking camp and marching on.

The movie crew swept out as fast as they had swept in, leaving coffee cups, tea mugs, water bottles, and drifts of scone crumbs in their wake. If this was a mere coffee break, what was serving a real meal going to be like?

Liza and Claire were back in the kitchen, trying to sort out the mess when Nick walked in. "Sorry to interrupt you. Is the kitchen off limits to guests?"

"Not at all," Liza replied. As if it would ever be off limits to Nick Dempsey! Was he teasing her? she wondered.

"Can I get something for you?"

"You can tell me the secret to those scones. I've already eaten two and I'd have two more . . . but we actors have to watch our weight."

"It's one of Claire's recipes," Liza told him. She glanced over at Claire, who stood at the sink, rinsing dishes.

Claire gave Nick one of her serene smiles. "It's a fairly simple recipe," was all she said.

Liza noticed that Claire did not offer to give him the recipe. This wasn't really a surprise. Claire was very protective of her recipes, even secretive about them.

"Really? I thought you must have brought them in from a special bakery." Nick Dempsey stared at her, as if testing the truth of her claim.

"They were baked right in this kitchen, Mr. Dempsey. We don't buy anything in a bakery."

"That's cool. I like to cook, too. And bake. In my spare time. It's one of my hobbies. Have you seen my website?"

"I'm not a computer person," Claire replied. Which Liza thought might be the understatement of the year. She wasn't sure Claire had ever looked at a computer screen.

"Oh, you ought to visit it. You, too, Liza. I'd like to open a restaurant, maybe a whole chain."

"That would be . . . impressive," Claire said evenly. *If it ever actually happened,* Liza knew she meant.

Nick merely smiled and puffed out his chest a bit, oblivious to Claire's meaning. "Well, thanks for the recipe, when you get a chance. You can e-mail it to me . . . or well, since you don't have a computer, just give a copy to Jason, my assistant. I'm sure you'll see him around."

Claire looked as if she was about to answer—to tell him she didn't give out recipes. But Nick didn't wait for a reply. He smiled again and disappeared out the kitchen door.

Once he was gone Liza said, "Looks like you've won another fan, Claire. Maybe *you* should have a website."

"Oh, that's not my style, Liza. You know that. Besides, there would be nothing to put on it. You know that I rarely give out my recipes."

Liza did know. She just wondered if the famous heartthrob Nick Dempsey would prove an exception to that rule.

CHARLOTTE walked down the long flight of stairs to the beach, following Nick and Brad. Brad wanted to speak to them about the scene before the first take. Charlotte took a few deep, calming breaths. She had her own ideas for the scene and didn't want to argue with Bradley. She tried not to bite her lower lip, which was her bad habit. She didn't want to ruin her makeup. It took a long time to get that natural look for the camera. Even her hair, which was naturally curly in humid weather, had been treated with salt spray and a blower to create loose, wind-tossed waves.

That step would prove futile. She could already feel her hair curling more tightly as she walked down the steps. Wisps of fog still clung to the shoreline, and piles of dark clouds had settled on the wide horizon. The fog was not going to clear, after all. If anything, the weather was getting worse.

Down on the beach, Bradley trotted over to the camera crew. She heard them murmuring, strategizing the camera work for the scene. Bradley came over to the actors next.

"Nick and Charlotte, sorry for those last-minute changes in the script. But I feel the dialogue is stronger now. Did you guys get a chance to look it over?" The two actors nodded quickly. "Any questions?"

"I'm ready to go. How about you, Charlotte?" Nick asked her.

"I'm good," Charlotte replied with a curt nod.

"Great. So, you'll start off there, in front of the rocks. We'll take a wide pan of you walking together down the shoreline. Then the camera will move in as you begin to argue. By the time you reach those big rocks, where Jerry is standing with the reflector, it should really be heating up. You stop and face each other. That's where you'll throw the ring," Brad said to Nick. "The water is very shallow there. So you go right in, Charlotte. It won't even be up to your ankles."

It would definitely be over her ankles, and probably freezing, but Charlotte nodded stoically. This was her job. She was too well paid to refuse to jump around in ice-cold water.

"This is the turning point of the film," Bradley went on. "Alexa has just found out that Tom has betrayed her. Everything that happens in the story comes back to this scene, this single conversation in their life together." He paused and looked at them. "Are you ready?"

Charlotte quickly nodded again, trying not to shiver. The wind off the ocean had kicked up, blowing a cold mist. She wore only a yellow sundress and a thin white wrap.

A gust of wind blew down one of the light reflectors, and a flock of technicians rushed to fix it. "Oh, this is going well," someone muttered.

Bradley wasn't fazed. "I know it's a little raw out here," he said, "but believe me, it will be worth it. You can't pay for weather like this. The way the clouds are gathering . . . it's a perfect metaphor for the end of this relationship."

Charlotte had to agree with that. Of course, Bradley wasn't the one in the skimpy sundress, she noticed. He wore a thick fleece pull-over, zipped up to his chin. He then retreated to his position behind the main camera.

Nick and Charlotte found their marks. "Are you okay? You look a little cold," Nick said quietly.

"I'm okay. But thanks." Charlotte shot him a quick smile, then went inward to focus on her character. She didn't take to Nick when she first met him. He seemed shallow and vain. But she soon realized that was just a pose. Underneath, he was a sweet, caring guy. A real family man, too.

"Alexa and Tom, start walking," Bradley said. The actors started down the beach, exchanging their dialogue as the waves swept in and out. The water and sand rushing at her feet was a little distracting, but Charlotte tried to work it all into her performance as her acting coach had taught her.

A camera and microphone on a special dolly that tracked through the sand followed on one side, and two handheld cameras were filming as well.

The argument between Alexa and Tom peaked at the big rocks, just as Bradley had directed. Nick's character pulled off his wedding ring and screamed at Charlotte's character.

"You want this? Here it is. Catch, Alexa. If you can find it, you can keep it." Nick angrily threw the ring into the ocean, right at Charlotte's feet.

She was standing knee-deep in water by now, the bottom of her dress drenched and dragging, her wrap lost somewhere in a passing wave.

"Tom, no . . . please . . . Why did you do that?" She delivered her lines as she knelt in the water, grabbing at the ring. Which, of course, was nowhere to be seen. Just as Charlotte had reached the end of her dialogue and action, a large wave rushed in and knocked her over.

"Cut! Cut!" Bradley called out.

Two lifeguards, who were standing by for just such an emergency, rushed in to help her.

Nick was there first, pulling her up from the water with both hands. It wasn't very deep, but her entire dress was drenched.

"Are you okay? Maybe we should tell him the water is too rough today for this scene. Don't worry, I'll back you up."

The offer was tempting. But the last thing Charlotte wanted was to be branded a prima donna, calling off the production schedule and costing everyone money because she got splashed by a wave or two.

"I'm fine, honest. Let's just keep going. I think we've almost got it."

As Charlotte and Nick reached the dry sand again, Meredith rushed up with a huge towel and wrapped it around Charlotte's shoulders.

Bradley was there in a heartbeat, too, full of concern. "Are you all right, Charlotte? That last wave really knocked you for a loop. I hope you're okay," he said solicitously.

"I'm fine, Brad. I just need to dry off a little."

"What a trouper." Brad patted her arm. "That wasn't bad. For a first take. Nick, I like what you're doing with Tom. You've got that pent-up thing going. There's real, understated intensity, like a bomb about to blow."

Nick seemed quietly pleased with the praise but was not one to gloat, Charlotte knew.

She shivered as Bradley turned to her. She could just tell from his tight smile that she was not going to get the same grade as her classmate.

"Charlotte, I love what you're doing with Alexa. We're feeling her shock and sadness. But I think you need to go deeper. Alexa is crying . . . but her real pain, her deep pain and shock at losing this marriage . . . I'm sorry, but it's not coming through to me. Can you play it some other way? With less anger at Tom, maybe? More shock and disbelief?"

Charlotte considered his suggestion. It wasn't the way she saw her character reacting. But she decided not to argue. "Sure, I'll try that way on the next take. No problem."

"That's all I ask. You're a trouper. I know that." He patted her shoulder amicably. "Sorry you're getting all wet. But there are plenty of fluffy towels up at the inn. If we all focus, we'll be back up there for lunch in no time."

Bradley strolled off to talk to the camera technicians again, and Charlotte was surrounded by a swarm of makeup and wardrobe staff, who whisked her off to a small tent. She quickly changed into an identical but dry yellow sundress and white shawl.

She sat in a canvas folding chair with her script book open in her lap, trying to rework her interpretation of the scene into what Bradley seemed to want.

Many sets of hands worked on her simultaneously, repairing her makeup and hair. Meredith handed her a cup of hot tea. "Thanks, pal. I needed that. Did you bring an electric kettle down here or something?"

The movie truck carried big generators so anything was possible.

"I called up to the inn and one of the ladies up there—Liza, I think—brought down a thermos for you."

"That was sweet. I'll have to thank her."

Warmed and fortified, Charlotte went back out to the beach. She'd grabbed a big sweatshirt in the tent and planned to keep it wrapped around her shoulders until the absolute last possible moment. The wind was even stronger now, and whitecaps tumbled one after the other into the shoreline. The wind had whipped up the sea and the tide was coming in.

A few minutes later, the second take began rolling. Charlotte pushed herself to give Bradley what he asked for—showing what her character was experiencing through her tone of voice, her physical gestures, her expressions and reactions.

Acting wasn't a costume and words on a page, her coach always told her. It was behavior. The transformation into another person from the inside out. Maybe she hadn't done a good enough job of that on the first take. Charlotte was determined to get it right this time.

But they hadn't even reached the moment when Nick threw the ring into the water before Bradley stopped them, yelling over the pounding waves. "Cut . . . Cut . . . That's fine, folks. Let's stop right there."

Once again the crew rushed in with towels and sweatshirts for Nick and Charlotte. They weren't nearly as wet this time, but Charlotte felt even more frustrated. It was not unusual to take several takes before a director was happy with a scene. But Bradley wasn't even letting them get warmed up.

Of course, it was Charlotte's performance he honed in on when he came to talk to them.

"Charlotte, we're just not going in the right direction here. Alexa is desperate. Shocked. Heartbroken. I'm sorry, but I'm not seeing you build toward that. When Nick throws that ring, you have to be there emotionally, one hundred and ten percent."

Charlotte thought she was there. If he would just let her play her part and stop talking, maybe she could show him how she interpreted this woman's feelings.

Charlotte sighed and pulled the big towel tighter around her shoulders. "I was trying for something a little more understated, Brad. This is how I interpret Alexa. She holds a lot inside."

He stared at her. "I'm sorry, I disagree. I think she's a woman of strong emotions. I think she puts it all out there. She acts out and regrets it later. That's why he's leaving her. See?" When Charlotte didn't answer immediately, he said, "Trust me on this, Charlotte. Please."

Charlotte took a deep breath. Now the entire crew was listening in as they milled about, acting preoccupied. She felt the pressure was all on her. If she started a big debate with him about Alexa or even showed her frustration, she would be labeled temperamental, unprofessional. She would be to blame for holding things up and the scene stalling out today. Never mind that it looked like a hurricane was moving in. She had to negotiate this impasse, or the whole crew would be annoyed with her.

"Maybe Charlotte needs a break," Nick said suddenly. "To think things through."

"Yes, I think a walk would do me good. I need a few minutes alone to get focused and centered again," Charlotte said quickly. "So I can process your comments, Brad."

"Sure, good idea." Brad nodded, looking grateful for her cooperative attitude.

Charlotte spared him a small smile and then caught Nick's eye. "Thanks, pal," she wanted to say.

She would thank him later, she thought as she marched down the shoreline, trying to put as much distance as she could between the set and herself. Nick was smart. She did need to cool off before she said or did something rash. Bradley could be difficult, but she'd dealt with hard-to-please directors before. She would win him over eventually, she thought. Or just bulldoze her way through. What choice did she have? She had to finish this film one way or the other.

She felt everyone watching her, their unified gaze boring into her back. She glanced over her shoulder, wondering if anyone was following a few paces behind. Like a Secret Service agent guarding the president. Thankfully, she was alone.

She quickly faced forward, the pounding surf quickly blocking the voices from the set. When she looked back again a few minutes later, she had turned a curve in the beach and couldn't even see them.

The beach was beautiful, even in the foggy weather. The sand near the water's edge was pounded smooth and flat, silky beneath her bare feet. The waves broke close to the shore, crashing with a thunderous roar, the cool greenish-blue water and foam rushing all around her, then just as swiftly, washing back.

Small white and gray birds on thin, stalky legs hopped about the damp sand, pecking at bits of seaweed and tasty bits of shellfish. Charlotte watched them, feeling herself calm down as she focused on their graceful movements and the sound and rhythm of the rushing surf.

She kept walking and walking. The shoreline gently curved

around a high cliff and a short distance ahead, a jetty of rough black and gray rocks stretched out into the waves. The rocks were flat on top, piled close together, their sides worn smooth by the pounding water.

She stepped up on one rock and then another, looking for a flat spot to sit. It was a great comfort and luxury to be this close to the waves. She felt the mere sight and scent of the ocean renewing her flagging spirit.

I'm going to get this dress wet again, Charlotte realized, *and I'll probably get a green slime stain on the back if I sit down. Oh, bother. I'll just stand here awhile,* she decided.

I just have to do the scene the way Bradley wants me to, she told herself. *Alexa ranting and wailing, even though I don't believe she'd do any of that. No point arguing with him. He's totally inflexible and I'll just come off as the spoiled diva. If I can just get this scene down to suit him, maybe he'll relax and lay off a bit.*

Charlotte stepped from rock to rock, considering the director's instructions and what she would do next in front of the camera. Lost in her thoughts, she looked up to find she had nearly reached the end of the jetty. It suddenly occurred to her that it wasn't safe out here. The waves struck with a booming sound, and the spray rose in plumes around her.

She stepped back carefully, feeling slippery green moss under her bare feet. *I went out too far. That was dumb. I'll have to be careful going back. Step by step, I can make it,* she coached herself.

She had made it halfway back, feeling almost home free, when a huge wave rose up beside her, curling over her head and crashing down on the rock where she stood. Charlotte would have screamed, but instead she stood mesmerized, watching the rushing water.

Seconds later, it knocked her off her feet and washed her into the sea. She had no chance to even take a breath. Her body was pulled under the water and churned like a pile of laundry in a washing machine.

The rocky jetty stood empty, foam ebbing back into the sea.

Chapter Four

SUBMERGED in the icy cold water, Charlotte didn't know which way was up. Holding her breath was instinctive. So was trying to swim back to the surface.

She fanned her arms and legs and felt a rock's jagged edge with her foot and quickly pushed off in another direction. She wasn't sure how she had escaped being dashed against the rocks, or how her bones had not been snapped like twigs by the force of the water.

She was a strong swimmer, but this was something altogether different. She couldn't hold her breath another second and felt a white-hot pounding in her head and deep in her chest. She felt desperate to open her mouth and gasp for air, as if she were being smothered. But she knew it would be fatal.

Was she going to drown? Was that what was happening to her? Was this really the way her life was going to end?

Oh, God . . . please help me. I don't want to die. Please . . .

Charlotte had not been to church in years, though she had gone as a child with her grandmother and still prayed from time to time. She wasn't sure where the prayer had come from, erupting from her desperate soul.

She wasn't sure if she'd actually heard an answer either. Or if it was just the kind of hallucination a person might have when they're dying.

Be strong, Charlotte. You are loved.

Had she really heard a voice, or was she getting hysterical? Hallucinating due to a lack of oxygen?

Was that the voice you heard at the very end? she wondered.

A current swept her up, tossing her around like a soggy rag doll. She tried but she couldn't fight it. She finally gave in, surrendering to its force. With all her strength she held her breath one more second. She knew when she let it go, it would all be over.

Another surge of water lifted her up, flinging her body like a leaf. Miraculously, her head broke through the surface. She tilted her head back, gasping for air and trying to tread water.

When she was finally able to get her bearings, she saw that she had been pulled far from the jetty. She was relieved that she wouldn't be dashed on the rocks, but she was so far from the shore now and could feel a strong current carrying her even farther out to sea.

The current was moving swiftly, parallel to the shoreline. She saw the crew on the beach, tiny specks in the distance. She tried to wave to them, but she was so far out and so tired, the simple gesture was impossible. And hopeless, she realized.

Stop panicking, she told herself. *You can survive this. What are you supposed to do if you're caught in a current?* She tried to remember her swim classes from childhood. All she could remember was that she needed to float, to save her strength. *Sooner or later, the current will weaken and you can swim to shore.*

If I don't get exhausted and drown first, she thought. *If a storm doesn't start up and a huge wave doesn't push me under again.*

Get a grip, Charlotte. Did you come this far in your life to just give up at a moment like this? What will happen to your family if you die now? Who will take care of them? What will happen to Lily? Think how much she'll miss you.

Thoughts of home and her family gave her a second wind. She would get through this. She'd get back to shore somehow or someone would see her. By now, she would be missed on the set. They would come looking for her and realize what had happened.

Charlotte tried to comfort and encourage herself. "Be strong, Charlotte. You are loved," she told herself, repeating the words she had heard in her head.

THE crew was due to return to the inn for lunch at one, but in the meantime, Judy had called, asking for hot coffee and tea down on the beach. Liza and Claire prepared two large percolators and a tray of donuts and more scones, and loaded it all in the back of Claire's truck, so they could serve it tailgate fashion. Then they drove the short distance across the road and parked at the top of the stairway that led to the beach.

Liza tried Judy Kramer's phone but didn't get an answer. "I'll go down and let them know we're here," she told Claire.

She started down the zigzagging flight of steps. The crew was nearby. She could see they weren't filming. The rolling camera apparatus was empty and the stars were not around. Everyone looked in a bit of panic. But that seemed to be their usual mode, Liza thought.

She saw Judy with her boss, Mike, and walked over. "I sent Zach down there to look for her," Judy was saying. "He walked at least a mile, to a jetty. He couldn't find her anywhere."

"She couldn't have just disappeared," Mike insisted.

"Maybe she's hiding somewhere. Maybe she's upset because I asked her to rethink the scene," Liza heard Brad say.

Nick stood by him, a towel slung around his neck. "Charlotte's not like that, Brad. I'm really worried. What if she walked out on that jetty and fell in the water?"

Liza felt her breath catch in her throat. They were talking about Charlotte. She was lost. Liza hung back, feeling this wasn't the time to interrupt about coffee and tea.

One of the cameramen was standing on a platform and scanning the horizon with a high-powered lens. "I see her," he called out excitedly. "She's out there, in the water. She must have been carried out by a wave."

Mike gasped. "Dear God. Get out there, what are you waiting for?" he screamed at the two lifeguards, but they had already grabbed their skiffs and raced into the pounding surf. They launched the skiffs and slipped onboard just past the breakers, then turned on a small outboard motor and plowed toward Charlotte. But the sea was rough and it was slow going for the small rescue boats.

Liza ran over to Judy. "Have you dialed 911? There's a harbor patrol that will come with a boat to rescue her." *If they can get to her in time.*

"Good idea. I'll do that." Judy frantically hit the keys on her phone. Nick shed his shoes and shirt, preparing to swim out to Charlotte. Brad grabbed his arm. "Don't be crazy, man. This isn't an action film. Who's going to rescue you?"

"We can't let her drown," Nick shot back.

"Don't worry, we'll get her," Mike insisted, his eyes fixed on the lifeguards. "We have to."

Standing nearby, Judy finished her call to the emergency number and was practically crying. "Poor Charlotte. Oh, God. I hope she can hang on long enough for someone to get to her."

Liza touched her arm, not knowing what to say. She couldn't see Charlotte out there at all.

"Look, a boat!" called out the cameraman who was holding the telescopic lens. "It looks like it's moving in her direction."

Everyone, including Liza, turned to look out at the sea again. She did see a boat out there suddenly. A fishing boat that was familiar to her, owned by a friend of Daniel's—Colin Doyle.

Did he see Charlotte? That was the question. Though it looked like he must be close to her from this point of view, out on a choppy sea Charlotte could easily be missed by a cruising boat.

Dear God, Liza prayed, *please let Colin or someone on that boat save Charlotte. Please let Charlotte survive out there.*

CHARLOTTE was so tired. She wanted desperately to float for just a few minutes of rest, but the sea was too rough. Every time she tilted her head back and tried to let her limbs go limp, her head went under and she got another lungful of salt water. She felt so weary from treading, she didn't think she could keep her head above the surface another minute.

She saw a small lifeguard's skiff far off in the distance, trying to make its way toward her. The sight gave her hope and a surge of energy. But all too soon she sensed that the current was carrying her along faster than the little boat could travel. She didn't see how it could ever catch up to her in time.

Suddenly she heard the loud sound of a big engine and turned to see a large boat, passing nearby. It took every once of energy she had left, but she managed to lift one arm from the water to wave and call out: "Help! Down here! Help me, please!"

The boat engine was so loud, she wondered if anyone heard her. She couldn't see anyone out on the deck. The boat kept going without changing course and Charlotte's heart sank.

That was it. Her only chance to be saved. Who else would come in time?

She started to cry, though it seemed insanely redundant to cry while you were in the middle of the ocean about to die. Thinking about this, she actually started to laugh at herself. *I must be hysterical,* she realized.

The sound of the boat's engine cut into her rambling thoughts, and she realized that the big boat had been turning in a wide arc, coming around to help her.

With an unexpected burst of energy, she paddled madly, trying to meet it. The boat stopped a few yards away, the engine quietly rumbling. A man appeared on the bow. He tossed a rope ladder over the side of the boat and then a line with a cork life preserver.

"Grab on to this and I'll pull you over to the ladder."

Charlotte managed to grab the lifeline. She tried to kick her legs as the man on the boat tugged the other end. She felt herself trembling when she finally managed to reach the rope ladder. She grabbed on to a rung and tried to pull herself up, but her muscles had no more strength left.

"I'm sorry, I can't do this," she cried as she slipped back into the water and flailed for the life preserver.

He didn't say a word. He just dove off the boat.

A moment later, his head popped up beside her. "I should have realized. I'll get you up. Just hook your arms around my shoulder."

Charlotte nodded, too exhausted to speak. Her arms felt like rubber, but she got them around him, and he wound one arm around her body and used the other arm and his strong legs to leverage up the rope ladder, carrying them both up the side of the boat as if it were a short flight of steps on dry land.

Some foggy part of Charlotte's brain registered how strong he was and how safe she suddenly felt. She had been saved. She wasn't going to die. She felt overwhelmed and thought she might start crying again.

Her body went completely slack with relief and exhaustion as he pushed her over the edge of the boat. She flopped onto the deck like a big fish, her hair a mess of tangles in front of her face as she coughed up seawater.

Her sweatshirt had floated off at some point in the ordeal and her dress clung to her body, her skin covered in goose bumps. She felt an uncontrollable shiver. Even her teeth chattered out loud.

Her rescuer jumped over the edge of the bow and knelt down quickly to help her. "Are you all right? Can you breathe?"

Charlotte nodded but couldn't speak. He wrapped a heavy gray blanket around her. It smelled moldy, but she felt warmer and snuggled into the folds.

"You must be in shock. You're shivering."

She finally lifted her head and looked at him. He was about her age, tall and slim with broad shoulders. He had dirty blond hair and a scruffy, unshaven look. His eyes were deep blue, the piercing color of the ocean on a sunny day.

She tried to answer him, but her stomach lurched and she ended up vomiting. She was so mortified, she wished she could just disappear.

He didn't flinch or seem repulsed. "You swallowed a lot of water. About half the ocean, I'd say. Feel any better?"

"A little . . . I'm sorry about that," she mumbled, turning her head away.

"No problem. Better to get it all up now."

She was still embarrassed and shaken to the core. "I-I'm probably in shock," she stammered. "I feel so . . . disoriented. As if this is all happening in a dream. Or I'm just acting in a movie . . ."

He gently took hold of her shoulders and looked into her eyes. "Can you stand? I'll get you belowdecks. It's much warmer down there."

Charlotte's legs felt weak, almost like liquid. She wasn't sure she could make it, but the word "warmer" was a lure. With the stranger's arm around her waist, supporting her, she came to her feet and stumbled the few steps across the deck and down a short flight of stairs.

The boat rocked from side to side and the smell of gas from the motor made Charlotte feel sick again, but she fought the urge, distracting herself by looking around the cabin.

The cabin space was close and rough. There was a small metal sink and counter area tucked near the steps, a wooden bunk on one side, and two small bench seats on the other. Charlotte was seated on one. At least she was out of the wind and rain and a little drier. That was all she cared about now.

"I'm going to take you to the dock. It's a short ride," her rescuer said. "I'm just curious. How did you fall in the water? Were you on a boat?"

"I was walking on a jetty, on the beach below the inn. It was so stupid of me, really. I slipped on a rock and fell in."

He looked amazed at her reply. "I know those rocks. You're lucky you didn't crack your head open."

"I guess I am." It was, she thought, just one of the lucky breaks she'd had that day.

She'd come so close to losing her life and the realization was stunning. Life was so fragile. It could be taken away in an instant, without any warning at all. Charlotte knew she took her life for granted, like most people, feeling as if she would live forever. But that just wasn't true. She closed her eyes and thanked God again for sparing her.

Life was so strange. So mysterious. What had led her to this island, to come so close to death today, only to feel the hand of fate pluck her up again?

Was there some meaning—some lesson she should learn from all this?

"Are you all right?" he asked quietly.

She opened her eyes to find him staring at her. "I'm okay, thanks. Just tired."

"You must be beat. You had the fight of your life out there. Would you like some tea? I think I have a bag or two around here somewhere." He rummaged through a drawer near the sink and pulled out a tea bag.

"That would be great. If it isn't too much trouble."

He put a pot of water on a burner and lit it with a match. "It's just a camp stove. But it does the job."

She smelled the Sterno and it reminded her of camping with her family, before her father died. They'd been too poor to take big vacations, but she hadn't realized that at the time. She thought camping was the best vacation and couldn't wait for the trip every summer.

The little boat cabin reminded her of the inside of a tent, rustic but cozy.

"So what are you doing around here? Are you a guest at the inn?"

"Not exactly. I'm in a movie. We're filming some scenes on the island this week."

"A real movie or a commercial? Are you a model?"

"I was for a short time . . . Now I'm an actress, Charlotte Miller." She paused, trying to gauge his reaction. But his back was turned as he fixed the tea and she couldn't see his expression. When he finally turned, he looked a bit surprised but didn't seem exactly overwhelmed.

"Sure. I've heard of you." He glanced at her over his shoulder. "How do you like your tea? I don't have milk or lemon but I have a packet of sugar around here somewhere."

"Plain is fine," she said. When he handed her the mug, she thought she noticed a spark of humor in his blue eyes. Was he putting her on? Did he really not recognize her or was that an act?

Lately, Charlotte enjoyed it when people didn't recognize her and she could walk around with some anonymity. But for some reason, she wanted this man to know who she was. She wanted him to be impressed. Just a little.

She held the mug in both hands and blew on the tea. Just holding the cup warmed her.

"Wow, Charlotte Miller . . ." He pulled a yellow slicker off a hook over the bunk and shook his head. "The guys on the dock will never believe me. I might get the prize for biggest catch of the summer. You even top the fifty-pound lobster Crawley brought in last August."

Charlotte felt weak and tired, actually dizzy. But she had to smile at the comparison.

"Gee, thanks. No one's ever compared me to a big crustacean before."

"Yeah, well . . . I think you beat the crustacean. But there will be some debate, I'm sure."

"Are you a fisherman?" She blew on her tea and glanced over at him.

"Yes, ma'am, I am. It's hard work. But it has its moments. You never know what's going to swim into your net, that's for sure."

He was teasing her again. Charlotte had to smile but wasn't up to any clever banter. She was so tired, she could hardly keep her eyes open.

He took a towel from another hook and handed it to her. "This one is clean. You can use it for your hair."

She glanced at him, suddenly feeling self-conscious. She touched her hair with her hand and felt a tangled, matted mess. She wouldn't doubt there was some seaweed stuck in there as well.

"I'm going above. We should be at the dock in a few minutes. If you need anything, just holler."

Charlotte nodded and watched him climb the short flight of wooden steps to the deck. A few moments later she heard the boat motor start and they were underway. The sturdy boat plowed through the choppy sea, bouncing as it hit the waves. Charlotte felt seasick again, but the hot tea seemed to help.

She wondered how long she had been gone from the film crew. It was hard to tell. Once she fell in the water, it was all a blur in her memory. It could have been hours or only a few minutes.

She wondered if everyone on the set knew she had been picked up by the fishing boat. Maybe the lifeguard on the skiff had seen her rescued. She hoped so. It would be awful if they all thought she had drowned.

Charlotte moved from the hard bench to the bunk and turned to look out the small window. It was still raining, and she couldn't see much through the thick, smudged glass.

She suddenly realized that she didn't know her rescuer's name. He must think she was horribly self-involved and rude. The man saved her life, and she hadn't even thanked him. She had to say something, right away.

Charlotte grasped the railing with one hand and her blanket with the other as she slowly climbed up to the deck. The waves were still rough, but the rain had tapered off to a fine drizzle.

She saw him up in the boat's cockpit, which was a few more steps above the deck. He stood at the wheel, staring at the sea. He was tall, Charlotte noticed. Tall and slender, wearing worn jeans and big boots. He hadn't changed out of any of his wet clothes, only pulled on the rain slicker, but he must have been accustomed to being wet, out on the sea all the time, she reasoned.

What a hard life. She could hardly imagine it.

He turned and smiled at her. "Need a little air?" Charlotte nodded. "Sorry for the bumps," he said. "It's hard to get a smooth ride today."

"That's all right." Charlotte had to shout to be heard over the boat engine. "I'm sorry, I didn't ask your name."

He flashed her a quick smile. She could tell that he had noticed but had written off her rudeness to either being a celebrity or being half-drowned.

"It's Colin. Colin Doyle," he shouted back.

Charlotte nodded again. She wanted to ask him more questions, but it was hard to shout over the engine. He seemed to realize that and beckoned with his hand.

"Come on up. I can't hear you. You're in the rain out there, besides."

Charlotte clutched at her blanket and went up. The cockpit of the boat was a small space, dominated by the steering wheel and a wooden panel of instruments. Sheltered on three sides by a flat glass windshield, it afforded a great view.

Charlotte gazed out at the ocean. "It's so empty out here. So vast and empty."

He glanced at her. "Does it frighten you?"

"No, not at all. I guess I should be frightened, after being lost out there. But when I look out now, I feel like it's just . . . such a relief."

He smiled at her answer. "That's the way I feel about it, too. The sea can be frightening at times and dangerous. You have to respect it." He paused. "You were lucky today."

"Yes, I really was," she said, thinking again about what happened to her. "I was very lucky that you came along and pulled me out. You saved my life. Thank you, Colin. I wish there was something more I could say or do for you."

He glanced at her then quickly looked away. He seemed embarrassed by her gratitude. "No thanks necessary. I was in the right place at the right time. My mother used to say everything happens for a reason. That's not even the usual place I cruise. I guess I was just meant to be there. To help you."

Charlotte just nodded. "I guess so."

He was silent for a moment, his gaze fixed on the open water ahead of the boat. "There's a legend about this island. People say angels live here and help folks in need, make things happen that seem impossible."

She glanced at him. "I'm not sure I believe in angels," she admitted. "But maybe I should start. I sure gave up hope of being rescued. It seemed impossible."

Before he could answer, the boat hit a series of high-cresting waves and Charlotte lost her balance as the deck below her feet tilted one way and then the other.

Colin grabbed her around her shoulder with one arm, steering with the other. "Whoa there . . . We don't want you to slip overboard again. That wouldn't do," he joked, his tone easy and affectionate.

Charlotte leaned against his warm, hard body for support as the boat continued to bounce on the water. With his strong arm circled around her shoulder, she felt secure and safe. She was glad, though, that she couldn't see his face or look into his eyes. She was used to the attention of attractive men, but she suddenly felt overwhelmed and self-conscious.

She felt drawn to him, unaccountably comfortable and relaxed with his arm around her. As if she'd known him forever.

Was that some strange reaction to being saved? Probably, she realized. Though it did feel like something more. Something very heady and real.

He turned his head to say something and suddenly, he was close enough to kiss her, if he wanted to. But the moment passed and he looked straight ahead again. His arm slipped from her shoulder as he slowed the boat down and then pointed to the shoreline.

"There's the dock. Looks like they're expecting you. Someone must have seen me pick you up."

"I guess so." Charlotte looked out at the throng of people from the movie crew who stood waiting for her. She waved to show she was all right, then felt surprised at her own reaction: She didn't want to get off the boat.

I should be happy, overjoyed, thrilled. I've been rescued and brought back to safety. People who know and care for me are waiting. I'll be stepping into a hot shower and dry clothes in no time. I may even snuggle under a quilt on that beautiful bed in my room at the inn.

Still, something tugged at her heart and she wished that the man who had pulled her from the icy cold water would turn the boat around and take her out to the vast quiet sea again.

Colin glanced over at her. He suddenly seemed different. It was in the way he held his tall, strong body and in the expression on his face. The easy intimacy between them had vanished. He seemed distant and more formal. And a little tense, she thought.

He cut the engine then steered the bow of the boat close to the dock. He jumped down to the deck, grabbed a line, and tossed it at one of the techs who stood near a piling, waiting to help them tie up.

The tech pulled the rope, bringing the boat alongside the dock's edge, then twisted it around a brass hook. The film crew was starting to crowd around, but Colin called out to them, "She's cold and wet and tired but otherwise fine. Give her a little room and I'll help her disembark."

Charlotte stood right behind him. He had one foot on the boat deck and the other on the dock. He took her hand and helped her cross over to the dock, where Meredith, Mike, and Judy were all waiting. Charlotte's legs felt rubbery as she stepped onto the dock, and Mike and Judy rushed to hold her up.

Meredith stepped forward and folded a thick wool blanket around her. "Oh, Charlotte, thank goodness you're all right. We were so worried. We thought you were going to drown." Meredith was crying as she hugged Charlotte.

"Are you sure you're okay?" Mike's voice was filled with concern. "I think we should bring you to a hospital and have a doctor look you over. You never know. There could be internal injuries."

"You don't get internal injuries from falling in the water, Mike," Judy said. "I don't think so, anyway."

"She fell on a pile of jagged rocks. Doesn't that count?" he said.

"I'm all right, honestly," Charlotte assured them.

Finally free of Meredith's hug, Charlotte found herself surrounded by the others. She looked past the crowd, wondering what happened to Colin. Then she saw him on the bow of his boat. He'd grabbed up the line and pushed off from the dock.

When she met his eye, he smiled and waved. She heard the boat's motor start and then he was sailing away.

"Wait!" she called to him. "Colin? Wait! I wanted to . . ." Her voice trailed off. If he could hear her, he gave no sign. The boat sailed and he stood looking out at the open sea, his back turned to the shore. She wished he would turn around just one more time, but he didn't.

She was sorry now she hadn't taken a moment to introduce him to everyone and praise his heroism. She had only been thinking about herself, with everyone swarming around, making sure she was alive.

Why, she wondered, hadn't Colin come off the boat with her? Was he shy? He hadn't seemed that way on the boat. Maybe shy wasn't the right word. Maybe he was just modest and didn't like to draw attention to himself—and didn't want his picture in the paper or on TV. Unlike everyone else she knew, who believed any publicity was good publicity. Of course, most people would love to be famous, especially for rescuing a movie star. But clearly, not Colin. He was different, and Charlotte had sensed that almost from the moment they met. She barely knew him and yet she was sure that she would never again meet anyone quite like Colin Doyle.

Judy twined her arm in Charlotte's, gently leading her toward the car that was waiting for them. "Let's get you back up to the inn. Then we'll decide about seeing a doctor. I think the nearest hospital is more than an hour away. Can you believe that? This place is almost too remote, if you ask me."

Charlotte hardly heard a word. As she dropped into the plush backseat of the limo, it suddenly hit her. *I'll never see him again.*

She felt inexplicably sad and empty.

Chapter Five

CHARLOTTE was shepherded into the inn and practically carried up the stairs, with Meredith, Judy, Mike, and Nick surrounding her. Brad followed close behind, trying to help as well.

"I feel absolutely terrible about this. I shouldn't have allowed you to walk off down the beach all alone like that. I'm so sorry, Charlotte."

Did Bradley Scott actually just apologize to her? She wished the cameras were rolling now. Perhaps she was hallucinating again. He rarely, if ever, acknowledged he was wrong about anything.

Charlotte managed to turn her head to meet his eye. "It wasn't your fault, Brad. I shouldn't have climbed up on those rocks. That was a totally dumb move. But I'm all right, honestly."

"By the grace of God," Charlotte heard Claire say. She stood at the top of the stairs, holding a pile of fluffy towels, a huge bathrobe, and a basket of fancy bath products. Charlotte wasn't sure how she had gotten up there so quickly. The big inn must have a back stairway, she reasoned. Still, it seemed as if the housekeeper had magically appeared in a puff of smoke. Or rather, a puff of scented bath salts.

Claire led the group to Charlotte's door and opened it for her. Thankfully, the parade ended there. Judy, Scott, and Mike clucked over her a bit and then went off to answer calls and text messages. Claire went into the room and set all her gifts in the bathroom. "You need a nice hot bath. Soak for a while. I'll be back with some soup and a mug of that tea you favor."

"That sounds perfect, Claire. Thank you," Charlotte said.

Only Meredith remained. "I'd better stay," she said. "I'll wait here while you're in the tub. Just in case."

"In case of what? I'm not going to drown in there. I think I've proved my unsinkability today." Charlotte nearly laughed at the idea. She started to strip off her wet clothes, but really wanted some privacy.

"You might feel dizzy, or even faint. You look very pale. You must have low blood pressure or something." Meredith grabbed her wrist.

Charlotte smiled, trying to reassure her. "I'm okay. I just look a wreck. Don't worry."

Meredith was not leaving easily, Charlotte realized, so she just gave up and went into the bathroom, firmly closing the door behind her.

When she caught sight of herself in the big oval mirror above the vanity, Charlotte wanted to scream. But she didn't dare, knowing Meredith would break down the door, fearing the worst.

No wonder Colin Doyle didn't recognize me, she thought, staring at herself in the mirror. *I look like some sort of ocean-dwelling zombie from a sci-fi film.*

She started running hot water into the big claw-foot tub and poured in some lavender-scented bath salts. Moments later, she sank into the deliciously warm water and finally felt the chill leave her bones.

Charlotte relaxed in the tub for a good, long while. As she washed her hair and dried herself off, she heard voices in her bedroom. She soon emerged wearing the long spa robe with another towel wrapped around her head.

Meredith and Judy stood waiting. Charlotte forced a smile, trying to keep her patience. She would have preferred her privacy right now. She didn't want to take a meeting on her condition.

"How do you feel now? Any better?" Meredith sounded anxious and concerned.

Charlotte felt exhausted and she ached all over. She could have slept for a week. But she didn't want to alarm Judy or sound like she was complaining.

"I feel a lot warmer and almost dry. I just need some sleep."

"That's good. But we think you should be examined by a doctor," Judy replied. "It might even be in your contract," she added quickly. "It's definitely in your best interest. We're just all concerned about you."

"Is there a doctor on the island?" Charlotte really didn't feel like getting dressed and going out. She just wanted to go to bed. Then again, she knew better than to violate the terms of her agreement. That would not be a good idea at all.

"Believe it or not, there isn't a real doctor on this entire glorified sandbar. I don't understand how people can live like that. The innkeeper called a registered nurse who lives on that farm next door. She works at an emergency medical clinic out here. If she thinks there's anything wrong with you, we'll take you to the best hospital in Boston, no questions asked."

Charlotte guessed that while she was in the shower, the brain trust—Judy, Mike, and Brad—had agreed on this plan. She didn't think she needed any medical attention but had to go along with their decision.

For some odd reason, the image of Colin came to mind, the way he'd looked standing at the helm of his boat, his face turned to the wind, his stance tall and strong as he pointed the bow through the wide, rough water, taking the waves head-on. She envied his freedom and independence.

Charlotte took the towel off her head and began to comb her hair, which was not an easy job. She found some conditioning spray and worked on the tangles. "I can call Noreen to do your hair, Charlotte," Meredith said, pulling out her cell phone.

Noreen was in makeup and styled Charlotte's hair for the film. "That's all right. I think I can get a comb through . . . eventually. She can work on it later or tomorrow. When is the nurse coming?"

"She should be here in a few minutes. She was busy on her goat farm when Liza called." Judy looked at Charlotte and raised her eyebrows. "That might be cute. If it didn't make me worry she won't know what she's doing."

Before Charlotte could respond, there was a sharp knock on the door. "Maybe that's her now." Judy jumped to answer it.

But it wasn't the nurse. It was Claire, who stood in the doorway, holding a tray. A warm, delicious smell wafted Charlotte's way.

"I've brought you some chicken soup with fresh vegetables," Claire said.

"Oh, I don't think she can eat yet, but thanks. You can put it down on that table, I guess." Judy spoke in an offhand manner while checking her cell phone.

Charlotte felt herself bristling. Judy was being rude to Claire, and she was treating Charlotte as if she were a child. *I'm perfectly capable of deciding whether or not I want to eat,* she thought.

She smiled at Claire and said, "It smells great. I think I'll try it." Charlotte pinned up her wet hair in a clip and walked over to the table. "All that swimming this morning made me hungry."

"I thought some soup would be just the thing to settle your stomach, along with some hot rolls and a cup of tea." Claire set her a place at the table, with fine china dishes, a linen place mat and cloth napkin, and a small bunch of pink roses in a glass vase.

Charlotte took a seat and started on the soup. She had such an awful feeling in her stomach from swallowing so much water, she hadn't felt any hunger at all. But the smell of food changed that in an instant.

"You need to get something in your stomach, dear. And drink a lot of fluids. You're dehydrated. A few hours of sleep should cure the rest."

Sensible advice, Charlotte thought. She glanced at Judy, who rolled her eyes. She obviously didn't trust homespun medical advice.

Judy's phone buzzed like a trapped insect. She quickly checked a new text.

"Come on, Meredith. We've been summoned," she said to Charlotte's assistant. Then she looked at Charlotte. "There's a meeting. You don't have to come down, of course. I'll bring the nurse up when she gets here."

A meeting to talk about the production delay she had caused by getting swept out to sea today, Charlotte realized. The schedule had to be changed, and the lost day of work had cost money. Charlotte tried not to feel guilty, but on some level, she did.

Judy and Meredith left the room, but Claire stayed, tidying up and removing wet towels from the bathroom.

"The soup is delicious, thank you," Charlotte said as she reached the bottom of the bowl. The rolls were delicious, too. Charlotte rarely indulged in carbs and never ate real butter, but she couldn't resist the hot, flaky bread. *For goodness' sake, you nearly died today. You can break your diet a tiny bit,* she told herself.

"Care for more soup? I can bring it up in a minute," Claire offered.

"Maybe later. I'm fine for now. I didn't think I could eat a bite today after all the water I swallowed. I was pretty sick on the boat. But Colin, the fisherman who found me, told me it was better to get it all out." Charlotte felt odd just saying his name out loud. Odd but good at the same time. As if she had a special secret now that made her feel happy inside.

"Colin was right. He knows about these things," Claire agreed.

"Do you know him? Does he live around here? I feel like I barely got to thank him. When we got to the dock, he just disappeared."

"Yes, I know Colin. He lives on the other side of the island, not far from my little cottage. There's a community over that way that used to be a fishing village. He's been there a few years now, I'd say. A very nice young man," she added.

"Yes, he was very nice." Charlotte would have described him in much stronger terms—brave, handsome, charming. She wanted to ask Claire how she could get in touch with him. But before she could work up the nerve, Claire spoke first.

"You were fortunate that he passed by and saw you in the water. And that he knew what to do."

"Yes, I am. Every time I think of what could have happened . . . I can't quite believe I survived. I am lucky. Even blessed," she added.

She suddenly thought of the voice she'd heard in her head when she was first lost in the water. *Stay strong, Charlotte. You are loved.*

For some reason, she had a feeling that if she told this woman about the voice, she wouldn't laugh at her or try to explain it away. But Charlotte didn't know the housekeeper well enough to confess that strange experience. She wasn't sure she had the nerve to tell anyone.

"It did make me realize how fragile life is," she confessed. "It could end at any moment, for any of us. It makes you realize that you don't appreciate your life the way you should. You don't pay attention to the important things, like friends and family, but also the sun and flowers, even fog. I know I don't. I'm always in a rush, pressing on to the next thing I have to do. And the next after that."

"That is a challenge for all of us," Claire agreed. "Perhaps in certain professions and lifestyles, like yours, it's even harder. But we can't let the demands of life steal the joy. Or what's the point?"

Charlotte knew that was true, because there was another issue in her life that stole the joy, one she couldn't confide to anyone. She got through each day by pushing it aside, refusing to look at it. Now, surviving the near drowning had brought it up to the surface, as if a sunken ship down there had come up alongside her.

She tried to make sense of it. "I feel . . . different now," she told Claire. "An experience like this makes you realize that time is precious and you wonder if you're really making the most of your life, using your time in a worthwhile way. It makes you think about mistakes you've made. Know what I mean?"

"We all have regrets, dear. I can't imagine a life worth living without a few regrets or mistakes along the way. That's all part of the journey. We must learn to forgive people who may have hurt us. And forgive ourselves. Life is too short to hold grudges or treat each other unkindly."

Charlotte nodded. She suddenly couldn't speak. There was someone in her past she couldn't forgive: her stepfather, who had treated her mother, and all of them, so badly. Charlotte knew she could never forgive him. Just as she could never forgive herself for running away and leaving her mother and siblings there with him.

Claire stood beside her and touched her shoulder. "My dear, it's only natural that all these big questions would come bubbling up to the surface right now. Look at what an ordeal you've been through. It's not entirely a bad thing. We all need to take account, from time to time."

Charlotte nodded. Claire's words made sense to her. They just felt . . . true.

"Thank you. And thanks again for the soup. I feel better already," she said honestly.

"Good." Claire nodded, looking satisfied. "That's what we're here for. If you need anything else, just let me know."

A few moments later, Charlotte was finally alone in her room. She stretched out on the bed, pulled the fluffy quilt to her chin, and closed her eyes. She thought about calling home. She wanted to talk to Lily just to hear her voice. But she didn't want to tell them what had happened today. Especially her mother. She was so frail emotionally, she would worry and fret for days even though Charlotte was safe. It didn't make sense to upset her. But Charlotte felt lonely not being able to confide in anyone.

Charlotte's thoughts turned to the past, to the memories that haunted her, the pages of her life story she hid from the world, like a secret demon locked in a closet. For years now she had lied about her past, sure it would radically change her public image if the truth were ever revealed.

Some days, she felt as if she were hiding out in her own life, in her own heart. The ordeal in the ocean had brought up all these memories and feelings. She tried to push them back and get some sleep, but it was very hard.

A knock on the door sounded. "Charlotte, it's Judy. The nurse is here. May we come in?"

"Yes, that's okay. Come in," Charlotte called from the bed.

Judy swung open the door. "How are you feeling?"

Charlotte sat up. "I'm fine. I just feel tired."

"That sounds about right, all things considered." A sturdy woman, carrying a medical bag, walked in behind Judy. Liza came in, too. The nurse was Liza's friend and neighbor, Charlotte remembered. She could tell they were close friends just by the way they glanced at each other.

"This is Audrey Gilroy," Judy said.

"Hello, Audrey. Thanks for coming." Charlotte shook her hand and sat on the edge of the bed. She could tell the woman was a bit in awe of meeting a "star" but was trying hard to hide it.

"I'm happy to help. Liza told me about your awful experience. It's a good thing that boat came. You must have been terrified. How are you feeling now?"

"Tired mainly and a little sore. I did a lot of swimming out there. I guess I'm out of shape."

Audrey asked Charlotte more questions about her physical condition and examined her, taking her blood pressure and listening to her lungs and her heartbeat. She also peered down her throat and into her ears.

"Wow, you were in the water a long time. There's a fish in there," she said from behind the instrument.

Charlotte turned her head. "You're kidding?"

Audrey laughed and leaned back. "Yes, I am. I did see a little water though. You probably hear it. You should see a doctor if it doesn't come out on its own tonight when you're sleeping."

Audrey turned to Judy as she put her instruments away. "I think she's fine. She just needs rest and fluids. It's counterintuitive, but staying in the water is extremely dehydrating. You would think it was the other way around. You should feel better in the morning, Charlotte, and back to your full strength in a few days. If you don't, then please visit a physician. Dr. Harding in Cape Light is an excellent doctor. I could call him for you, if you like."

"Dr. Harding. All right, I'll make a note of that. But if she takes a turn for the worse, we'll probably bring her into Boston," Judy answered.

Charlotte gave Judy a look. "I'll be fine. But I will remember about Dr. Harding," she promised. Audrey began to pack up her medical bag. "I've been curious about your farm," Charlotte told her. "I can see it from the window. Liza told me you raise goats?"

"Yes, we do. And we make cheese and other good stuff."

"Really? I'd love to come visit if I have time while I'm here."

"Please do." Audrey looked amused at the idea. "My husband, Rob, would just faint if he ever saw you in person."

Charlotte smiled graciously. "Better get some smelling salts on hand. I could surprise you."

When the women finally left her, Charlotte lay down again. It was only late afternoon, but the weather outside made it seem almost as dark as night. The shades were drawn and she turned off the lamp on the bed stand. She closed her eyes and felt herself drifting off to sleep.

It was frightening at first. For some reason, she resisted the feeling of losing consciousness. It was as if she were out in the water again, struggling to hold her breath and stay alive.

Finally, she fell into a deep, dreamless sleep.

AUDREY was so excited by meeting Charlotte Miller, she practically floated down the stairs and into the kitchen, where Liza and Claire were hard at work, fixing dinner for the movie crew.

"I didn't really believe you, Liza. But it's true. Charlotte Miller is just as nice in person as she seems in the movies. And even more gorgeous, if that's possible. She nearly drowned this morning, and she still looked better than most women do on their best day."

"Now, now. We all have our charms, Audrey," Claire insisted.

"Sorry, ladies. Of course we do." Audrey took a carrot stick from a platter of crudités and noisily crunched down. "It's just that some women seem to hit the jackpot. If Charlotte ever does visit, I'm not sure whether I should give Rob any warning, or let it be a surprise. I'd love to get a picture of his face when he sees her—up close and personal—stepping around the goats."

Liza laughed at the image. "That would be some picture. You could probably sell it to some fan magazine."

"No, I don't think so," Audrey said with a grin. "It goes against my professional ethics. Nurses shouldn't hawk photos of their patients. But speaking of stepping around goats, I'd better get back home. Have to feed the livestock—and the husband—soon."

Once Audrey left, Liza got back to work again. Since there had been no work on the film today, dinner would be served early. Then the crew members who weren't boarding at the inn would go back to their hotels in Cape Light or the rented waterfront mansion in Newburyport, where the studio executives and stars were staying.

Serving dinner to the large number of guests had its challenges. Liza and Claire decided on a buffet and set up tables in the downstairs rooms with enough seating for all the guests. It was a lot like catering a wedding or other type of large party, Liza thought. There just wasn't any music. And there certainly wasn't a festive mood. Charlotte's near-drowning experience had cast a somber, tense mood on the entire crew.

Dinner ended with a spread of Claire's delectable desserts. There wasn't a crumb left, Liza noticed as she cleared away the platters. Luckily, she had saved some of the dinner and a few slices of the chocolate cake and peach pie for Charlotte.

As the executive group got ready to leave, it became apparent that they intended to wake Charlotte and take her back to Newburyport with them. "Did you knock on her door?" Mike asked Judy.

"Of course I did, but she didn't answer," Judy told him. "I hate to just barge in there."

"I think you have to. It's getting late." He looked at his watch. "She's slept long enough, hasn't she?"

Liza glanced at Claire. They were standing nearby and couldn't help but overhear. Claire looked upset. Not that she ever lost her temper, but now she seemed as close to it as Liza had ever seen.

"No, she hasn't slept long enough." Claire stepped into the circle and answered the producer's question. "She's suffering from exposure. She nearly drowned today. She's exhausted, dehydrated, and probably still has the chills. She's perfectly comfortable right now, snug as a bug. She should stay here with us. We'll take good care of her," Claire promised. "Won't we, Liza?"

"Absolutely. My room is right next door. I'll hear her if she needs anything during the night."

"My room is upstairs but I'll check on her, too. And she can get a few more minutes of sleep in the morning if she doesn't have to travel down from Newburyport."

Liza could see that the producer didn't enjoy being overruled by the inn's housekeeper and cook, but he valiantly held his tongue. Perhaps because Claire was a dignified older woman and he wanted to be polite and respectful. Or maybe because he knew she was right.

With a little more conversation, they finally deferred to Claire and decided Charlotte should stay. A few minutes later, the trio was gone, along with the others who were not staying at the inn.

Meredith decided she should stay, too. She clearly considered herself the star's shadow though, from what Liza had observed, Charlotte didn't seem to feel the same close connection. Liza found a room for Meredith across the hall from Charlotte's, which seemed to satisfy her.

THE inn emptied out and the movie crew scattered, most going off to their own rooms, some staying downstairs and using the common areas to watch TV or play cards and chess.

It was about nine o'clock when Liza heard someone at the front door. She was in the kitchen with Claire, going over menu plans for the next day. "Who could that be in this rain?" Claire asked. "Is Daniel dropping by tonight?"

"I don't think so. It's his night to work at the clinic." Liza went to answer the door, expecting to see one of the movie people, coming back for a forgotten cell phone or iPad. Or even, for Charlotte.

When she pulled open the door, she found Colin Doyle. He looked a little wet, especially his hair, which was combed back from his forehead. Otherwise, he was hardly recognizable from the man who rescued Charlotte earlier that day. Dressed in jeans and a dark blue sweater with a white polo shirt underneath, his scruffy beard was gone and he was cleaned up from head to toe.

He carried a bouquet of flowers close to his chest, trying to shield them from the rain with his large hand.

"Hello, Colin. Come on in," Liza welcomed him.

"Hey, Liza. I just wanted to see how Charlotte is doing. Is she around?"

He looked around the inn, seeming self-conscious. Liza felt for him. Wow, he had some crush. Who could blame him?

"Charlotte's been sleeping for hours. She's exhausted but otherwise seems fine."

"Oh, that's too bad. I mean, it's good that she's getting some rest."

"She's coming along." Claire had come out of the kitchen and was walking toward the door to meet him. "Charlotte asked me if you lived on the island. I think she wants to get in touch—to thank you for helping her."

Colin shook his head. "I just did what anyone would do in those circumstances. I don't deserve any medals."

"Well, she seems to think you do," Claire countered with a twinkle in her eye.

Colin looked pleased to hear Charlotte had talked about him, Liza noticed. But he was trying to hide it.

"I'm glad she's okay. Just tell her I stopped by. And you can give her these, I guess. If they have any petals left." He started to hand over the wet, drooping bouquet, then gave it some consideration.

Liza heard someone coming down the staircase and turned to see who it was. "I guess you can give them to Charlotte yourself," she said, turning back to him. "Here she comes."

They all turned to look at Charlotte making her way down the stairs, a disheveled but gorgeous mess, wearing a pair of gray yoga pants and a sweatshirt Liza had left in her room that read: "Save a Chicken's Life . . . Eat a Lobster."

Charlotte's thick reddish-gold hair hung in long, wild curls. She brushed them back from her cheek with a graceful motion then lifted her head and saw Colin in the foyer. She stopped and stared at him, her eyes opening wide.

"How do you feel, dear?" Claire called out to her.

"Better, thanks." Charlotte smiled but had not spared Claire a glance. Her gaze was fixed on her surprise visitor.

Liza thought she actually heard Colin sigh. He definitely cleared his throat but didn't say anything.

"You have a visitor," Claire said, though it was perfectly obvious. "Why don't you two go in the sitting room? I'll fix you something to eat, Charlotte. Would you like some more soup?"

"That would be perfect." Charlotte turned to Claire a moment, then looked back at Colin. "Good to see you. Are those for me?"

He nodded and stepped forward, handing her the flowers. "They got a little wet."

"Seems about right, considering the occasion." She bent her head to smell the bouquet. "They're beautiful. Thank you. I'll put them up in my room."

"Oh, I'll do that," Liza offered. She took the bouquet and headed for the kitchen with Claire while Charlotte and Colin walked into the sitting room.

Charlotte was glad to see that the room was empty. She didn't want to feel as if the entire crew was listening in. She sat on a small love seat near the hearth, and Colin chose an armchair. She was surprised to see him. And secretly thrilled. She had planned to get in touch with him somehow, if only just to thank him again. But this was even better. She had been thinking about him so much, she felt as if her wishes had summoned him here.

"I won't stay long, but I came to see how you're doing," Colin said.

"I'm much better now," Charlotte told him. "A hot bath and a nap can work wonders."

Colin nodded. "I'm glad you feel better. Do you have to go back to work tomorrow?"

"I do, if I can walk and talk—or anything close. Time is money in this business. You'd be surprised what some actors have endured while filming. Marilyn Monroe worked when she had appendicitis. She had a doctor freeze her appendix so she could finish a film before getting an operation."

"I had no idea Marilyn was so tough. So fighting for your life out in the ocean for an hour or so is no big deal for a beautiful actress, I guess." He shrugged, his eyes sparkling. He was teasing her, of course.

"It was at the time," she countered, feeling herself blush at his compliment. She was used to having men tell her she was beautiful. At times she was even bored by it. Why did she feel so giddy with this guy? Like a teenager with her first big crush.

Settle down, Charlotte, she chided herself. *Say what you have to say and try to sound like a grown-up.*

"I don't know how I can ever thank you for saving my life. Honestly. I know I said it before, on the boat, but I feel as if I can't say it enough."

He met her gaze for a moment then quickly looked away. "I happened to be nearby and heard you cry out. It was . . . a fluke. No pun intended," he added, turning the serious moment into a lighter one. "Anyone would have done the same. It was really just luck."

Charlotte nodded. "Lucky for me."

"Oh, lucky for me, too, I have to say. How else would I ever have gotten to meet you?" he countered.

Charlotte had no answer to that, at least none that she would dare voice aloud. A small voice inside her insisted that some way, some day, their paths would have crossed. It wasn't just chance or luck that had brought Colin into her life. She suddenly felt deep inside she was meant to come to this place and meet this man.

Her brush with death had shaken her to her soul and made her think about so many things. Some of it may have been silly—like believing in fate and destiny. But her life was a case study in being in the right place at the right time, in being very, very lucky. Coming out of Nowhere, Ohio, with no connections and no real knowledge of the movie business and ending up one of the most famous faces in the world—that was enough to make anyone believe there was something more going on in the universe than meets the eye.

And this wild, dangerous, amazing day had had the same effect on her. She just didn't know what it all meant yet.

All I know right now is that Colin is the most attractive guy I've met in a long time. He looks so handsome tonight, he could easily take a place on the other side of the camera with me.

But she didn't dare tell him that.

"So . . . I guess you like lobster," he said suddenly.

She was puzzled, then realized he was looking at her sweatshirt. "Oh, the shirt . . ." She laughed. "I borrowed this from Liza. I didn't have any warm clothes with me. But I do love lobster, now that you mention it. I grew up in the Midwest, and fresh fish was not part of our diet. I was about sixteen before I realized fish didn't swim around in little rectangles with breading on top. All we ever got at home was fish sticks."

Colin laughed. "You're kidding, right?"

"No, really. It's true," she insisted. "Now I can't get enough lobster."

"The Midwest is a big territory. Where did you live?"

"In Ohio, Greenwood, a small town, not far from Toledo."

"I've never been to Ohio. I hear it's very—"

"Flat?" she asked with a laugh.

"That wasn't what I was going to say. But I've heard that, too," he admitted. "I hear it's a very friendly place. A lot of presidents come from Ohio."

"Yes, I know. We heard all about them in school. I think that's the only thing I can remember from my history classes."

"Do you have sisters and brothers?" he asked curiously.

"Two sisters and one brother. I'm the oldest. How about you?"

"Me? Two sisters. Both older. I'm the baby of the family, couldn't you tell?" He smiled at her again, and she noticed a deep dimple in his chin.

"Yes, come to think of it. I was just about to say that," she teased. "But I didn't want to offend you."

"No offense taken." He laughed again, seeming pleased that she kept up with his verbal sparring.

Charlotte was pleased, too. He had a quick wit, which she liked about him. And she enjoyed talking to him. She didn't feel obliged to impress him in any way. She could just be herself.

Now it was her turn to ask some questions. "Were you raised around here, Colin?"

She recalled that Claire said he'd been on the island a few years. She was curious about where he grew up.

"Not too far away. In Concord. It's about an hour or so inland. My folks used to take us camping on the island when I was growing up. That's how I learned about this place."

He sounded as if he had a happy childhood, a happy family life.

She was glad for him, though she couldn't help but feel a bit envious for anyone who sounded like that. She wondered how he decided to become a fisherman, but didn't feel comfortable enough yet to ask.

There were a lot of questions she wanted to ask him. She wanted to know everything about him. As if she were the one giving some movie star an in-depth, super-personal interview. She sure knew the questions by heart by now.

But what was the point? It didn't seem logical to get too involved, no matter how attracted she felt or how much she wished they could get to know each other better.

He was probably thinking the same thing about her, she guessed.

He leaned back in his chair and gazed at her. She was used to people looking at her every day, filming her every move. But his appraising look somehow made her self-conscious. She wanted him to like her, she realized. For some mysterious reason, it was important that this man she barely knew like her. Maybe it was because she already liked him.

"How long will the movie crew be in Cape Light?" he asked.

"Oh, about two weeks, I think. It depends on how well we can keep to the schedule. We lost a whole day of work today, but maybe we can make it up somehow, shooting extra hours on one or two days. When we get back to California, we'll shoot a few more interior scenes on a movie set."

"You must travel a lot, going from place to place to make all these films."

"I do," she said. "I just filmed a movie in Japan and last year, let's see . . . I was in London, Cairo, Budapest, and New Zealand."

"Wow, that's quite an itinerary."

She suddenly felt bad, as if she had been bragging. He probably didn't get to travel much beyond his fishing routes. "I'm usually working most of the time and don't get to see much," she explained. "I'd love to take a long trip sometime as an anonymous tourist. A long train ride through Europe, or a cruise around the Greek Islands in a private little boat."

"The Greek Islands are breathtaking. I crewed on a private yacht for a while. We sailed the Mediterranean for a year. You should do that, in between your movies sometime."

Charlotte was impressed. "Sounds like a real adventure. If you find a boat and crew, maybe I will."

Had she just said that? Wow, she was never that forward. He was really getting to her, wasn't he?

"Anytime, just let me know. Even some parts of the Caribbean are beautiful. Or the islands off the coast of Venezuela, like Bonaire."

"Did you sail around those places, too?" she asked curiously.

"I crewed sometimes, and other times I just took odd jobs in the cities and worked my way around, mostly in Europe and South America. I took two years off after college and just bummed around with a backpack and no reservations, as the expression goes."

"No schedules, no itinerary, no one telling you where you had to be?"

"That's right. That's it exactly."

She suddenly pictured him sailing in the Caribbean. He was very suntanned and had on a billowing white shirt. There was also a woman with him. Charlotte didn't like that part of her fantasy, but she couldn't imagine him alone on such a romantic trip. She wished she could be the one to visit places like that with him.

"That's the kind of trip I'd like to go on. Someday," she added wistfully.

"I hope you do." He smiled softly at her and she smiled back.

She suddenly wondered if he believed her. After all, why would she ever travel in such a rough, basic fashion? She was accustomed to the very best—the most luxurious hotels and spas, the most exclusive restaurants. But that level of luxury was, in a way, like a thick, soft wall that blocked her from the real world. It was a wall that sometimes felt like a prison.

Colin experienced the real world, head-on. She could already tell that much about him. Whether out on his boat in the middle of the sea, or hitchhiking through the French countryside.

She suddenly envied him and anyone who could do those things with him. The truth was, their lifestyles were so different, they might as well be living on separate planets. Charlotte hated to face that fact, but there was no getting around it. It was the truth.

She looked up and met his deep blue gaze. Every rational thought about how different their lives were vanished. Maybe she shouldn't dismiss this attraction so quickly. Maybe this could work—in some improbable, unimaginable way?

Meredith walked into the sitting room, carrying her laptop. She didn't seem to even notice Colin and made a beeline for Charlotte. "There you are. Liza told me you were up. How do you feel?"

"Better. I got a good rest. I think that's what I really needed."

"Great. Judy's been texting me all night. Now I can finally report some good news. Do you think you can work tomorrow?"

Charlotte nodded. "No problem. I'll be out there."

"Great. I'll let her know." Meredith opened up her laptop and started to type.

Charlotte glanced at Colin, trying to send an apologetic look. She was sorry they'd been interrupted. She hoped Meredith would go do her work someplace else so that they could talk more.

"Meredith, this is Colin Doyle, the man who pulled me out of the water. Colin, this is my assistant, Meredith Pope."

Meredith looked up and blinked at him. "Oh, hello. I thought I recognized you."

Colin just nodded at her, but he suddenly seemed uneasy. He looked as if he were getting ready to leave, but Charlotte didn't want him to go. Not yet.

Meredith glanced up from her screen. "Oh, Charlotte, there's something I have to show you. I don't know how it got out, but somebody already reported on the incident. They got it all wrong, of course, and said we were filming on a boat and you fell overboard . . . I bookmarked it. Just give me a second." Meredith tapped away on the keyboard.

Colin stood up and put his hands in his pockets. "I'll be going now. I'm glad to see that you're all right."

Charlotte stood up, too, and smiled at him. "Thank you for coming. I'll see you out."

"That's all right. I know my way." Then he stuck out his hand, a rather formal gesture, she thought. In Hollywood, everyone hugged lightly and gave air kisses. Even if you despised the person. But she took his hand and shook it, grateful for that contact at least.

"Good luck with the movie. Don't get into any more trouble, okay? I had to send my superhero cape out to the cleaners."

She laughed. She loved his sense of humor. "I'll try to be careful. But keep your phone on, just in case."

They actually hadn't exchanged cell phone numbers or e-mail addresses or anything like that. Charlotte suddenly wanted to offer, but caught herself. It would be pointless. He seemed to know that, too.

Once Colin left, she was alone with Meredith, who had finally found the link to an Internet story on Charlotte's watery adventure. Charlotte sat beside her on the love seat, watching the short video.

She hardly heard a word. She was thinking of Colin. She had been wondering all day if her attraction to him was just the excitement of the moment, a crush on her rescuer, the way it always happened in the movies.

But it wasn't that at all, Charlotte decided. Or more precisely, it was not *only* that. There was something about Colin—his strong, quiet manner, his gentle humor—that drew her more strongly than any man she'd ever met.

And that was something else to think about.

"AUDREY? When are you going to do something about this dog? I think she just stole half my breakfast off the table."

Audrey's husband, Rob, had done his usual early morning chores in the barn while Audrey fixed breakfast. He had just come in and washed his hands and now stood by the table, looking at his plate. Which was missing the pile of whole-wheat toast Audrey had left on the plate beside his eggs.

"At least she didn't eat the eggs. I'll make some more toast."

"Thanks, but you didn't answer my question." He sat down and reached for his coffee mug.

"I know, I know. I've just been really busy the past few days and with all that rain, I didn't feel like walking around with a pile of soggy flyers."

Audrey sat down across from him. They were eating at the picnic table on the porch. The dog wandered over to her blanket in the corner of the room then lay down and began licking her paws. *She knows we're talking about her,* Audrey thought. "I'll take care of it today," she said. "I'll take her to a shelter. I think there's one in Essex."

Rob looked at her as he wolfed down his scrambled eggs, not

bothering to wait for the toast. "Why don't you just take her up to the General Store? Maybe someone there will recognize her."

"Good idea. I'll start with that. I just have to weed the garden before it gets too hot," she added. And she had a list of many other things to do, too. Such as more research about fertility issues, so she could ask the right questions at her appointment with the specialist on Tuesday. It was painful to look up those articles and read about everything that could go wrong and even face the fact that she might never be able to give birth to her own baby.

Dealing with new doctors was also draining, as was explaining her story to receptionists and nurses. It was the most pressing issue in both their lives right now and ironically, it was the one she most avoided thinking about. Any excuse, even this silly dog, was enough to pull her attention away.

Audrey sighed and started on her breakfast. Rob looked over at her. "Something wrong?"

Nothing more than the fact that she couldn't seem to get pregnant. She shook her head and forced herself not to be so glum. "Just thinking. I'll take care of the dog thing, I promise."

"Good, I hope you do. She's getting very comfortable around here. It will just be harder for the dog if she has to go into a shelter, or go back to her real home."

Audrey knew that was true. The dog *was* getting comfortable with them. She followed Audrey around all day and when Audrey returned after going out for an errand, the dog ran to the door and nearly knocked her down with her ecstatic welcome.

Audrey was starting to understand the difference between cats and dogs. Not that she necessarily liked the dog, but the animal was amusing. She was also a lot of extra work that Audrey didn't want or need.

When they finished breakfast, Audrey took the dishes to the sink and scraped off the crust of toast and egg. The dog sat right behind her, so close she could feel her panting on the back of her legs. "All right . . . here's the scraps. I know I shouldn't have given you any people food. That's my own fault, right?"

Audrey scraped the leftovers into the dog's bowl and received a quick lick on her hand in thanks.

She returned to the sink and finished the dishes. The kitchen floor had been much cleaner the past few days; she had to give the dog credit for that.

Audrey went out and got to work. She had a lot to do before taking the dog to the village center, and it was getting late. The dog followed her to the garden then lay down in a shady spot under a blueberry bush and watched Audrey work.

When Audrey finished in the garden, she washed her hands at the hose and the dog ran over to have a drink. Then they walked over to the barn to tend to the goats. Audrey let the herd out into the meadow to graze, and the dog chased them in all directions, causing a din of hysterical brays. But the dog was just playing, Audrey had realized after the first day. The goats could be so stuffy at times, and there was no harm done.

I wonder if I could train that dog to help me round them up and get them in the barn. I guess I could . . . if we wanted to keep her. Which we don't.

Audrey didn't know much about dogs, but this one was very nosey. She had to investigate everything: the goats' food and water, the chickens in their henhouse, the old blanket where the cats curled up and slept.

While Audrey cleaned the goat stalls and put down fresh hay, the dog disappeared from view. *Probably taking another nap,* Audrey thought. Then she heard an unholy racket—loud, hysterical hissing, the dog barking wildly, the chickens in an uproar, and the watering can being knocked across the yard. She ran out to see what had happened and saw the big orange tabby, Sophia, up on the roof of the henhouse, calmly stretching in the sun. The chickens were hopping about, flapping their wings, bereft of a few feathers, but otherwise unharmed. The dog, however, was running toward the house and dashed under the back porch.

The cat and dog had been circling each other warily for the past two days. Audrey guessed there had finally been a showdown—and Sophia had won, paws down. Audrey considered letting the dog pout and lick her wounds in private, but that solution didn't sit well. After a few moments, she put down her rake and walked toward the house.

She called to the dog, but she didn't come out. "Dog, come! Come on out. I have a treat for you," she fibbed. Finally she got down on her hands and knees and looked under the porch. The dog was lying down, panting. A little bit of blood was trickling down from her muzzle.

Sophia had used her claws to make her point. Audrey suddenly felt sorry for the silly dog, who was probably only trying to play, the way she did with the goats.

Audrey went into the kitchen, got a piece of turkey from the fridge, and came out again. It only took an instant of waving the enticing treat under the steps, and the dog magically appeared.

"What happened to you? Let me see your nose. What did that bad cat do to you?" Audrey petted the dog as she fed her the turkey. Her nose had a big bloody scratch on one side. It must have hurt. Wasn't a dog's nose its most sensitive body part? Audrey brought the dog into the kitchen and gently cleaned the scratch with water then dabbed on some antibiotic ointment. More turkey was required for this medical procedure.

"Good girl." The dog just wagged her tail. "I have to finish my work and then I'll take you to the village. Do you think you can stay out of trouble until then?"

The dog stared at her, and Audrey could have sworn she smiled. Audrey smiled back, then caught herself.

I really have to stop talking to this dog. I sound like a lunatic.

That was another reason the silly canine had to go.

LATER that afternoon, Audrey fashioned a homemade leash from a piece of rope and led the dog to the passenger side of the pickup truck. She did not need to be asked twice to jump in and seemed delighted to be going for a ride. Maybe someone would recognize her in the village center. After all, everyone wound up in the General Store sooner or later, and Walter and Marion never forgot a face or a name—or a dog. Hopefully, the old couple who ran the store would remember who owned this dog.

In case that didn't work, Audrey had made a flyer on her computer. It was pretty basic, but she had caught a good photo of the dog with her digital camera and put it together with their phone number. Who knew? Someone might see it today and the dog could be gone by tonight.

Audrey glanced over at her passenger, who was, of course, oblivious to Audrey's mission. The dog rode with her big head hanging out the window, her tongue hanging down, and the breeze blowing through her fluffy ears.

Audrey had to smile. Whatever else you might say about their canine houseguest, she sure knew how to enjoy the little things, like a truck ride.

When they reached the village center, the dog hopped down and followed Audrey without the slightest tug on the leash. "I can't see how you got lost. You must have been well cared for by somebody," Audrey told her. "Do you know where you are? Did your owner ever bring you here?"

The dog looked up at her attentively and panted. *Of course she couldn't answer. She'd be home by now if she could,* Audrey reminded herself.

There was a narrow, shaded porch outside the store, where Audrey tied the dog's leash to a post railing. Maybe Marion or Walter would come out and take a look. They would surely let her hang up a flyer or two.

"I'll be right back. Stay right here and don't get into any trouble," Audrey told the dog. The dog seemed to understand. She sat down and watched Audrey walk away.

Audrey turned to enter the store and nearly walked right into a woman coming out, pushing a double stroller. "Oh, I'm so sorry."

"That's all right. I just got this stroller. I'm not the best driver with it yet."

Audrey smiled politely but her gaze was fixed on the babies. They were heart-wrenchingly cute. Twin girls dressed in pink and white polka dot one-piece outfits with matching hats. They were sleeping, side by side, their plump baby fists tucked up to their rosebud mouths.

Audrey stood staring at them, not even realizing she was blocking the woman's way.

"How old are they?" she asked suddenly.

"Three months. Thank goodness I had them right before the

summer. I was miserable enough. Out to here," the woman gestured, showing Audrey how far her pregnant belly had extended.

"Oh, I'll bet." Audrey tried to sound sympathetic but what she really wanted to say was, *What are you complaining about? I'd do anything to have a huge pregnant belly—shoveling snow barefoot in Antarctica the whole nine months.*

"Well, it was definitely worth it," she said instead. "Your babies are gorgeous. Good luck," she added kindly.

"Thanks a lot. See you around."

Audrey was about to help her down the steps with the stroller, but the woman deftly turned the vehicle around and steered it down a handicap ramp near the stairway. The babies were facing the storefront and Audrey caught one last glimpse of them before turning away.

Your time will come, don't worry. Good things come to those who wait, Audrey reminded herself. But somehow the soothing slogans did little to fill the empty place inside.

She walked into the General Store, focusing back on her errand. An overhead fan spun in lazy circles, wafting the warm air with its distinctive scent: a mixture of ripening fruit, soap powder, and pickles. The building was so old that the plank floor creaked as customers walked down the aisles. Walter and Marion seemed to carry a little of everything on the shelves, from penny nails to nail polish remover.

They were both behind the counter in their crisp white aprons. Walter was in the deli section, making a customer a big sandwich and Marion was standing staunchly at the register. She was helping another customer mail a package, since the store also doubled as the island's post office. Audrey gathered up her items—a few peaches, a pint of blueberries, and laundry detergent—and brought them to the checkout spot.

"Hey, Audrey. How are you?" Marion greeted her as she began to tally up Audrey's goods. "The sun finally came out again. I thought I'd never see it."

"It's hot but I'm not complaining. It's so good to see some sunshine. When we had that big storm on Tuesday night, a dog wandered into the yard. It doesn't have a tag or any ID. I was wondering if you or Walter might know who she belongs to." Audrey showed the flyer to Marion. "Here's her picture. She looks like a mix between a golden retriever and . . . oh, I don't know, a pony?"

Marion put on her glasses and checked the photo. "Gee, she's pretty. But she doesn't look familiar. Maybe Walter would know."

"She's right outside. I brought her with me to show around," Audrey explained. "Would you mind stepping out to take a look?"

"Sure, I love dogs . . . I'll tell Walter, too."

Marion walked out with Audrey, and Walter soon followed.

They both looked down at the dog, who had been lying in a shady spot but now stood up and greeted them with an eager expression, her tail wagging.

"She's pretty. Nice dog," Walter said, holding out his hand. The dog stepped over and licked his fingers. "Dogs always like me. I don't know why," he said proudly.

"She smells the cold cuts," Marion reminded him.

"Do you recognize her at all?" Audrey asked.

The couple looked at the dog a moment or two longer then shook their heads. "Sorry," Walter said. "Wait a minute. I'll bring her out a scrap of bologna. She looks hungry."

Marion laughed. "He can't help it. We had three dogs when the kids were growing up. Now we're down to a little Jack Russell. Spoiled rotten," she confided.

Audrey nodded and smiled. She had hoped the Doyles would be

more help in finding the dog's owner. She put up her flyer on the bulletin board inside the store and one on the porch near the entrance. The dog wolfed down her bologna scraps, and they headed across the street to Daisy Winkler's Tearoom and Lending Library.

The Tearoom was a small cottage, painted pale yellow, with a violet door and gingerbread trim on the sloping eaves and porch. It looked like something out of a fairy tale, or perhaps, a child's playhouse. But it seemed to suit its proprietor perfectly.

Audrey, with the dog alongside, opened the creaky wooden gate, then walked through the wild, untamed garden to the door. A small sign in a window read, "*Closed. So Sorry. Come Back & Have Tea With Me Soon!*"

Audrey peered through a glass pane in the door anyway. She could see the small tables where tea and sweets and finger sandwiches were served, the walls lined with bookcases up to the ceiling. In another small room farther back, where there was a thrift shop, Audrey caught sight of Daisy's shadowy form, carrying an armful of clothes.

Audrey pulled the chain on a brass bell that hung near the door. The tinkling sound hardly seemed loud enough to alert anyone, but she soon heard steps approaching.

Finally, Daisy appeared in the doorway. As usual, the tearoom proprietor looked as if Lewis Carroll, the author of *Alice in Wonderland*, had dressed her. Her hair was piled haphazardly on her head. A long chiffon sash wrapped around her forehead and trailed down her back. Several yellow pencils stuck out of her hair like strange ornaments. Audrey knew she used them to write and was so absentminded, she probably didn't even know they were there.

Oblivious to the heat, Daisy wore one of her long dresses with a round neckline and full skirt, complemented by a neck full of beads, an armful of jangling bracelets, and many rings, large and small, adorning her crooked fingers.

Daisy was the island's very own self-proclaimed Emily Dickinson, though she was not a recluse, and Daisy's many volumes of poetry were self-published. She had never married, dedicating herself to her writing and promoting the arts at her tearoom, a tiny cultural outpost.

It was a long shot that Daisy might recognize the dog, Audrey realized as soon as the woman appeared. In fact, even if she knew the dog, her memory was so vague, she might not remember who the owner was. But it was worth a try, Audrey thought.

"Hello, Daisy. I'm sorry to bother you. I hope I didn't interrupt your writing."

"No bother, dear. Come in, come in. Would you like some tea or a look around the shop? Maybe there's a book you need." Daisy motioned toward the tiny rooms of her cottage filled with books.

"Not today, thanks. I just stopped by to see if you recognize this dog. I'm trying to find her owner. She wandered into our yard Tuesday night, during the thunderstorm."

Daisy peered down at the dog through her half glasses, then crouched to get a better look. She held the dog's face in her hand and stared into her eyes so that they posed nose to nose. Audrey was glad the dog was so gentle. She hardly reacted but did look very puzzled.

"Oh, poor dear. Are you lost? What soulful eyes you have. Can you tell me where you belong, darling?" Daisy cooed.

Then she held her ear very close to the dog's muzzle, listening. Audrey stood by, wide-eyed. *If this works, then I'll really be worried.*

Finally, Daisy stood up and shook her head. A pencil slipped out from her hair, but she caught it. "Sorry, she didn't say. But she is very content and likes you very much."

"Well . . . thanks." Audrey smiled awkwardly in answer.

"A dog is the only thing on earth that loves you more than you love yourself," Daisy told her. "I'm not sure who said that. Someone named Josh Billings, I think. I do think it's true."

"Quite possibly," Audrey replied, not knowing what else to say. She took out one of her flyers. "Would you mind hanging this in your shop? I'm hoping her owner will see it and call me."

Daisy looked over the flyer. "No trouble at all."

Audrey gave the rope leash a tug, and the dog rose and followed her. "Thanks, Daisy. I'll be seeing you."

"Come again soon, dear. Come for tea. You can bring your dog inside. I won't mind," she added.

Audrey just smiled. Daisy was confused. *She's not my dog. That's the whole point.* But she didn't bother to correct her.

Next, Audrey stopped in at the emergency clinic, where she volunteered a few hours a week. Again, she left the dog outside. It was busy, with a few patients waiting. She noticed that Daniel was on call, but he only had time to wave from an examining room.

She hung up the flyer and walked to her truck with the dog trotting beside her. "Okay, what now, pal?" Audrey asked as the dog jumped into the truck. "Shall we head to Essex and the dog shelter? Or give the flyers a little time to work?"

The shelter did seem a harsh fate, and Audrey really hadn't tried very long to find her owner. Just as she was trying to decide what to do, her cell phone buzzed. It was a text from Rob. He needed her help to move a heavy piece of equipment in the cheese-making room and wondered when she would be back.

Audrey texted that she would be home in a few minutes. As she stuck the phone back in her purse, she glanced at her four-legged companion. "Okay, you're off the hook for now. No dog shelter today. You wait here while I go back in the store. I forgot dog food. Looks like you'll be hanging around with us a few more days."

"LOOK at these lobsters . . . Where did they come from? Liza, did you order lobster for tonight?"

Charlotte had wandered into the kitchen, looking for a glass of iced tea when Claire came through the back door carrying a large cooler.

She set it down on the floor near the refrigerator. Liza, who was stirring something on the stove, walked over to take a look. "I didn't order lobster, not for tonight. We were making halibut with leeks and tomatoes. Don't you remember?"

"I do. Then what is this?" Claire lifted the lid on the cooler, and Charlotte let out a little scream. "Ahh! They're alive! I mean, I know you have to cook them live, but I didn't realize they were so wild."

Claire laughed at her. "We grow them lively around here. They don't go down without a fight."

"A few even still have some seaweed stuck on," Liza observed.

Charlotte grabbed her courage and peered into the cooler again. A pile of dark green and black lobsters squirmed in a pile of ice, writhing and snapping their claws. One very brazen specimen hooked a claw to the edge of the cooler and began to lever itself out.

"Whoa there . . . back inside. You aren't going anywhere except into a pot of boiling water." Liza grabbed the lobster's tail and it slid back under the ice. Then she slammed the lid on the slithering creatures.

"They're real beauties. A pound and a half or even two pounds each, I'd say," Claire guessed. "Looks like at least a dozen. That should be enough for everyone left, don't you think?"

"I do," Liza agreed. "Scratch the halibut, we don't want this bounty to go to waste."

"Where do you think they came from, if you didn't order them?" Claire asked, peering under the lid of a pot. She turned to Charlotte. "We were told that you like lobster by the powers that be," Claire explained. "But I wasn't planning on making that dish for this group. I would have needed a truckload."

"It could have been a fan," Liza suggested. "Maybe they read somewhere about your favorite foods."

"Maybe. People do send me presents," Charlotte said, though she had a feeling it was a new friend. It had to be Colin, she decided, thinking back to their conversation two nights earlier. These might even be lobsters he caught in his own traps today. If so, it was an incredibly sweet and thoughtful gesture. The only thing that could have made it even better was if Colin stopped by to share them. He had shown up uninvited the other night. Maybe he would return? She hoped so.

"So . . . how many people are here for dinner tonight?" she casually asked Liza. "The inn seems pretty empty."

Charlotte knew that after the filming had wrapped up for the day, Brad headed back up to the rented mansion. He never liked to eat dinner with the staff. Mike and Judy had left at noon for Boston. They had a business meeting and would go straight to Newburyport tonight.

After her first night staying over, Charlotte had decided to remain at the inn. She liked her room and loved the atmosphere. She also liked having some space away from Brad and the other higher-ups on the film.

There had been some concern about leaving her here alone and the lack of conveniences. But she had finally persuaded them that she could focus better on the film if she stayed. The island was less accessible to the press, and the inn's atmosphere helped get her into character. Finally, they gave up and let her have her way, though Meredith insisted on staying like a faithful shadow.

"Oh, we're down to a handful tonight," Liza explained. "All the crew members staying here decided to go to Spoon Harbor for a Friday night on the town. So it's just us three and your assistant. We can easily fit at the table on the patio. This dinner is best enjoyed outdoors."

So she didn't expect Colin.

"Let me help you. Just tell me what to do," Charlotte offered.

Liza looked surprised but nodded. "Maybe you can set the table later, when we're ready."

"She can chop these vegetables until then," Claire called out. She pointed with a long wooden spoon to a chopping block on the table where a strainer of freshly washed vegetables and salad stood draining in a colander.

"There's a knife on the table. Don't cut yourself," Claire warned her. "You'd better grab an apron. I bet that outfit cost a small fortune."

Claire looked over at Charlotte's casually chic halter top and swingy, summer skirt. It had cost a small fortune, by most standards, but her closets were full of such clothes. When she was a teenager, she loved fashion but hardly had any nice clothes. That all changed when she started modeling. Now that she had more money than she could even count, shopping for new clothes was her greatest indulgence. It was something she could do in private, surfing the Web for new fashions and accessories. She knew she used it as a distraction, too.

"Do you ever cook, Charlotte?" Claire asked, breaking into her rambling thoughts.

"Once in a while . . . not that much, though I do know how to cook. Simple things," she added.

"Simple dishes are often the best. In my book, anyway," Claire said.

Charlotte agreed, though she ate at the finest restaurants and had sampled the most complex and exotic of dishes.

She took the apron Claire handed her, wrapped the strings around her narrow waist, then set to work on the vegetables. She fell into the rhythm easily. Growing up, she'd had to help out at home with the cooking, cleaning, and watching her younger siblings. Her mother worked hard at home but often seemed overwhelmed and depressed. Charlotte was always the one to step in and take over. She was no stranger to housework, though it had been a long time since she'd had to do any.

With so many helping hands in the kitchen, dinner was soon ready. Though Charlotte loved eating lobster, she'd never cooked it herself and got an informative lesson from Claire.

"I like to stun them before putting them in the pot. Like this." Claire showed her how to strike the lobster at the back of the head. "I think it's just more humane that way."

Charlotte agreed. She was not a vegetarian and ate all kinds of meat. But it was hard to see a living thing dropped into boiling water.

The small group of women made for relaxing company, Charlotte thought. She had come to know both Liza and Claire a bit over the past few days. They were both interesting and intelligent. She was impressed by Liza's decision to quit her safe but boring job in an advertising agency, and stay on the island to run the inn. And Claire was, well, unique. She was the only person Charlotte ever met who didn't seem to be the least bit impressed by actors or the film crew. Charlotte had the sense that Claire would treat any guest with the same brisk but genuine consideration that she showed them.

Though she enjoyed the evening's conversation, Charlotte had been secretly watching and waiting for Colin—right up until Claire served dessert, a lemon Bundt cake with homemade strawberry ice cream on the side.

Charlotte helped clean up and then sat with Liza and Claire on the front porch, enjoying a last cup of tea and the ocean breeze. Claire took out her knitting.

"That's beautiful yarn." Charlotte reached out and fingered the heather-brown strand. "What are you making?"

Claire was counting the stitches in the row but smiled before she answered. "It's a shawl. For myself, for once. I plan to wear it on chilly nights about the house or even over my coat when it gets wicked cold outside. Do you knit, Charlotte?"

"I usually do when I'm shooting a movie. It makes the downtime on set go faster. But I forgot my knitting bag on this trip. I was in the middle of a sweater for my sister. I'm starting to miss my needles."

"You should have said something. There's a lovely knitting shop not far from here, in Cape Light. Tell the owner that I sent you. She'll find everything you need."

Claire wrote down the name and address of the store. Charlotte decided to go into town tomorrow after they finished filming. She loved to read, but was running out of books and needed some other diversion.

Besides thinking about Colin.

She had given up on seeing him tonight somewhere around the homemade ice cream. She was disappointed, but maybe it was for the best. After all, how far could their relationship go? Not very, Charlotte reasoned. It was hard for her to have a relationship with someone outside the entertainment business, even if the man was at the same economic level. Which Colin definitely was not. Was that a cold way of looking at it? Yes, but it was also realistic. Besides, she was on the West Coast a good part of the time or traveling for her work. And Colin was here. Fishing.

If things ever got serious between them, she could certainly afford to fly him out to California to see her. But she wondered how he would feel about that. Was he the type of man who felt uncomfortable with a woman who was far wealthier? She knew it was old-fashioned of her, but the truth was, that most of the men she'd met who did enjoy that arrangement were not worth getting involved with.

There were so many obstacles to anything long term between them. Maybe Colin had come to that conclusion, too, Charlotte thought. They could never have anything more than a romantic fling during the filming here. If the press ever found out, they would have a field day. Charlotte cringed, imagining the headlines of the trashy, grocery-store tabloids or even worse, the gossip columns on the Internet—how they would slander her and make a mockery of Colin.

Colin was a great guy. One in a million, she had no doubt. But she never wanted to hurt him, or turn him into prey for the paparazzi. That would be no way to repay the man who had saved her life.

Chapter Six

"A UDREY, did you see my other boot? I left it right here by the door when I came in last night."

Audrey cringed at her husband's question. She didn't know where the boot was, but had a good idea who did.

Audrey was at the kitchen table, sorting out labels for the cheese packages that she had just printed out from her laptop. Saturday was usually a busy day at the shop, and she wanted to be prepared with fully stocked shelves. The dog lay under the table, at her feet.

"Oh, here it is. I found it under the couch."

Rob hobbled back from the living room, one boot on and the other in his hand. Audrey glanced over at it quickly. Not too much damage, though the cowhide laces were chewed to bits.

"Look at this. Look what that dog did."

Audrey sighed and took the boot. "Thank heaven she didn't chew the leather. I have some new laces in the sewing box. I think they'll be long enough."

"Great. But you promised to take that dog to the shelter in Essex. Remember?"

"I know. But I've been so busy. Every time I plan to go, something comes up." That much was true.

He stared at her a moment then walked into the pantry to look for the sewing kit. "Do you want me to bring her in?" he asked quietly.

"I can do it. You have enough to do today." There was a farmer's market at the Cape Light village green every Saturday morning, from Memorial Day to November. They had a spot there to sell their products. Rob usually took care of it while she stayed at the shop. He was getting a late start and had to get a move on.

Rob reappeared with the new laces. He sat at the table, taking out his frustration with the dog on his boot.

Her husband was so sweet. It was hard for him to get mad at anything. He liked the dog, too, though he would never admit it. She had caught him petting her more than once, when he thought she wasn't looking.

"I wonder if the shelter is open on Saturday."

"Why wouldn't they be? A lot of people work during the week. That's the only day they could look for a pet."

"Right." Audrey nodded, counting out the labels to make sure she had enough of each type—plain, herb-coated, and roasted garlic. The last one was a new flavor that was catching on.

"The shop will be busy. I'll have to close early."

"I'll be back by three. That should give you plenty of time."

She finally looked up at him but didn't say anything.

"Audrey, if you want to keep her, we'll keep her. But we never talked about it. You don't even like dogs."

"I know." She felt the dog's head come to rest on her bare foot.

Then the dog sighed. Oh, brother, this dog was too much. Rob didn't know the half of it.

"I just wish someone had answered the flyers. I only put them up yesterday. We could give it a little more time?"

Rob tied his other boot and stood up. "Some dogs have a little microchip implanted that will locate their owners. Did you know that?" Audrey had never heard of that technology and shook her head. "If you bring her to the shelter, they can scan her and maybe find her owner that way."

"That would be great. I hope she has one."

"Me, too," Rob said sincerely. He leaned over and held her shoulder while he kissed her good-bye. Then he leaned back just a little and stared into her eyes. "If she's here any longer, you'll really get attached. Then what?"

Audrey didn't know what to say. "Have a good day. Sell a lot of cheese," she called as her husband walked out.

The dog stirred and stretched out, obviously relieved her nemesis had gone and she had Audrey all to herself again.

She was a pretty dog, Audrey thought. Not that badly behaved either—except for the boot laces and a few socks. Her company had been a big distraction the last few days, even her bad behavior. *Keeping my mind off the appointment with the specialist on Tuesday*, Audrey realized.

But there was a family somewhere who missed her. It wasn't fair to keep her. For that reason alone, Audrey knew she had to do the right thing and keep trying to find the dog's owner.

The farm's shop was busy all day, as Audrey had predicted, keeping her mind off the onerous chore facing her. By the late afternoon, Audrey's resolve had melted, but Rob appeared promptly at three and she couldn't make any more excuses.

She carried the dog's rope leash, but didn't even bother fastening it to her collar. "Come on, sweetie. Want to go for a ride?"

The dog eagerly followed her to the truck and hopped in.

If only you knew what was coming, Audrey thought, glancing at her happy passenger as they left the farm.

She found the dog shelter in Essex easily, but the entrance to the office was not marked very clearly. On the way, she passed an open kennel filled with rows of dogs in wire cages, barking nonstop and jumping at the bars of their cages when she passed—or, worse, looking sad and disoriented, slunk back in a dark corner.

She walked by quickly, trying not to dwell on the dog's possible fate. She finally found the entrance and led the dog into the building. There was a small reception area that smelled strongly of disinfectant. A receptionist sat behind a glass window. An air conditioner hummed loudly, but Audrey could still hear the barking dogs in the background.

"This dog wandered onto our property. I'd like to have her scanned for a microchip," Audrey explained.

"Have a seat. Someone will be out for you shortly."

Audrey took a seat in a hard plastic chair, and the dog sat next to her, leaning on her leg and panting. *The dogs outside must have scared her,* Audrey thought. *Or maybe she just senses where she is.*

"Audrey Gilroy?" A veterinary technician called her name from another doorway. Audrey stood up and followed him, leading the dog into an exam room.

"When did you find her?" He crouched down to examine the dog.

"She found us, Tuesday night. She was barking in our yard during a thunderstorm so I took her in. There weren't any tags on her collar or any other ID. I put up some flyers yesterday, on Angel Island, where we live, and my husband brought a few into town this morning. We haven't heard from anyone yet."

"It might take a while. You'd be surprised. She may have come to the area with someone who was vacationing around here."

"Oh, right. I didn't even think of that."

"She seems to be in pretty good health, though she has a little skin rash on her belly."

Audrey had noticed it and put a bit of antiseptic lotion there but didn't know what else to do.

"I'll scan her for a chip and see what we find."

The dog was too big to lift onto the exam table. The vet tech kept her on the floor and asked Audrey to hold her head while he swept the scanning wand around the dog's body.

Audrey felt anxious but the dog was happy to be held by her, resting the full weight of her head in Audrey's hands. She stared up with total trust and adoration.

Audrey sighed and petted her silky fur. *Do you really have to make this so hard for me?* she nearly said out loud. Half of her wanted the vet to find a chip, and the other half screamed, *No-o-o-o! Stop!*

He finally leaned back and shook his head. "I'm sorry, I didn't find one. It's usually in the hindquarters or shoulder. I searched her entire body. Nothing."

"Oh, that's too bad," Audrey said, feeling surprisingly relieved. She patted the dog's head one last time and stood up.

The dog stared back and panted as if asking, "Time to go, right?"

"Do you plan to leave her here? Or keep her?" he asked.

"I'm not sure," she said honestly.

Rob would not be happy if she came back with the dog. But he would get used to the idea. Facing his annoyance seemed a small price to pay at that moment. What chance did the poor thing have here? She was so big and shaggy, no one would adopt her. No one with a nice home would want all that dog hair flying around. At least on the farm, it didn't matter . . . that much.

"It's a big responsibility," the vet tech said, cutting into her thoughts. "I'm not trying to pressure you."

"I understand." Audrey knew she had other things to worry about now, more important priorities. If she had to get fertility treatments, she would be away from the farm a lot and Rob might be, too. The dog would just be an extra worry.

As she tried to decide, the dog leaned against her leg and turned her head to look straight up at her. Audrey automatically gave her a reassuring pat. Just outside the window of the exam room, she heard the lonely, excited dogs, barking in their cold, bare cages.

Could she leave this sweet animal here to face that fate?

"I guess I'll take her back with me. I'm going to try a little harder to find her owner. Can I come back if I can't find her home?"

The vet tech smiled; Audrey could tell he was happier with that decision, too. "Absolutely. But if you're going to take her, she needs a few shots and some ointment for that rash."

The shelter gave her a discount on the medical costs because the dog was a rescue, but Audrey hadn't expected to pay any vet bills today. They also gave her a real leash and a few pamphlets on dog care and training.

Back in the truck, they headed for the island. "Well, here we are again," she said to her cheerful passenger. "I think you knew you didn't have a microchip. You just let me bring you anyway."

The dog leaned over and licked her ear.

"Okay, if you're going to hang around awhile, we need a few

ground rules. No chewing shoes or socks. Or stealing the goat food—or people food either," she added.

The dog seemed to be listening, Audrey noticed. Or maybe just humoring her.

"You'll hear more from Rob on this subject, I'm sure," she warned her.

The dog was not fazed. She appeared to smile and stuck her head out the window for the rest of the ride home.

THE crew was filming two scenes on Sunday in town. But Charlotte wasn't needed for either. She was glad to have some downtime. The inn was very quiet and even Meredith had gone off for the afternoon to explore Newburyport with a few other staffers who were not scheduled to work.

After lunch, Charlotte sat on the porch with her script, reviewing her lines for Monday's shooting schedule. Liza was out but had promised to take her for a ride around the island when she came back. All Charlotte had seen so far was the beach below the inn, where they had done most of the filming. And the ocean, of course.

She couldn't seem to focus on the script, and turned her attention to knitting instead. She had found the shop in Cape Light Claire had recommended and picked up yarn and a few supplies to start a knitting project. She had picked a pattern for a hat and matching scarf, a project she could complete before she left the island.

Charlotte was so immersed in her needles and yarn, she didn't notice Liza, cruising up to the porch on her bike. A crunch of gravel announced the innkeeper's arrival, and Charlotte suddenly looked up.

"Sorry, didn't mean to startle you." Liza slipped off the bike, then took a package from the basket in back. "So you found the knitting shop," she said, coming up the steps.

"Yes, I was so glad Claire told me about it. Knitting is sort of like meditation for me, except you have something to show for your efforts afterward. Besides, I like to think of the person I'm knitting for when I work on something. It's like sending waves of love in the stitches."

"How sweet. I never thought of knitting that way. I should try it. Maybe Claire can teach me."

"It's not hard," Charlotte encouraged her.

"What are you making? Looks like a hat," Liza observed.

"Yes, it will be," Charlotte said quickly. She glanced at Liza and changed the subject. "Do you ride your bike around here a lot?"

"When I'm not in too much of a hurry. It's good for my hips and the environment."

"I haven't been on a bike in years."

"You can take mine out if you like. You'll get a really good tour of the island on a bike ride," Liza suggested.

"I'd love that." Charlotte had reached the end of a row and capped the needles. She liked the idea of seeing more of the island, up close and personal—and incognito. It would be hard to recognize anyone under a bike helmet and sunglasses, she thought. And she could use the exercise, since her personal trainer, who often traveled with her on location, hadn't been available for this shoot. Charlotte couldn't afford to return to L.A. flabby. Her next role was a sultry nightclub singer in the 1940s, and all of the costumes were close-fitting.

"Would you like some company? I can come with you," Liza offered.

Charlotte sensed Liza was just being polite, and a bit overprotective.

"That's okay. You've already had your workout. You probably just want a cold drink and shower."

"I do," Liza admitted. "It might be more fun to wander on your own, anyway. There are only two big roads on the island. One goes north and south and the other, east and west. You can't really get lost, even if you try. I'll give you a map, and you have your cell phone—"

"I'll be fine, honestly," Charlotte cut in. "All I need are some water bottles."

"No problem. I'll bring them right out for you."

A few minutes later, Liza adjusted the bike seat for Charlotte's long legs and gave her a map with the island's best sites circled and her cell number written on the bottom of the page.

Charlotte set off, turning right at the bottom of the inn's long drive and heading for the village center. She glided past the Gilroy Farm and remembered her promise to Audrey to visit. But she was enjoying herself too much to stop. Maybe on the way back, she thought.

It was such a relief to have some time completely on her own. She was always surrounded and even smothered by her coworkers and helpers. The downtime was a real luxury, and she relished the feeling of the sun on her face and the sea-scented breeze that kept her cool as she pedaled along. Even the uphill climbs on the road were invigorating, forcing her muscles to kick into gear.

With the view of the ocean and blue sky to her left and the rolling green meadows of the farm on her right, Charlotte felt elated by the beauty all around her. There was so much open space here, endless blue sky arching over the sea and green spaces. Even though she owned a home on the water back in California, this place felt completely different. It was so empty and untamed. No mini-mansions and postmodern glass boxes marring the landscape.

She thought again about the island legend Colin had told her. She could understand why people here could believe in a story like that. This place was totally enchanting and the more she saw of it, the more she felt it casting its spell on her.

As she pedaled along her mind kept circling back to the idea of angels. She had never given much thought to them before—except to maybe think of them like Santa and the Easter bunny, sweet stories having very little to do with reality. But here the entire notion seemed more believable. The landscape was flat and empty; the sky seemed so vast, merging with the sea. Even the air seemed clearer and full of soft, radiant light.

The island was a unique place, she had no doubt, and she could easily believe it was a place touched by the powers above, a place that was closer to heaven somehow than the rest of the world. She did think there was something to the legend of healing here. She had felt it herself, the day she'd been rescued from the sea. The experience had touched her deeply, transforming her in some way she couldn't quite understand, and couldn't deny.

Charlotte pedaled along and soon came to the island's village center. Seeing the General Store, she decided to go in and explore. She stopped her bike then took off her helmet and sunglasses. She was about to go inside when a group of cyclists swooped into the village, swarming the small square. Dressed in black spandex shorts and colorful biking shirts, the group rode up to the store and dismounted, grabbing their water bottles. She lingered at a distance until one of them pulled off his helmet and waved to her.

Charlotte waved back, then put on her helmet, turned her bike, and kept going. The cyclist stood staring at her, wide eyed. Charlotte wasn't sure if she'd been recognized, but she didn't want to take any chances. She pushed on the pedals for some speed and headed on, passing the little tea shop and the medical clinic.

A few minutes later, when it seemed safe to stop, she took out a water bottle and consulted the map. Liza had circled the fishing village at the other end of the island as a spot worth seeing. Liza mentioned that Claire lived there.

The village was on the southwest coast of the island, along a little peninsula called Thompson's Bend that stuck out in the ocean. Charlotte stared at the circled spot. That was where Colin lived, too. If you didn't count the lobsters, she hadn't heard from him since Wednesday, the day he rescued her. And she hadn't stopped thinking about him since. If she rode out there, maybe she would run into him.

But as she considered the idea, she began to have her doubts. *Have you caught some weird bug from all your crazy fans and stalkers? You'll be doing the same thing to him that you hate people doing to you.*

Charlotte suddenly understood the crazy impulse. It wasn't really stalking. She just wanted to see where he lived. She probably couldn't pick out his house, but it would be fun to see the neighborhood. *Besides,* she reasoned as she started off, *he'll be out on his boat on such a perfect day anyway. He'll never even know I rode by.*

Charlotte knew it would have been much better if she could just douse the attraction she felt, not feed it like a fire that was growing inside her. But she just couldn't resist. Not as long as she was on this island.

The ride to the fishing village wasn't as short as it appeared on the map, but the scenery was breathtaking and well worth the effort. She finally saw a small wooden sign for the little community stuck to a post in the main road. Charlotte turned down a narrow lane, following the arrow.

Cobblestone streets were not the best for bike riding. As soon as she steered onto the stones, the bike bounced wildly under her and pedaling became much harder. She steered onto a narrow road flanked by tall beach grass and trees, and a mass of low cottages came into view. The main road branched off into narrow lanes, with quaint names, like Teapot, Fish Bone, and Hasty. She was fascinated. She had never seen anything quite like this place, which felt as if it had emerged unscathed from the nineteenth century. It was better than a movie set.

She turned at the corner of Fish Bone Lane and rode along. Some of the mailboxes at the side of the road bore names, but most had only numbers.

She spotted the name North on a mailbox and realized it might be Claire's cottage. It was just as Charlotte imagined Claire's home would look, only better. The low white cottage was covered with rambling pink roses on one side and had a brick chimney on the other. The windows were flanked by dark green shutters and offered window boxes full of summer flowers. A few steps led up to a small porch that covered the front of the cottage. The front door was painted bright yellow and some wicker furniture, lanterns, and more flower-pots filled the space. But most remarkable was the garden that filled one side of the front yard and overflowed into the side of the property. Charlotte paused, straddling the bike to get a better look at the rows of carefully tended vegetables and flowers, all mixed together but probably in a carefully considered arrangement. Rows of sunflowers bowed their heavy golden heads in her direction, as if bidding a respectful greeting. Charlotte spotted big ripe tomatoes, curling green squash, and other ripening treasures she couldn't identify.

Where did Claire get the time to work on this huge garden? she

wondered. She seemed to be working at the inn twenty-four hours a day. But she was a remarkable person in her quiet way; Charlotte was coming to see that.

She rode farther along, hoping Colin's cottage would be as easy to pick out, but she did not see any mailboxes with the name Doyle. She wound her way around the narrow streets, stopping twice to take photos with her cell phone. Then she headed in the direction she had come, hoping she could find her way back.

She was pedaling slowly, feeling every bump of the cobblestone lane. *Maybe I should get off and just push the bike awhile. I'm going to pay for this adventure tomorrow morning,* she realized, nearly laughing out loud. Still she pedaled along, at a slow, shaky pace, slowing down even more as she came to a corner.

Do I need to make a left here . . . or right?

A big red pickup truck drove up behind her. Charlotte hadn't even heard it coming until the last second. She felt a hot blast of air as it drove by. It came so close and she got so rattled, she lost her balance and felt the bike slip out from under her as she tumbled to one side.

It all happened so fast. She put her hands out to brace herself as the ground suddenly rushed up to meet her. The bike went forward and she slipped off sideways, tumbling onto someone's lawn.

Finally, her flying body came to a stop. She felt the hard ground under her and smelled fresh grass and dirt; she even tasted some in her mouth. She felt a little stunned but pushed herself up just as the truck came to a screeching stop. Her knee stung and her chin hurt. She took a deep breath and bent her leg to take a look.

The driver of the truck jumped out and ran toward her. "Hey, are you all right? Should I call an ambulance?"

She looked up, about to give the guy a piece of her mind, when she suddenly saw that it was Colin.

He stared at her in total shock. He obviously hadn't recogn.
her either, under the bike helmet and sunglasses.

"Charlotte? What are you doing out here? On a bike, no less.
He stared at her a long moment, shaking his head. "Can't we just
meet like normal people—without some life-threatening crisis?"

Despite her injuries, which she knew were minor, Charlotte had
to laugh. "Good point. We need to work on that."

"I'm so sorry," he said. "I should have been paying more attention. I must have been daydreaming or something." He caught sight
of her leg and winced. "That must hurt. You scraped your elbow, too."

Charlotte bent her arm to look at her elbow. "Whoops, I'll need
a little extra makeup on that one. As long as there's nothing on my
face," she said, feeling suddenly alarmed. "Do you see anything on
my chin? I think I banged it on the handlebars."

She held her face up to him and he leaned close to check. "Looks
good to me." He stared into her eyes a little longer than was necessary. Her heartbeat quickened.

"I'll be in trouble if I look banged up on camera," she explained.

Colin gave her a thoughtful look. She could tell he had no idea
just how closely she was watched and micromanaged.

"Come on, let me help you up." He stuck out his hand and she
grabbed it, then was lifted off the ground with a single tug. "Can you
get yourself over to the truck? I'll get the bike. You can come back to
my cottage and clean up."

Her knee hurt a little as she limped over to the truck, but it was
a small price to pay for a visit to Colin's house. Despite her little
aches and pains, she almost laughed out loud, realizing she had acci-
dentally achieved her goal—though not at all the way she planned.

Colin drove a short distance, making a few quick turns, and
finally pulled up to a whitewashed cottage that was set back from

the road and surrounded by tall trees. She caught a glimpse of sparkling water through the foliage and realized the back of the house faced the sea.

The driveway was coated with crushed white bits of seashells and made a crunching sound as the truck pulled up to the house. Colin climbed down from behind the steering wheel but Charlotte was slower, trying not to jostle her knee. Before she managed to get down, Colin had come around to her side.

"Here, let me help you. I feel so bad about this. It was so stupid of me."

He put his hands on her waist and gently swung her down to the ground. They stood like that a long moment. Charlotte swallowed hard, unable to look up at him. She'd had her fair share of romances and wasn't all that shy with men, but for some reason, it was very different with Colin.

He stepped away and cleared his throat. "Do you need help getting inside?"

"I can manage. All I need is an ice pack. My knee is just a little sore."

Charlotte's voice was light, but the blossoming bruises brought back bitter memories. She knew how to care for this type of injury all too well. She'd had a lot of practice hiding black and blue marks over the years. She was a pro at it, and so were her sisters and brother and her poor mother.

She found herself biting down on her lip, fighting back the sudden rush of memories. Colin glanced at her. "Actually, it hurts a lot, right? You just don't want to tell me."

He gently took her arm and led her to the front door. Charlotte stepped into a small foyer. A low wooden trunk with a cushion on top sat near the door. Above it she saw a row of hooks covered with

Colin's jackets and sweaters, and above that, a shelf that held hats. A staircase faced the front door, leading to an upper floor. Charlotte guessed the rooms up there had pitched ceilings; from the outside, the cottage looked too small to have two stories. She also saw openings to several rooms: a sitting room, a kitchen, and another room with a closed door. The walls were whitewashed with dark wood molding that made her feel as if she were in the Irish countryside. The low ceilings and wooden floors topped by area rugs added to that effect.

"Let's go in here and you can sit down," Colin said, leading her into the sitting room.

Charlotte's knee hurt more now, and after a moment or two of limping, Colin slipped his arm around her waist and practically carried her to a cushy leather chair next to the fireplace.

"Watch out for the books. I don't want you to break a leg or anything."

Charlotte feigned a smile at his mild joke. The truth was, she had only noticed the books in a distant, foggy part of her brain. His hard, strong body pressed close to hers was wildly distracting. By the time he set her down, she felt a bit light-headed. And she knew it wasn't from the tumble off her bike.

She made herself focus on the room and saw a fireplace built of round gray stones with a stained-wood mantel. There were pictures on it and built-in bookcases on either side of the hearth. More books were scattered on every surface, on the tables and in stacks on the floor. There were even a couple of books on the couch.

Colin gently lifted her leg up on a hassock. "Stay right there. I'll get some ice and a cloth."

Charlotte nodded. She felt a bit overwhelmed by all this atten-

tion. So far, all he did was take care of her. This was getting embar-
rassing. *He probably thinks I'm some sort of flailing, damsel-in-distress,*
she thought. Though the truth was Charlotte had taken charge of
her own life at eighteen and had been running it quite successfully
ever since.

No help for that now, she thought with a sigh. *He won't know me
long enough to realize I'm not like that.*

She glanced around, noticing the room seemed very much like
him. Comfortable but masculine; orderly but not too perfect. It was
a lot like the cabin in his boat. The décor wasn't any one style; it
was sort of a cozy mishmash, but what could you expect? She was
sure the good folk of Thompson's Bend didn't hire decorators, like
all her friends in L.A.

Her eyes were drawn to the framed photographs on top of the
fireplace mantel. She wished she could get a closer look at them, but
she didn't dare get up and bend her knee again. The bleeding had
just about stopped.

On the other side of her chair, she saw a tan couch with loose
throw pillows, and a rocking chair. She could easily picture Colin in
the rocker, stretching out his long legs, or taking a nap on the couch,
his feet probably hanging off the armrest.

At the opposite side of the room, a long wooden table stood in
front of several windows that framed an ocean view. The table was
obviously used as a desk, its wood surface displaying a laptop, a
brass reading lamp, neat piles of papers and folders, and yet more
books.

She wondered if he was going to school part-time, in between
his fishing trips. It looked like a lot of books and writing going on
here, for a man who made his living on the sea.

He soon returned with a tray that held two glasses of iced tea and a pile of first-aid supplies. It looked as if he had emptied out his entire medicine cabinet.

Charlotte nearly laughed. "Does it really look that bad? Just a bandage and some antiseptic cream would do."

"I have it here somewhere," he promised, setting the tray on a low table that appeared to be made from an old battered door. "Here's a washcloth. You can clean out the scrapes. I don't want to hurt you," he admitted.

Charlotte took the damp cloth and got the dirt out of her cuts. Then she dabbed on some antibiotic cream and covered her knee with a big bandage. Her elbow had already stopped bleeding and only needed the antiseptic. "Thanks," she said when she finished. "You run a good clinic here, Dr. Doyle."

Colin winced. "This place is a mess. I wasn't expecting company."

"It looks fine to me. You do have a lot of books, enough for a library," she added. She leaned over and sipped her iced tea. "I guess you like to read. I do, too. I've loved books ever since I was a kid. It was a big escape for me," she added, though she stopped short of admitting just what she needed to escape from.

"Me, too. I hate TV. I don't even own one. You don't get very good reception out here anyway. I'd rather read a good book. There's plenty of time for that in the winter."

"Because you can't fish?"

"Not unless I go south. Sometimes I do, but fishing year-round is not really my plan."

"Your plan? Hmm . . . That sounds mysterious. I guess I did sense something else going on with you. Do you lead a double life?"

He made a mock mysterious face, then moved closer to whisper his answer. "Not so loud. You'll blow my cover. I do lead a double life. I fish in the summer and write in the winter. I moved out to the island after I got my MFA in creative writing."

He had a master's degree? Charlotte was impressed. She had only finished two years at a community college in California, and taken some acting classes.

"I had a job at a boating magazine for a while after school and I tried to write at night," he explained. "But that was too draining and boring. So I came out here and decided to earn a lot of money fishing in the summer, then live off it the other months and write. It's been working out all right so far."

"That's an original solution." Charlotte knew a lot of fledgling writers, working on screenplays mostly. They all faced the same problems: bringing in an income to support their creative work and having enough energy left to write after a workday.

"What kind of writing do you do?" she asked.

"Fiction, mainly. I've had some short stories published. I'm working on a novel. It's almost finished. I've been trying to work on it a little this summer, but I hardly have time. I'm looking forward to getting back to it soon. It should be done by spring."

"That's exciting. What's it about? I know some writers don't like to talk about their work," she added quickly. "They think it will jinx it or something."

Colin laughed. "I'm not superstitious, but I still don't like to talk about it," he admitted. "I feel like, if I keep telling the story out loud to everyone, I won't feel like writing it anymore."

Charlotte nodded. "That makes sense. That's the way I feel when a director asks for too many takes of the same scene. It squeezes all the juice out or something."

"Exactly."

"Do you have a publisher yet?"

"No. But an editor who likes my short fiction said she would take a look."

"Hey, maybe if it's made into a movie, I could play one of the characters. Is there a part for me in the story?"

His smile grew wide at the suggestion. "I'm not sure . . . but I could write one in that would suit you. It's not too late."

The way he looked at her made Charlotte's face feel warm. Was she blushing? Was that even possible?

She looked away and smoothed out the bandage again. She had sensed there was something special about Colin. He was not only independent and unconventional but creative, a combination that she found incredibly attractive. The more she learned about Colin, the more she felt drawn to him.

The sound of her cell phone brought her back to reality.

It was a call from the inn; she heard Liza's worried voice on the other end.

"Charlotte? I'm just calling to see if you're all right. Did you have any trouble with the bike? Maybe I should pick you up. You must be tired."

Before Charlotte could answer she heard Meredith in the background. "Is she all right? I don't think she should have gone out biking all alone. That wasn't smart."

"I'm fine. Can you hold on a minute, please?" Charlotte pressed the phone to her chest. "They're about to let the bloodhounds loose. I have to go back."

"I'll drive you, no problem."

That would be the fastest solution, Charlotte thought. It would also require the fewest explanations.

"I can get back on my own, don't worry. I'm not far," Charlotte told Liza. She felt a little guilty fibbing, but the island was so small, she really wasn't far.

Charlotte hung up and slid her cell phone back into her pocket. Then she got up slowly from the chair.

"How's your leg? Need any help?"

Colin held out a strong arm. The offer was tempting but Charlotte shook her head. "I feel much better, thanks. I'm sure I won't even notice it tomorrow. Thanks for the tea and the first-aid kit." She looked around wistfully. She had enjoyed her little escape so much, it was hard to see it end.

"You have a really nice house," she said as she started toward the door. "It's really . . . you."

He laughed. "I'm not sure if I should take that as a compliment, but I think you meant it that way. You'll have to come back when you have more time."

It was the kind of casual, automatic invitation anyone might extend, but it made Charlotte feel deeply happy. "I'd like that," she replied. "I'd like that very much."

They walked outside and Colin helped her into the truck, then got behind the wheel. It was a short ride to the inn. They breezed past the village center and drove along the coast. The edge of Gilroy Farm soon came into view.

Charlotte had been asking Colin questions about fishing, but suddenly touched his arm, interrupting him. "I'm sorry, but you'd better drop me off here. I'll just walk the bike the rest of the way."

He glanced at her, looking puzzled, but slowed the truck and began to pull over. "Why can't I bring you up to the inn?"

"I know it seems strange, but if you bring me back, there will be a lot of questions. It's been such a perfect afternoon, driving around on my own. Even getting mowed down by your truck," she teased him. "I just felt like a normal person for a few hours," she tried to explain. "It would get spoiled completely."

She glanced at him, wondering if he understood. She could see he was trying to. She wanted to protect the fragile connection growing between them.

"I guess you don't have much privacy," he said finally.

"I don't have any," she said glumly. "Reporters follow me everywhere. Nothing feels off limits to them. The more outrageously intrusive the photo, the more money they're worth. The producer has some security people chasing them away when we film, but I know they've staked out the inn with their high-powered cameras. They caught me on the dock, coming off your boat, and they'll catch me again. They could even be hiding in that tall grass, disguised as goats." She pointed at the meadow, trying to make a joke out of it.

He stared out at the goats and rubbed his chin. "Which one do you think is part of the paparazzi? That white one? Is that a bell around his neck—or a digital camera?"

She laughed but felt sad inside. "I'm sorry. I know it sounds like I'm exaggerating, even paranoid. But it's almost that bad."

"I believe you, Charlotte. You're just so nice . . . and normal. I keep forgetting that you're so famous."

Of all the compliments he could have come up with, that one pleased her the most. "Well, thanks. I hate when people treat me like some exotic creature in a zoo. I'm a regular person, just like everyone else."

He smiled at her reply. "I wouldn't go that far. You're not like anyone I've ever met before."

Then he looked suddenly serious. He took her face in his hands and kissed her so sweetly it made her toes curl. The kiss was long and deep, and Charlotte wished it could go on forever.

She sat back feeling stunned, while a rare kind of happiness bubbled up inside. She lifted her hand and pressed it to his cheek. "You're not like anyone I ever met before either. I really mean that."

He took her hand and dropped a kiss on her palm. "When can I see you again?"

Charlotte didn't answer. She just stared into his deep blue eyes, wondering if they should see each other again. Where could this lead, except to both of them feeling hurt and frustrated?

"You *don't* want to see me again?" His voice was light and teasing, but she saw the first shadow of hurt in his eyes, and she couldn't bear it. She couldn't hurt him, especially not for a lie.

"Yes, I do. Very much." She told him the truth. "I don't know when though. The filming schedule can be so crazy, especially with the weather. It's hard to know when I'll be free," she explained. "Give me your cell phone number. I'll call you."

"All right. Just make sure you do." Colin grinned and quickly gave her his number, and she gave him hers. Then he jumped out of the truck and took her bike from the back and set it on the road.

With a little sting in her scraped knee, she was able to get back on the bike and start pedaling toward the inn. Colin watched her a moment from inside the truck, then waved and drove away in the opposite direction.

The inn was only a short distance from the farm and soon came into sight. Charlotte saw Meredith watching out a window in the sitting room. By the time Charlotte reached the front steps of the inn, her assistant was on the porch, looking frantic. "Charlotte, we were worried about you. Where have you been and what's that on your knee? Did you fall?"

Charlotte parked the bike near the porch, checking it over for any dents or scratches. She didn't want to leave Liza with a damaged bike. But it looked all right. It had fallen on the grass, she recalled.

"I had a little spill," she told Meredith. "But a very nice couple helped me and drove me part of the way back." Meredith eyed the bandage. "They had a first-aid kit in their truck," Charlotte added.

"I hope it doesn't leave a mark," Meredith said. "You'd better stick close to the inn until we go. This cute little island is hazardous to your health."

Charlotte smiled. "Don't worry, I think I'll survive."

Charlotte was glad it was dusk and the fading light of the sun hid her expression. She felt as if she were glowing like a firefly. She wanted to sing and dance and run out on the beach and scream at the top of her lungs, to shout out to the whole world, "The most wonderful man in the world just kissed me. I can't wait to see him again!"

But of course, that was out of the question. Though she might sneak a song or two in the shower.

Meredith was watching her closely. "Are you all right?"

Charlotte nodded and swallowed back her happiness. It was hard to keep a normal tone. "I'm fine. I think I'll just sit out here a minute and watch the sunset."

"Okay, see you inside. Liza is going to serve dinner in a few minutes. She was waiting for you."

"I'll be right in," Charlotte promised.

She had never asked Colin about the lobsters. She had to remember to ask the next time she spoke to him. Soon, she hoped. Maybe even later tonight.

She knew the whole idea of falling for Colin was insane. There were a million and one reasons why nothing would come of it. But she couldn't wait to hear from him. She couldn't wait to see him again. She couldn't deny it.

Chapter Seven

Dusk was falling when Audrey and Rob returned from Boston. Audrey was the first one in the house. She knew the dog was waiting for her. The poor thing hadn't been out all day. Rob went straight to the goats, stopping just long enough at the barn door to pull his rubber boots on over his good pants.

Audrey opened the back door to the house and, as she expected, was greeted by ecstatic barks. The dog was desperate to go out but still had time for a happy-dance greeting, jumping around Audrey and wagging her tail so hard she nearly knocked over a chair. She tried to lick Audrey's face, acting as if they had been separated for weeks.

Audrey was trying to teach her better behavior, but so far she was more of a Dog Shouter than a Whisperer.

"Down, girl. Go out. Go ahead." Audrey opened the back door again, and the dog finally took off. Audrey didn't worry about the dog running away. The property was bordered by sturdy fences, keeping the goats in and unwanted creatures out. Audrey filled the dog's bowl with kibble and gave her fresh water. Moments later, she found her at the back door again, eagerly sniffing through the screen for her dinner.

Well, that was easy. People food was another story, unless she was serving cold cereal tonight. Audrey felt exhausted, too tired to cook, but she did have some tasty leftovers on hand and stuck them in the microwave while she worked on a green salad.

The visit to the fertility specialist in Boston had taken all day. The drive was only about two and a half hours but by the time they had the appointment, got some lunch, and did a little shopping, it was late afternoon before they started home, hitting commuter traffic to the North Shore villages all the way.

She knew that Rob felt tired, too, the fatigue more emotional and stress-related than physical. They hadn't done a bit of work, just driven around in traffic, then been poked and prodded by a doctor. They would get the results sometime next week. Audrey hated the waiting. So much of her life these many months seemed to be about waiting: Waiting for the best time to conceive. Waiting to see if she was pregnant. Waiting to try again.

She wanted a baby so much. Being childless was becoming more and more painful. It seemed everywhere she looked, there were babies, like the other day at the General Store. It seemed like a baby conspiracy. Sometimes it felt as if she were surrounded by babies dozing in strollers, riding in car seats, or lugged along in snuggly little packs, strapped to their mothers. So heart-wrenchingly sweet and beautiful.

Friends and acquaintances would call and casually report that they were expecting. All of her friends and siblings who had gotten married about the same time, and some who were recently married, had children by now. In their late thirties, she and Rob were getting a late start. That was part of the problem right there. But it was just easier for some couples, no question. Her friends and relatives didn't mean to hurt her feelings with their happy reports. They had no idea what she and Rob were going through.

Audrey usually wasn't a very prayerful person, but she had become one lately. Sometimes she asked God why this was so hard for her and Rob. She asked God to help them—or at least, help them understand why they weren't among the fortunate ones. So far, nothing was clear to her.

As a medical professional, she knew there were amazing advances these days to help couples conceive and have a child. She just wasn't sure yet if she wanted to exhaust the possibilities of medical intervention in order to start a family.

She wasn't sure if Rob wanted that either. The doctor had outlined a few courses of treatment with them. He couldn't say yet which was the most appropriate or even necessary. A lot depended on the test results. More waiting, Audrey thought. More hoping and praying.

By the time Rob came in, the food was ready. They went out to the porch to eat, and Audrey lit a large candle. The summer days were winding down, and darkness was already starting to fall earlier each evening.

"My, my. Very romantic." Rob sat down and unfolded his napkin.

"You say that now. You haven't seen the menu. I just heated some turkey chili that was left over from the other night. Maybe we should have eaten in town."

Rob picked up his fork and dug in. "Darling, I'd take your turkey chili over a gourmet meal in Boston any day."

"You only say that because it's cheaper. And because you're so hungry, you'd eat the tablecloth with a little shredded cheddar and chopped onions on it."

"That, too," he admitted between mouthfuls.

Audrey laughed at his expression as he met her eyes. They could always find something to laugh about. That's what she loved about Rob, why she loved being married to him. They could always talk things out in a reasonable, calm manner—ninety-nine percent of the time, anyway. They would get through this with God's help, she was sure.

She sighed and began eating. They had carefully avoided discussing the doctor's visit on the ride home but had to sort it out sometime. She let out a breath but wasn't quite ready.

"So, what do you think?" Rob asked finally.

"Shouldn't have left the chili in the microwave that long. It's a little dry."

"Audrey." Rob gave her a look. "About what the doctor said."

Audrey shrugged. "He didn't say much, did he? It all seems to depend on the test results. Did you hear something different?"

"We have to wait for the results, that's true. But he did say he suspects we'll need to go the full route, with intense treatments. I think he just wants the tests to confirm it."

There was a small chance their challenges weren't that extreme and the problem could be addressed with the help of local doctors, with drugs and hormone therapy. But that hope was slim. Rob was right, as usual. They pretty much knew the answer they'd get.

"I know we don't know for sure yet, honey," he went on. "But we ought to talk about possibilities. If we need to go the major fertility treatment route, it would make a big impact on our life. We would probably want you to be treated in Boston, and you'll need to be close to the doctor's office. During some phases of the treatment, you have to see the doctor every day."

"I know that," Audrey said calmly. "I figured I would have to stay over in the city when we get to that part. Maybe I can stay at my sister's house. She doesn't live that far out."

"Maybe," Rob said, though his tone was doubtful.

Audrey could guess his concerns. Her sister lived in Belmont, which was thirty to forty minutes from the city. So it was definitely close enough, but it would be odd staying over more than a night or two. The house wasn't very large, and Audrey would have to sleep on a pullout couch in the living room.

Rob was quiet for a moment. He was done with his dinner and pushed aside the plate. "You would be gone weeks at a time, honey. What about your work here? You know this place needs two of us to run it. We could hire someone to take over your work, but I'm not sure we could afford that and the treatments, too."

"Yes, I know the fertility treatments are expensive, but you do wind up with a baby," she reminded him. "Or," she said more honestly, "there's a good chance that we will. I know nothing's guaranteed." She sighed. It was hard to ask the question but she had to. "You do still want a baby, right? I mean, what the doctor said, about how hard it might be for us, that didn't change your mind, did it?"

Rob looked alarmed at her question, then took her hand. "Of course I want a baby, as much as ever. We're in this together, sweetheart. I'm just sorry that I can't share more of the physical burden with you. Especially hearing all you might have to go through." He squeezed her hand. "We will have a baby, honey. Don't worry. That's going to happen for us. Nothing can change my mind. It's something we've both wanted for a long time and it will be worth any sacrifice. Right?"

She nodded, feeling on the verge of tears. She was so weepy lately. She didn't know what was wrong with her, especially when they got into this subject.

"We just have to figure it all out," he continued. "We have to be realistic about it—about where you would get the treatments, what it will cost, and how this will all work out with us running the farm. That's all I'm trying to say."

Audrey nodded. She didn't know the answer to any of those questions. "I guess we should check with the insurance company. Maybe some of this is covered?"

"I did. They don't give much for fertility issues under our plan. We went for the no-frills coverage, remember?"

When they both worked in the city, she as a nurse and Rob as an accountant in a big firm, they had excellent health coverage. But once they went into business for themselves, they had skimped on insurance. They were relatively young and in good health, so they decided not to pay for a lot of coverage they would never use. Which had turned out to be the correct guess—with this sole exception.

"I'm just not sure how we're going to afford everything, honey. The farm is doing all right, for a new business. But you know what the books look like some months. One unexpected vet bill blows us out of the water. If you have to stay in Boston for weeks at a time, not only will I miss you, but who will do your chores? No one's going to do it for free."

Audrey felt an aching hollowness in her heart. "You're saying that we might have to give up the farm?"

"Audrey, I'm sorry, honey. Maybe it's too early to even talk about this. But I've looked at the costs and our finances. I don't think we can pursue fertility treatments *and* run the farm, too. Even if we could somehow scrape by and worked twenty-four seven to hold it together while you were working on the baby project, do we really want to start a family feeling so economically unstable, possibly in debt?"

In more debt than they already carried, she knew he meant.

Audrey held her hands under the table so Rob wouldn't see them trembling. She knew fertility treatments were expensive. She just hadn't stopped to work out the math—or look at what these choices might really cost them.

Rob reached for her hand, and she felt hers stop trembling in his strong grip. "Giving up the farm would be the very last option. We can try to get a loan or a second mortgage, but I'm not sure we'd qualify. We don't have much equity here yet. We can try to lease out the land, but that would have to cover our mortgage."

"It wouldn't be as bad as having to sell the place," Audrey said quickly. "But we'd have to do something with the goats, I guess."

"The goats are an asset. I'm sure we can sell them."

"Sell them? Do we have to? Can't we put them in storage or something?" She was half joking but half serious, too. The goats were like pets to her. She knew them all by name and knew their personalities—which ones liked carrots and which liked to be scratched under the chin.

"Audrey, come on." Rob couldn't help laughing at the suggestion.

"Maybe some other farmer would watch them for us for a while. If we paid board, I mean."

Rob didn't answer. He didn't have to. She knew what he would say: That would be another expense. Best to just cash in the goats if they decided to leave the farm.

"Hey, we don't have to figure this out tonight," he said gently. "I just wanted to start the conversation rolling. We have options, Audrey. Don't worry."

"I know. We do have options," she repeated, though it didn't sound to her as if they had many.

Rob rose and touched her shoulder, then picked up their plates and carried them into the kitchen. "Sit a minute, I'll clean up."

He was finished talking about this for now. She was thankful for that. She felt drained and downhearted. There wasn't too much to say or do until the test results came back.

It was the first time in their marriage that they had faced such a big question. Coming out to the island and having the farm had been a dream for both of them, but mostly for Rob. It had been his idea. Audrey loved the life they had made on the island these past years and always imagined raising their children here. Could they really trade their life here to start a family—and take away Rob's happiness in the bargain?

He might work out all the facts and figures now and even be the one proposing the solution. But down the road, years from now, she was afraid he might regret giving up the farm and all they'd built here. She worried that he might grow to resent her.

It was all so complicated. She felt the familiar frustration. She and Rob were good people. They would be good parents. It just didn't seem fair.

The dog had been lying under the table during dinner, as she usually did. Now she stood up and nudged Audrey's hand with her muzzle.

"Did you miss me today, is that it?" Audrey asked, stroking her silky head. "Or are you just looking for leftovers?"

The dog rested her head in Audrey's lap and let out a long sigh.

Audrey sat petting the dog and realized she was crying a little. She sniffed and shook her head. Silly. No reason for that.

We'll get through this, one way or another, she told herself. *It will be hard but we'll figure it out. There are always hard choices in life and unexpected changes.*

"We'll be okay as long as Rob and I stick together," she told the dog. "We love each other very much. That's the most important thing."

The dog licked her hand. "You're sweet," Audrey told her.

A sweet distraction from sad thoughts. I don't know where you came from, dog, but at least I have you.

On Wednesday morning, Audrey found a message from Liza on her cell phone. "Hey, Audrey, I was just wondering when you wanted to come over and meet Nick Dempsey. He usually gets back to the inn around four p.m., so I thought you could just be hanging out here, blocking the doorway or something, so he can't get up to his room without talking to you. Let me know what you think of my subtle plan. Any day this week is good for me. And by the way," she added, "did I tell you that he loves goat cheese and is an amateur chef?"

Audrey was still feeling drained and blue about their visit to the doctor and her conversation with Rob; she didn't feel up to a visit to the inn to meet her favorite heartthrob movie star. Besides, she still had to catch up on her work. Even one day away from the farm left double the chores. Audrey called Liza back a few hours later and thanked her for the invitation. "I can come tomorrow. Will that be okay?"

"Perfect. He should be back again between three thirty and four, so just come a little before that," Liza told her.

"I'm not sure if I can get my hair and nails done and lose ten pounds by three fifteen tomorrow. But I'll try. See you then," she promised. "And I'll bring plenty of cheese. I've got that one covered."

"I'm sure you do," Liza replied.

Liza was the crafty one, Audrey realized the next day as she dressed and put on makeup for her sneak attack on Nick Dempsey. It was as if her friend had guessed she was feeling low and had figured out the perfect distraction. Well, it seemed to be working, Audrey thought as she fluffed out her auburn hair and checked the tie at the back of her sundress.

I'm no Beverly Hills babe, that's for sure. I look like a country girl, plain and simple. But that's who I am and it will have to do, she decided with a smile.

Down in the kitchen, she grabbed the basket of gourmet cheeses and treats she had prepared for her idol and started for the door.

The dog, who had been following her around all day as usual, trekked close behind. Audrey didn't see any harm in that. Liza wouldn't mind, as long as the dog stayed out on the porch.

They soon arrived on Liza's property. As Audrey walked through the gated trellis in the fence, she saw Liza waiting on the porch. The dog bounded up the stairs, eager to make new friends, her tail wagging wildly.

"Down! Don't jump up on Liza!" Audrey commanded, jogging now to catch up with the dog.

"So you kept her, I see." Liza was laughing as the dog tried to lick her face.

"She kept us, you might say. We didn't get any calls from the flyers yet. And Rob likes her, too. Neither one of us wants to take her back to the shelter. So here she is, in all her furry glory," Audrey added. "Stay down, silly. Don't jump on Liza. Please? Here, let me put your leash on now."

Audrey set the basket of cheese on a table and quickly fastened the dog's leash, then tied it to a porch rail. "She'll settle down in a minute. She's just very social."

"I can see that. Here, I'll give her some water." There were a few pretty china dessert bowls on a tray alongside a larger bowl of berries and a pitcher of iced tea and another filled with ice water. Liza poured some water for the dog and set it down for her.

"Liza, you don't have to serve my dog from your antique china," Audrey said.

"Don't worry, it's not the really good stuff. Just some pretty odds and ends I found in the basement. Besides, it's a tradition of the inn. My aunt used to serve all her pets with the antique Wedgwood."

"You're not getting the same treatment at home, Millie. So don't get used to it," Audrey said to her dog.

"So you gave her a name—Millie?" Liza asked.

Audrey nodded. "Yes, we decided this weekend we couldn't just keep calling her *dog*. I called her Silly a lot because she's always doing something to make us laugh. But Rob thought that name would be bad for her self-esteem. So we decided to call her Millie. She looks like a Millie, I think. And it's close enough to 'silly' to fit her personality."

"I think it's a perfect name for her," Liza agreed, petting the dog's head as she sat between them.

"She's a handful, but also a big distraction, and she has to be the happiest animal on the face of the planet," Audrey added honestly. "Never in a bad mood, always ready to play, never needs coffee to wake up in the morning. And she never holds a grudge if we get mad at her." Audrey shrugged. "I can really take a lesson from this dog most days. And I can use all the distraction I can get, too."

"How did the doctor's appointment go?" Liza asked.

Audrey quickly filled her in. "We have to wait for the test results, of course. But it sounds like we'll need to go through a pretty involved treatment process—hormone shots, egg harvesting, the works." She sighed. "I know a lot of couples face this and go through it, but it's not going to be easy. It makes me angry at myself, for waiting so long," she admitted. "But it just didn't seem to be the right time before this, you know?"

"I do," Liza said quietly. "I'm afraid sometimes that I'm waiting too long to have children, too. But what can I do? I knew that I didn't want to start a family with my first husband. And I'm glad now that I didn't. Having a baby seems like the most natural thing in the world, but it's still a miracle. I think it will just happen for you when the time is right."

When God thinks it's the right time to send a baby, Audrey knew her friend meant. She did agree with that. *Everything good in this life came from God, no question about it. But you still have to help yourself, don't you?*

"I know what you mean, Liza. But it's hard for Rob and me not to try to push the process along. Doesn't God help those who help themselves? We can't just sit by and hope for the best. It's too frustrating."

Liza's expression was sympathetic. "I understand. I didn't mean to sound as if I didn't. I think you're doing all the right things. I hope it happens faster than you expect. Faster than anyone expects," she added.

"Thanks. I know you're in my corner," Audrey said, patting her friend's hand.

Liza served the tea and berries. There were also some small peanut butter cookies, one of Claire's specialties. Audrey enjoyed one with her tea.

The conversation about her baby problem had taken her mind off the main event completely. She glanced at her watch. "It's almost half past three. I guess he'll be back soon, right?"

"Very soon," Liza promised.

"So how is it going, having all these movie people here? You've hardly said a word about it."

"It's been an experience," Liza replied. "They've mostly been very polite and easy to deal with. Charlotte is a real sweetheart. You would hardly know she's famous."

Audrey had to smile at the casual way her friend referred to the megastar. "How about Nick—or do you call him Nicky?"

Liza laughed. "We call him Nick. Or Mr. Dempsey. He's very nice, too. Lovely manners. A little fussier than Charlotte at times. But he adores Claire. We can hardly get him out of the kitchen. He watches her every move as if she were a walking, talking cooking show."

"Oh, she must love that," Audrey said dryly. Claire was notorious for blending in with the wallpaper. She was the last person in the world who would want that kind of scrutiny.

"She's managing. You know Claire. Nothing ruffles her."

"And how about Daniel? I bet he's not in awe of the movie stars at all."

"He's not, though he joked around about it before he left for Canada."

"Canada? What's he doing up in Canada?"

Liza looked surprised at Audrey's reply. "Oh, I thought you knew. I thought he probably saw you at the clinic before he left and told you he was going out of town."

"I wasn't at the clinic last week. I had to miss my shift." Audrey and Daniel both volunteered at the island's medical clinic and often saw each other there. "Did he go on vacation?"

"Not exactly. A college friend asked if he would help finish a summerhouse he was building on Prince Edward Island. All the framing is done, but the friend was worried he wouldn't get the interior finished before the fall weather set in. So Daniel went up to help him. It should take about two weeks, maybe a little more."

"Two weeks? That's a long time. Won't you miss him?"

"I will. But I've been so busy with the movie people, we've hardly had a chance to get together. And he needed the work, so . . ." Liza shrugged. "I hope it goes faster than he expects."

"Me, too, for your sake." Audrey smiled at her friend but didn't say anything more. Liza and Daniel were perfect for each other. You could see them together for a minute and you could just tell. They still had issues to work out, that was for sure. But Audrey secretly hoped that she and her good friend would someday be pushing baby strollers side by side down the beach road. With Millie trotting alongside, of course.

Before she could confess this happy daydream, the sound of cars coming down the gravel drive made her turn around.

"There they are. They're back," Liza said quietly.

Audrey's mouth got suddenly dry and she took a sip of tea.

She had already met Nick Dempsey in person last week when the group arrived. But this was way different. She was actually going to talk to him.

She heard car doors slam, and two men and a woman got out of the first car. "Those are the movie execs, the producer, the production associate, and the director," Liza whispered as she got up to greet her guests. Audrey rose and followed.

"Hi, everyone," Liza began as other cars parked and emptied out. "There are some refreshments out here for you and more inside. Please let me know if you need anything before dinner."

The movie execs were all talking intensely to one another and barely acknowledged her as they headed into the inn.

Audrey heard someone else coming up the walk and turned to see Nick Dempsey. Her heart pounded in her chest and she felt so light-headed, she had to hold on to the porch rail for support. She heard Millie whining behind her, obviously unhappy at being tied up. But Audrey couldn't move. She felt riveted to the spot.

Nick Dempsey was even more handsome than she remembered from last week. He still wore some makeup from the set, but it only seemed to enhance his good looks. Liza stood next to her and held her arm. "Nick, I'm so glad you got back early today. This is my friend Audrey. She and her husband run the farm next door. She just stopped by for a visit, and she was dying to meet you."

Audrey was afraid he would be annoyed to have a fan hanging around. If he was, he hid it well. He flashed a flawless white grin and stuck out his hand to greet her as he came to the top of the steps.

"Audrey, how nice to meet you. I've been admiring that little farm from my bedroom window. You raise goats there, do you?"

Audrey smiled back shyly. She couldn't quite find her tongue. "Yes, we do. For their milk. We make cheese mostly. Goat cheese. And fudge and soap," she added quickly.

"How nice. I love cheese." He smiled again. Audrey nearly sighed out loud.

Millie barked, then made a long, funny whining sound that made them all look at her. "That's my dog. She's a character," Audrey said.

"She looks sweet. We have three dogs at home. I miss them," Nick confided. Audrey already knew that from all the articles she had read about him and the clips she'd seen on entertainment gossip shows. He walked over to Millie and began petting her. "What's her name?"

"Millie, rhymes with silly," Audrey explained. She knew the names of Nick's dogs but didn't want to admit it. She didn't want him to think she was a totally crazed fan.

"Have you had her long?"

"Not very," Audrey admitted. "She sort of wandered onto our farm and adopted us."

Nick laughed at her joke and she felt very clever. "Dogs are very intuitive. They know who likes them." He suddenly noticed the iced tea. "This looks good. It was hot out there today." He poured himself a glass of tea and began to drink it thirstily.

Audrey was mesmerized, watching his Adam's apple as he swallowed the tea. She never watched Rob drink a glass of iced tea, or a glass of anything, for that matter. But everything Nick Dempsey did seemed . . . superhuman.

"Would you like some berries or a peanut butter cookie?" Liza offered. "Please help yourself."

He looked tempted then turned away, patting his waistline. "I'll wait for dinner. After hanging around this place, I'll need triple workout sessions when I get home."

You look fine to me, Audrey wanted to say. But of course, she couldn't.

"Well, ladies, nice to chat. I'd better grab a quick nap. We're working again tonight, shooting a scene in town."

"Really? That's exciting . . . for the people in town, I mean," Audrey said.

He smiled at her. "There will be a few onlookers, I'm sure."

Try the entire town, Audrey thought. She wondered if Rob would consider driving over to Cape Light tonight, but decided that was too much to ask. Too much Nick Dempsey up close and personal in one day. Even for her.

"Great to meet you, Audrey," Nick said politely.

"Very nice to meet you," she replied, sensing he was ready to go inside. She suddenly felt Liza jab an elbow into her side. What in the world?

Then she remembered. The basket. She hadn't given it to him.

"Wait, I brought you a present." Audrey grabbed the basket she brought over and handed it to him. "It has a selection of cheeses and other products. And a cookbook."

"Thank you very much. That's beautiful. It all looks delicious. I love to cook. It's my hobby. I'm hoping to open a restaurant in L.A. soon," he added proudly.

"Liza told me. I think that's great. It will be mobbed," she said, sounding very sure of it.

Nick looked pleased by her prediction. "I hope you're right. If the food is good enough, people will find you. That's what the professionals say," he added. "I'm trying to learn every angle of the business right now, especially the food side. For instance, I've always wondered how cheese is made. Would you mind if I popped by sometime and saw your operation?"

Audrey could hardly breathe. "N-No. Not at all. I mean, of course. Please come. Any time. I'll give you the grand tour and a cheese-making lesson."

"That sounds great. I will take you up on it the first chance I get." With the basket in one hand, he winked and waved. "See you soon, Audrey. Thanks again for the treats."

Audrey waved back, feeling light-headed again. "You're very welcome. See you, Nick."

All too soon the screen door slammed behind him, and he was gone.

"Well, what do you think?" Liza's voice came to her as if in a dream. "Do you still think Nick Dempsey is awesome and amazing—or just a mortal human being?"

"The former. Even more awesome than I imagined," Audrey said happily. "Not quite as tall," she whispered, leaning closer to her friend. "But does that really matter? Nah . . . ," she said, answering her own question. "Do you think he'll really come to the farm?"

Liza shrugged. "I think he might if he has the time. He seemed really interested."

"I think he might, too," Audrey agreed. She walked over to Millie and untied her leash. It was almost five, time for them to head back to the farm. "Wow, wait until I tell Rob. He won't believe it. Do you think I should do anything special to get ready? Like, wash the goats or something?"

Liza gave her a look. "You're kidding, right?"

Audrey was kidding, but partly serious, too. "Well, whether Nick Dempsey actually comes to the farm, the very idea that he might has certainly given me something to think about. Aside from my baby woes," she admitted to her pal. She leaned over and gave Liza a quick hug. "Thanks for making that happen, Liza. I definitely owe you one."

"Oh, you don't owe me anything. You engineered that invitation yourself," she added in a hushed tone, glancing over her shoulder. "But I do hope he comes. I can already see the autographed photo hanging in the cheese shop."

"So can I," Audrey admitted. "I'm going out to buy a really nice frame for it tomorrow. You know what they say about movie stars."

"If you have a frame for the photo, they will come?" Liza improvised.

Audrey smiled and nodded. "Something like that."

A few minutes later, she hopped off the porch and headed back to the farm with Millie trotting alongside. She was feeling far more positive and upbeat than she had for days, that was for sure.

CHARLOTTE returned to the inn a little later on Thursday afternoon than her costar and the studio executives. She had to stop in town to meet with the wardrobe mistress. There was a problem with the dress she was to wear for the scene they were filming that night, and she had to have a special fitting.

When she got back to the inn, she quickly headed for her room to relax and freshen up before dinner. As she unlocked the door, she felt her phone buzz in the back pocket of her jeans. She opened the door, went inside, and checked the number, then quickly closed the door behind her and locked it. She didn't need Meredith poking her head in right now or even Liza, trying to be helpful.

She pressed her back against the locked door and hit the Answer button, then heard Colin's deep voice on the other end.

"Hey. I thought I was going to get your voice mail again. Did I catch you at a bad time?"

"Not at all. I finished a little late today. I just got back to the inn. Just in time for one of Claire's delicious mega-calorie meals," she added.

"It all looks good on you, Charlotte," he teased her. "How did it go today?"

Charlotte had told Colin about her difficulties working with Bradley. Now as she gave him today's installment, she could feel the tension leave her. It wasn't what she was saying. It was knowing that Colin was there listening that gave her a calm perspective she'd never quite had before.

"So it wasn't too bad," she finished. "But the day isn't over yet. We're shooting a scene in Cape Light at the harbor tonight."

"Cool. Maybe I'll stand in the crowd behind the barriers and gawk at you."

Charlotte laughed and sat back against the headboard of her bed, hugging her legs to her chest. "Don't do that. You'll make me nervous. I'll flub my lines."

"Me? Make you nervous? I doubt that. But I won't come and gawk if you don't want me to. Though the entire rest of the town will be there," he reminded her. "How else am I going to see you? Can't you steal that bike again and take a ride? It won't be dark for hours." His tone was charming and very persuasive.

Charlotte glanced out the window, feeling tempted. They had spoken a few times since Sunday, and each time Colin had entreated her to meet him again. Charlotte wanted to very much. The note of longing in his voice made her wish she could sprout wings and fly straight to his cottage. But work demands had kept her too busy to break away and now her old reservations surfaced, warning her to pull back.

"I want to see you, too. You know I do. I just don't think it's a good idea," she admitted.

"Because you're a movie star and I'm just a fisherman? I thought we got past that."

"We did," she said quickly. "Way past. It's just that I'm not going to be here much longer. How will we ever get to see each other after that?"

If it were someone else, almost anyone else, Charlotte wouldn't have cared about the future. She dated casually all the time, not worrying if the relationship had any lasting potential. But for some reason, with Colin it was different. She had hardly spent any time with him and already knew that when she left here, she would miss him very much. She would miss what might have been.

"I could come out to California to see you. Planes fly both ways, you know."

"Of course you could. But I'm hardly ever there. I'm away on location more than half the year," she explained.

"We can get around distance," he told her. "That's just logistics. What is it really, Charlotte? Do you have a boyfriend or something you haven't told me about? You can be honest with me. I won't get mad," he promised.

"There isn't anyone."

"Seriously?"

"Honestly," she said. "I've dated a lot, but there hasn't been any-one serious. But what about you?" she asked, suddenly daring to pose the question she'd been wondering about. "I never even asked. You must have a girlfriend somewhere."

"I don't have a girlfriend or anything close to it," he assured her, but his voice sounded troubled.

"What's wrong?" she asked.

He was silent a moment then said, "It's not that I think you're lying to me. I just don't get it. How could a gorgeous woman like you be roaming around unattached? Are all the men in Hollywood blind?"

"Not blind, just quite enamored of their own reflections," she explained.

"Maybe I should search the question on the Internet." His tone was teasing again.

"What? You mean you don't read the supermarket tabloids? If you did, you'd know I'm going out with every guy in L.A., including Elvis."

"And you're not?" he asked, a soft laugh behind the question.

"Not even close," she said. "I barely have time to talk to my own assistant." Not that Meredith was high on her list of people she wanted to converse with. Charlotte sighed. "That's just the problem. I don't have a normal life, and I don't want to make your life miserable, too."

"Hey, it's my life. Don't I have some say? If I'm willing to be miserable, I think you should let me. Misery loves company, right?" He was half joking, trying to make her laugh again and almost succeeding.

She didn't answer. She was trying to do the right thing. She didn't want to drag this perfectly wonderful, totally normal guy into her celebrity fishbowl. He had no idea what a nightmare it could be. "I think you might be getting in for more than you bargained for," she warned.

"Undoubtedly," he said, his tone easy. "But it doesn't scare me."

"It scares me," she said quietly. Actually letting Colin into her life seemed the surest way to lose him.

"Okay," he said after a moment's pause. "I take your point. And I'll think about it. I also think, since I saved your life, you can do me one little favor, Ms. Miller."

"And what might that be?" Charlotte asked, though she already had a good idea.

"See me one more time before you go. Then I'll leave you alone forever."

You don't need to go that far, Charlotte nearly cut in. Of course she didn't want him to leave her alone forever. Her feelings were just the opposite.

"If you can't meet me tonight, how about tomorrow?" he asked. "Or tomorrow night? Any time that would work out with your schedule, you tell me."

When he put it that way, it was hard to refuse him. The truth of the matter was, she did want to see him. One more time wasn't too much to ask, was it?

"We're going to shoot very early tomorrow. Brad wants to catch the first light on the dunes down by the cliffs. But I should have time off again in the afternoon," she said finally. *Meredith will be hanging around, but I'll get rid of her somehow,* Charlotte told herself.

"Great." Colin sounded happy. "If you can borrow the bike, ride down to the dock where I dropped you off last Sunday. Think you can find it?"

"I remember." How could she ever forget?

"I'll bring my boat around and wait for you. It will be good weather. We can go out on the water for a while. We'll have plenty of privacy in the middle of the ocean, don't you think? I don't know that much about photography, but a telephoto lens can only see so far."

Charlotte had to smile. Finally a man who understood what she really needed. "I think the middle of the ocean should definitely be private enough. You may have actually figured out a way to stump the paparazzi."

And once again amazed me.

They agreed on a time to meet, and Charlotte promised to text him when she left the inn. When she finally put the phone aside, she had a moment of doubt. Was she doing the right thing?

Charlotte pushed the question out of her mind. She didn't care if it was wrong or right. She just needed to see him.

Chapter Eight

THE morning scenes went quickly. For once, Brad had no sug-
gestions to make about her performance. Charlotte wondered if
she was actually starting to understand what he wanted—or if he
was just getting tired of correcting her.

There were more scenes on the schedule, to be shot in the afternoon, but Charlotte was not in any of them. Just as she had hoped,
she was back at the inn by noon. She wanted to run straight up to her
room and get ready to see Colin, but she forced herself to slow down
and avoid drawing attention to herself. She had lunch with the cast
members and crew who were hanging around the inn for the day,
their schedules as free as hers. Of course, this included Meredith,
who sat next to her at the table, her laptop at the ready.

Just as Charlotte was wondering how she could keep her assistant off her trail for the day, Sally Ann, who worked in wardrobe
spoke up. "Judy loaned me her car for the day. I was thinking of driving up to Newburyport and looking around. I hear there are some

really cute shops and antique stores up there. Want to come, Meredith?"

Meredith looked interested but glanced at Charlotte.

"Oh, I don't know. Don't you need to run through your lines for tomorrow, Charlotte? Brad made some changes to the scene."

"Don't be silly. You deserve a few hours off. You go along," Charlotte encouraged her. When Meredith still didn't look convinced, Charlotte added, "Maybe while you're out you can pick up a few things for me. I think there's a shop up there that sells the French moisturizer I like. And I'm running out of that Moroccan Argan oil. I'd love it if you could find me another bottle or two."

Meredith looked pleased to be assigned a real errand, which kept the trip from being purely for fun. "I'll take care of that for you, no problem."

Charlotte nearly sighed with relief. How easy was that? She went up to her room and got ready to meet Colin, dressing in shorts and a tank top for the bike ride and packing her bathing suit, towel, and a long-sleeved top. She already knew how cool it could be out on the water, even on a hot, sunny day.

From her bedroom window she saw Meredith leave the inn with Sally Ann and another crew member. A few minutes later, Charlotte came downstairs with her pack. Liza was clearing up the dining room and glanced in her direction. "Heading out?"

Charlotte nodded. "It's such a beautiful day. I thought I'd take a bike ride and maybe stop someplace to sit on the beach. If I can borrow a bike again," she added politely.

"Of course, help yourself. You have your cell phone, right? I don't mean to sound like a mother hen, but just in case you have trouble with the bike," Liza added. "You might not be as lucky as the last time."

Charlotte was puzzled a moment then remembered her fib about the elderly couple who had helped her on the road. Oh, dear, she hated to lie—especially to someone as nice as Liza. That was the downside of having a secret relationship.

Not secret, Charlotte; private. You have a right to some privacy in your life. Even if the rest of the world doesn't think so.

"Don't worry. I'll be okay." She smiled briefly at Liza and headed to get the bicycle from the shed behind the inn.

A few minutes later she was out on the road, with the sea breeze in her hair and the brilliant sun warming her skin.

She paused on the road, to check if she was being watched or followed. She didn't see a soul in sight, no cars or other boats in view. She even scanned the tall marsh grass that grew along the side of the road. She saw a few chirping birds, hopping from stalk to stalk but no reporters crouching in the grasses. Not today, at least.

She steered the bike the rest of the way to the dock, then chained it to a wooden bench. Colin's boat looked empty and she felt a moment of dismay. Then he suddenly appeared from below deck and smiled at her, a smile that seemed familiar by now and never failed to move something deep inside her.

She grabbed her pack and ran to the boat, feeling as if she wanted to jump right into his arms.

He stepped up to the dock and met her. "I was worried for a minute that you weren't coming. You said you'd send a text when you left the inn."

"You're right. I totally forgot. I was so focused on getting rid of Meredith and sneaking out." Charlotte felt bad for giving him even a moment of doubt. She could tell from his expression he had been worried that she was going to stand him up. "I'm sorry," she added.

"That's all right. You're here now."

"Yes, I am." Impulsively, she put her arms around him and hugged him. He hugged her back, pressing his face in the crook of her neck for a moment before pulling back.

"Come on. We'd better get going."

He jumped onto the boat and helped her down. Then he untied the lines from the dock and pushed off with a long wooden pole.

"Is there anything I can do to help you get going?"

Colin grinned. "You can be my deckhand. Roll up these lines nice and neat, like those on the other side, so nobody trips over them." He pointed to bunches of rope that were secured in neat figure eights and fastened to the side of the boat on brass hooks. "Then you can take out the bench cushions from the seats and tie them on. Like this . . ." He showed her where the cushions were stored, under the flap lids of the bench seats along the bow. "I'll be up in the cockpit. Come up when you're done."

Charlotte had only been trying to be polite. She hadn't expected to actually work. "Aye-aye, sir." She saluted, her tone teasing.

"No need to be so formal, swabbie. As long as you follow orders."

Charlotte had to laugh at the last remark and the nickname. She happily set about rolling up the rope and pulling out the cushions.

A few minutes later she joined Colin, standing beside him in the small sheltered space as he stood at the controls. The boat was moving quickly now; it bounced a bit as it hit the waves. Sea spray blew up and lifted her hair.

Colin smiled at her and brushed a strand of her hair from her cheek. "Are you all right? The bumps aren't bothering you?" he shouted over the engine.

"I'm fine." She turned and looked back. The coastline had already receded into the distance. She could hardly see the dock.

"We're almost there," he said a few minutes later.

"Where is . . . there?" she asked curiously.

"You'll see. I think you'll like it," he added, smiling at her mysteriously.

Charlotte's curiosity was piqued. She had thought they were just going out on the water, not heading for a destination. It didn't matter, she decided. She was happy just being with him.

"What are all those screens and dials for?" Charlotte asked, pointing to the boat's dashboard. "It looks like a spaceship."

"That's my high-tech fish-finder equipment. The poor fish don't have a chance." He pointed to one of the screens. "The sonar sends a sound wave through the water, so I can see where the schools are feeding or find my lobster traps. Sometimes I drop them without a marker. Like that one." He pointed out at the water, and Charlotte saw a flag marker bobbing in the water.

"There are a whole string of traps tied to that marker, on a long line. Every lobsterman has his own special pattern on the flag, so we can tell them apart. The boat swings by and yanks them up with a pulley. I only have a few pots. I put them out for special occasions."

He turned to her and grinned. "Or if I want to give someone who likes lobster a surprise."

Charlotte gave him a look. He was all but admitting he had left the lobsters at the inn last week. "An anonymous surprise?"

"Sometimes," he admitted. "That's the best kind. Don't you think?"

"It can be," she agreed. "But then the person who gets the surprise can't thank you."

"They usually figure out some way to thank me." He gave her a sly smile, and Charlotte didn't know what to say.

Colin slowed the engine and glanced at her. "Want to drive the boat?"

"Can I?" Charlotte thought it looked like fun. "I don't need a special license or anything?"

Colin shook his head. "For better or worse, you don't. Anybody can get behind the wheel of a boat. You drive a car, right?" Charlotte quickly nodded. She didn't drive herself around very often, but she did have a license. "It's not much different. Come here, I'll show you what to do."

Colin stepped away, and Charlotte stood at the helm and put both her hands on the steering wheel. Colin stepped back and stood behind her. He was very close, resting his hands on her shoulders.

"That's the compass. Just keep the needle hovering around the W. We want to travel due west."

Charlotte nodded, but felt totally distracted by his nearness. "Whoops . . . I lost it . . ." The compass needle drifted to the E for east, and Charlotte made a quick, sharp correction with the wheel.

Much too quick and sharp.

The boat swung to one side and the deck shifted underfoot. Colin quickly wrapped one arm around her waist to keep them from falling, and with the other, held the steering wheel and righted the boat.

"Oh . . . I'm so sorry. That was dumb," Charlotte said, trying to regain her balance.

Then she felt Colin hugging her close for a moment. He dipped his head and kissed her cheek. "That's okay. Everybody does that when they first try it. Slow, small corrections, that's all it takes."

Charlotte was tempted to turn in his arms and kiss him for real but didn't dare. No telling what would happen then.

She nodded, staring straight at the horizon again. Suddenly, a small landmass came into view. It was a tiny island, complete with a sugary white shoreline and small trees that filled the center. Charlotte didn't see any structures, not even a shack. Though there wasn't room for much. The entire island would probably just fill a football field.

Colin reached around her and cut the power even more, so that the boat was just chugging along. "Here we are. It's not the exact middle of the ocean, but it will have to do, considering I can only take you out for a few hours. I will guarantee that it's totally private."

Charlotte smiled at him. "It looks like paradise . . . a postage-stamp-size one," she added.

He laughed at her description. "Let's just swing around and make sure no one else is tied up out here today. I tried to reserve it, but no one answered the phone."

She glanced at him then realized he was joking. Of course, there was no one to call out here—no phones, no people. Nothing but the deep blue water and brilliant blue sky.

The boat cruised around the island quickly. There were no boats tied up on the other side. Colin seemed pleased. He steered the boat into shallow water and cut the engine completely. "This is as close as I can get. I'm going to drop the anchor," he said. He pushed a button then headed for the back of the boat. "Would you like to go ashore? We can do a little fishing and I brought a picnic."

"That sounds great." Charlotte was dying to go onto the island and explore. Or just sit on the beach and soak up the sun.

"We have to wade and carry everything over," he added. "Still up for it?"

She nodded. "Sure. I even brought my suit."

"Good thinking." He looked pleased by that announcement, enough to make Charlotte blush a bit. She headed below and changed while Colin gathered what they would need for their island adventure.

When she came above, she saw that he had put on his trunks and had assembled a few canvas tote bags.

"I'll take these two—they're the heaviest—if you can take this one. Just put it up to your chest or on your shoulder to keep it dry."

"No problem."

A few moments later, Colin helped her over the side of the boat. The water was clear and warm, up to her hip. There were small waves but not strong enough to knock her over. With the canvas bag pressed to her chest, Charlotte made her way to the shore. Colin quickly followed.

They set up a large blanket in a fringe of shade from the scruffy trees. There was a cool breeze off the water, which kept the beach from feeling hot.

Charlotte took off her T-shirt and stretched out on the blanket. She felt totally relaxed and even a bit sleepy.

Colin was busy emptying out the rest of the bags. "Are you hungry or thirsty? I brought enough food for a week," he confessed with a laugh.

I could spend a week out here with you very easily, Charlotte nearly replied.

"A cold drink would be great," she said. "Just some water if you have it."

"Coming right up." Colin pulled out two frosty bottles of water, and Charlotte caught one easily.

"How did you ever find this place? It's magical," she said.

"Just by chance, cruising around, looking for fish. I camped out here once or twice. It was great. There are a few wild creatures in that little woods behind us. You'd be surprised. I can't figure out how they got out here."

"There just smart creatures, I guess. They know how to find the most perfect spot in the area."

He walked over and sat down next to her. "I'm glad you like it so much. I've never taken anyone out here," he added.

That made it feel even more special—and made her feel special, too. She had just assumed this was a place where he took his dates.

"I love it. I feel as if we're castaways or something."

Colin laughed. "We could be. Maybe you could use it as a movie set someday."

Charlotte turned and met his gaze then shook her head.

"Never. That would ruin it. It would ruin my memory of coming here with you."

He stared at her a moment, then took her face in his hands and kissed her. Slowly at first, softly tasting her lips. Then the kiss deepened. His mouth moved on hers, his lips tasting salty and sweet at the same time. Charlotte wound her arms around his back. She felt the hard ridges of the muscles in his shoulders. His skin felt smooth and warm.

She felt his hands in her hair as he slowly moved his head back. "You take my breath away," he said quietly.

Charlotte felt the same, but wasn't able to answer.

"And it's not because you're famous. It's because . . . you're you," he added. His tone was calm and certain. As if he had given the question some thought and had come to this conclusion.

"I know I haven't known you very long. And I don't know you that well. But I feel as if I do," he added. "As if everything that's happened between us is just meant to be. I'm sorry, that sounds really crazy, doesn't it?"

Charlotte swallowed hard then shook her head. His face was so close, and his brilliant blue eyes seemed to be the only thing she could see. "It doesn't sound crazy. Not to me . . . I feel the same about you. Though I couldn't find the words to say it as well. Just the way we met, out in the middle of the ocean. The way you saved my life. I do feel it's all happening for a reason," she agreed. Though she wasn't sure yet what that reason was. Or if it meant they could be together, some way, somehow.

He took her hand and twined his fingers around hers. "I'm glad. That means I'm not imagining it . . . or we've both gone over the edge."

Charlotte thought it could be a little of each. She was certainly way over the edge for him. Still, a small part of her held back. This all seemed so perfect—and unreal. Like a dream. But reality would set in pretty quickly. She had only agreed to see him this one time. The last time, she thought. It wasn't the beginning of things for them.

"What's the matter, Charlotte? You look worried."

She sighed. "I don't want to be. I just don't know how this could ever work out for us," she said honestly. "I'm leaving here very soon, within a week if the crew keeps to the schedule."

What would happen after that? She didn't know how they could keep a relationship going at such a great distance—and with such wildly different lifestyles.

"I know, I know." He nodded and sighed. "Let's not worry about that now. Let's just have our day, okay? Our great day together?"

She nodded. He had gone to so much trouble, and it was a perfect day. Or would be, if they didn't think about the future.

"Want to do some fishing? We could probably catch some striped bass out here, just fly casting."

"That sounds like fun. Just show me which way to point the pole."

Colin laughed and tugged her up by the hand. "Which way to point the pole, huh? You'll probably have beginner's luck and catch way more than I do."

A short time later they were set up for fishing. Colin showed her the basics and baited her line. His prediction proved true, and Charlotte soon felt the third or fourth tug on her line.

"That's it, play with the fish a little, tire it out. Are you sure you've never done this before?"

"Not fly casting." Charlotte followed his instructions, reeling in another good catch, which they tossed in a bucket. "My father took us fishing once or twice, on a big lake not too far from our house. We never caught very much, but it was fun. My family didn't have much money. So we always went camping in the summer."

"That sounds like fun. Do your folks still live in Ohio?"

"My mother does, with my two sisters and little brother. My father died when I was about ten. But my mom remarried. My stepfather died about three years ago, I guess."

"Oh, that's too bad. I'm sorry," Colin said politely.

Charlotte just nodded and kept fishing, turning toward the water so he couldn't see her expression.

It was hard to tell him there was nothing to be sorry about. Her stepfather had been a cruel, sick man who had abused her mother and terrorized Charlotte and her siblings for years.

Early on in the marriage, before anyone could see his real nature, he persuaded her mother to let him legally adopt the children. Charlotte's mother had thought that very generous—until she wanted a divorce and realized her second husband could win custody of her own offspring. A cold, shrewd man, he used the threat to control Charlotte's mother and the entire family.

Charlotte wished she could tell Colin the real story of her family life. The magazine and TV interviews that she had been giving out for years painted a warm, rosy picture that was a complete lie. She carried the truth deep inside her, a bitter, sad secret. It was all part of the unspoken deal she had made for fame and fortune: No one— not even the people she was closest to—would ever really know her.

For one insane second, she wondered if Colin was the one person she could trust with this secret. No, she realized at once. The story was surely worth money to the tabloids and entertainment shows. It could tarnish her name if twisted about. Even worse, it would make her mother's years of humiliation public. Charlotte felt deeply guilty that she'd left home at age eighteen, right after high school graduation. She had left her siblings and her mother to fend for themselves, as if diving off a burning ship.

She turned to Colin. He was baiting his line and didn't seem to notice that she had been totally lost in her own thoughts for a while now. But, like her, he wasn't the type of person who needed to talk constantly. Which made her feel even more comfortable with him.

"Do you get to see your family much?" Colin asked suddenly.

"Not as much as I'd like to. But I do what I can for them. I bought them a nice house and pay all the bills. My mother doesn't have to work anymore or take care of the housework either. She's not that strong. She's been through a lot. It's been good for her to be able to retire." Charlotte glanced at Colin, wondering if he thought she was bragging. She really wasn't. She was just being as honest as she could with him.

"It sounds as if you take good care of them."

"I try. I want to give my sisters and brother the advantages I never had. I know it can't make up for everything, but it makes life easier for them. Which is why I work so hard, I guess. I think I'm a pretty good actress, but the public is fickle. That's what my agent is always telling me. Sooner or later, I'll be bumped by another pretty face. I have to make the most of my fifteen minutes of fame," she joked.

Colin smiled briefly then looked serious. "I think your career will last much longer than that. But it's good of you to do so much for your family. You're young to take on that role. I admire that a lot. It sounds like you miss them."

"I do. Especially my sister Lily. She's almost ready to start college. I want her to come out to California, so I can see her more. Lily is so great. I wish you could meet her," she added.

"I'd love to. Maybe someday I will."

Charlotte glanced at him. They were starting to talk about the future again. Hadn't they agreed not to do that? She sighed. It was hard not to look ahead. Especially when you felt so wonderful just being around someone. It was hard not to want this feeling to last and last.

A short time later, they packed up the fishing gear and Colin spread out their picnic. The sun was making its slow path to the horizon, and the breeze on the island had shifted. Charlotte pulled a gauzy long-sleeved shirt on over her bathing suit and Colin put on a T-shirt.

They sat side by side on the blanket, enjoying the feast of fruit, cheese, crackers, and a bottle of white wine. "Not that original a menu. But this is all gourmet stuff . . . from my aunt's general store," he joked with her. "She traded me for some striped bass."

Charlotte laughed and bit into a juicy ripe peach. "Your aunt owns that general store, the one in the island center?"

Colin nodded. "My aunt and uncle, Marion and Walter. They're quite a pair. That's why my family used to come out here in the summers, to see them. That's how I got to know this place. The Doyles are pretty famous around here," he said, puffing out his chest. "I mean, it's not Hollywood."

Charlotte laughed. "It's definitely not."

Colin looked shocked, acting as if he were insulted. "Some people," he said under his breath. Then he smiled and slung his arm around her shoulders, pulling her close. "Some people are so . . . amazing," he said quietly. He glanced down at her. "How's that peach, any good?"

She nodded. "Very good. Want a bite?" She held it up for him to taste.

He smiled and leaned closer, but instead of biting the peach, he kissed her. "Mmmm. That is good," he murmured. "I'll have some more."

The peach dropped to the sand as they continued to embrace. Charlotte fell back against the blanket and held him tight. It felt so wonderful to be close to him like this, so true and right. It was more than just physical attraction between them. She had never felt this way about anyone before. And doubted she ever would again.

Suddenly a rustling sound from the woods made them jump. Colin sat up suddenly and looked around. Charlotte sat up, too, feeling dazed and slowly coming to her senses. She turned, expecting to see someone with a camera pop out of the woods. "What is it?" she asked anxiously. "Did someone find us?"

"Looks like they did. But if we toss him some crackers, maybe he won't take any pictures."

He pointed and Charlotte saw a huge seagull sitting on a piece of driftwood, its beady black eyes fixed on their food.

She laughed and playfully pushed Colin to the side. "You really scared me. That wasn't very nice."

Colin grinned. "I know, but it was fun to see your expression."

He got to his feet and pulled her up by the hand. "It's getting late. We'd better get back before someone does find us. I expect your friends at the inn will be sending out the Coast Guard again."

Charlotte had lost all track of time and was shocked when she checked her cell phone. "You're right. I'm going to call Liza and tell her I'm fine. Just sat on the beach too long."

He smiled and shrugged. "Well, that's not entirely a lie. We have been on the beach a long time."

Not nearly long enough, she wanted to say. But she just smiled back. Along with the cool breeze and soft late-afternoon light, Charlotte also felt reality setting in.

As they rode back to the dock in Colin's boat, Charlotte went below and changed back into her clothes. When she came above, it was almost dark out on the water, and the sun was setting on the very edge of the horizon, giving off a last flare of brilliant light, the clouds all around tinged with rose, pink, lavender, and gold.

"When the light streaks the clouds like that, I used to say to my parents, 'Look Dad, that's God in the sky.'" Colin told the story with a little laugh.

Charlotte held his arm, standing close to his side. "But that's what it looks like. Like God is trying to remind us He's still there, watching over everything. What else could look so brilliant and beautiful?"

Colin nodded but didn't answer. He took her hand and gently kissed it.

When the dock came into view, Charlotte felt a knot of dread in the pit of her stomach. She didn't want to leave Colin. She didn't want their time together to end. And she didn't want to answer the inevitable question: When will we see each other again?

Colin tied the boat to the dock and helped her off. "Well, here we are, safe and sound."

"Thank you for a beautiful day. I'll never forget it."

He put his hands on her shoulders and gazed down at her.

"I hope not." He sighed and kissed her. The kiss ended much too quickly, she thought. "So . . . what now, Charlotte? What should we do? Is this it? Really?"

She looked up at him, then looked away. "I don't know. I don't know what to do. What if we tried to make this work and it just ruined everything? If we ended up just hating each other? That would be worse, I think."

"I think it would be worse not to try. Not to try at all." His voice, his eyes, the expression on his face—everything about him pulled at her heart.

When Charlotte didn't answer, he said, "I'm sorry . . . I just don't understand it. It seems so good between us. So easy and perfect. Too good to just toss away."

She felt the same about being with him. It was just so easy and wonderful. Like stepping into another world entirely—or maybe just a tiny island in the vast blue sea—but a place they shared together where everything felt right. Still, sooner or later, she'd have to leave that place and return to her own more difficult reality.

"I know, Colin. I know exactly what you mean. And I cherish that. I really do," she said quietly. "But you don't know what my life is like. I know you think you do but . . . it's harder than you imagine. Let's be honest. How would we even get to see each other? How would this ever work out? Would you fly to L.A. or wherever I was stuck making a film to be with me? To squeeze yourself into my schedule? How about being in the public eye all the time?" she rushed on. "With strangers constantly speculating about our relationship, putting all kinds of false rumors in the media whenever we're apart. Reporters hunting you down out here, knocking on your door, following you everywhere. Would you like that? Because that's how it would be, just for starters. Just to even try."

She could see from his expression he hadn't really considered that side of the question, and the scenario disturbed him.

Finally, he shook his head, as if shaking loose her negative rebuttal. "We could work it out. If we really wanted to."

Charlotte sighed. He was breaking her heart. She knew he didn't mean to. Why couldn't he just be reasonable, logical? Why did she have to be the mean one? Her phone rang. It was Judy, looking for her. Charlotte stuffed her phone back in her pocket and looked up at him. "I'm so sorry . . . I have to go. We said it would be just this one time. You told me that would be all right. It's not what I really want either," she added, feeling ready to cry. "I never meant to hurt you. But I thought you understood."

Charlotte didn't know what more to say, how to explain her feelings and fears. She felt tears spilling from her eyes but didn't want him to see her cry. She turned and ran to the bike, unlocked it, and started to ride away.

She thought Colin might try to follow her. But he didn't. When she turned to look at him, he had jumped back on the boat and stood on the deck, watching her.

It was too dark now to see his face.

Charlotte pushed on the pedals, tears blurring her vision. She felt as if her heart had just been torn into a million pieces. There was no way she'd ever be able to put it back together again.

Chapter Nine

AUDREY hated waiting for the doctor to call, but there was no help for it. There was no sense calling his office to try to speed things up. She tried once and received a short, sharp reply from the nurse in charge. "The doctor will call you when he has the results. It will definitely be a few more days, Mrs. Gilroy."

Half of her was dying to hear, and the other half didn't want to know. So far, she and Rob were able to plod along without having to make a real decision about what to do. But once they had the results, there would be no avoiding it.

By Saturday, Audrey was starting to feel the strain, jumping every time the phone rang though, logically, she knew the doctor would not call on a Saturday. He probably wouldn't call before Tuesday or even later in the week. It would take at least a week for him to get the lab reports. He had already told them that. Still, she couldn't help hoping he would call sooner. She just wanted to know.

Rob felt the same way, she was sure. He wasn't a talker, tending to hold everything inside. But she could tell her husband was on edge from waiting, though he always presented a calm demeanor. She tried to follow his lead, going through her daily routine, acting as if everything was normal and always would be. But she was still rattled from the discussion they had right after the appointment when Rob had raised the possibility of giving up their farm and moving off the island.

Rob was the first one up on Saturday morning. When Audrey came down she smelled coffee and pancakes. Rob stood at the stove, flipping a stack onto a platter. The dog sat right beside him, looking up alertly, waiting for one to miss the plate.

"Wow, those look good. What did you put in them?"

"Peaches and blueberries," Rob said proudly.

"You could be a TV chef, honey."

"Sounds good to me. Maybe that will be my next career." Rob turned and smiled at her. Audrey wasn't sure if he was just making a joke or thinking about their unsettled future. She poured herself a cup of coffee and sat at the table.

"Audrey, have you been giving this dog table scraps again? She hasn't left my side since I turned on the stove. I practically tripped over her."

"She's a watchdog. She's just watching you cook. Right, Millie?"

The dog tore herself away from the pancakes long enough to trot over for a quick head pat.

Rob brought the pancakes to the table. "Here you are, madam. Dig in."

Audrey slipped a few pancakes onto her plate then fixed them with syrup and cinnamon. That was one thing she loved about living on the farm. She worked so hard every day and walked so much, she hardly had to worry about dieting and could eat just about anything she liked. She would definitely miss that if they moved back to the city.

They ate in silence. Rob opened the paper and glanced at the headlines. The phone rang, and Audrey waited to hear who it was on the message machine. She didn't always screen calls, but she didn't always get the chance to enjoy such a good breakfast that someone else had cooked for her.

"Hi, Audrey. It's Tara. Are you there? I have some news for you guys."

"It's my sister. I'd better get it." Audrey picked up the phone. "Hi, Tara, I'm here. We were just eating breakfast," she added to explain why she was talking with her mouth full. "What's up? Is everything okay?"

"Everything's great." Her sister paused a moment. "Guess what? I'm pregnant. Isn't that wild? We just started trying."

Audrey felt a lump in her throat. She knew her sister wanted another baby. Tara had told her when they came for a visit on Memorial Day weekend. But she didn't think it would happen so quickly.

Audrey glanced at Rob. He had put down the newspaper. "What is it—bad news?" He mouthed the words so her sister couldn't hear.

Audrey shook her head and briefly covered the receiver. "No, good news. I'll tell you in a minute," she whispered back. She forced a smile, but could tell her eyes had filled with tears. "I'm sorry. Rob was just asking me something. But your news, that's so wonderful. When did you find out?" she asked quickly, trying to remember the right things to say.

"Just last night. I was late. But I didn't think much of it. Ever since Christopher was born, I've never quite gotten back in sync."

Christopher was Tara's three-year-old son. Time passed so quickly. It felt as though her nephew had been born just yesterday.

"I have the same problem. Guess it runs in the family," Audrey replied. Though so far, her erratic schedule had not meant she was expecting. "When is the baby due?"

"In late April. That seems like a lot of time, but it's really not. This house is so small, I don't know where we're even going to put the new baby. Dave thinks we might need to set up a crib in the laundry room," Tara joked.

"The laundry room? No way. I'll take that baby," Audrey quickly replied. "We have plenty of room. Just until you get a new house or build an extension," she added in the same joking tone.

Inside, her heart had twisted into a triple knot of longing, self-pity, and unfair anger at her dear little sister and any woman anywhere who was having a baby. While she was most definitely not.

"Oh, Audrey, you're too much. Watch out, we may take you up on that offer. At least for some babysitting."

"I'm here for you, honey," Audrey said sincerely, feeling guilty for her mean thoughts. Audrey suddenly felt overwhelmed by emotion and swallowed back some tears. "Listen, I have to get off but I'll call you back later, okay?"

"Uh . . . okay. Is everything all right?" Tara sounded concerned, and Audrey worried that she might have heard the tears in her voice.

"Everything's fine. I've got some late-summer allergies, that's all," Audrey added. "Ragweed or something. Gets me every year at this time. Talk to you later. Give my best to Dave and Chris," she said.

Audrey hung up. Then she stood by the kitchen counter, staring into space, trying to get a grip on her emotions.

"Your sister is expecting again, right?" Rob had left the table and stood right next to her. She turned to him.

"That's what she said. She just found out. The baby is due in April. Great news, right?"

Rob nodded, but wore a sad, sympathetic expression. Then he opened his arms to her and Audrey stepped into his warm embrace. "It's all right, honey. You don't have to pretend with me. I mean, I'm sure you're happy for your sister and wish her well. But I know it hurts, too."

Audrey nodded, her face pressed against his chest. "It does hurt. A lot. It seems so unfair. She already has a child—and she's younger than me. She's gotten pregnant so easily. Why did I have to get stuck with the bad baby-making genes?"

"Hey, you can't blame yourself, honey. Even if that is the problem, or just part of it. It's not your fault. Or my fault, for that matter. It's just the hand we've been given. All that matters now is how we deal with it."

Audrey nodded again and picked up her head. She dabbed a tissue to her nose and tried to compose herself.

"You're right."

"It's going to work out for us," Rob promised. He lifted her chin and stared into her eyes. "We just need to have some patience—and some faith."

Audrey let out a shaky breath. "I'm trying. At least there's one golden lining to this cloud. I couldn't go through all this with anyone but you. I'm so thankful that you're my husband. I don't know what I'd do without you," she confessed.

"Oh, you'd manage," Rob said, hugging her close again. "But it's nice to hear you say that. I don't know what I'd do without you either," he added, kissing her forehead.

Audrey was about to kiss him back—a real kiss, not just an affectionate peck—when she felt a nudge against her leg. She looked down to see Millie edging her way into the embrace, her muzzle caught under the hem of Audrey's bathrobe.

Audrey leaned back and looked down at her. "Millie, what are you doing? Feeling left out, are you?"

The dog gazed up at her, then pressed her big head against Audrey's leg. Audrey couldn't tell if she just wanted to be included in the affectionate moment, or was offering comfort; Audrey was pretty sure that Millie could tell when she was feeling blue.

Audrey reached down and patted her head, and Millie sat up alertly and offered her paw. Audrey shook her head with a smile. "Do you want to be petted, or are you still thinking about the pancakes?"

Rob laughed. "What a question."

Millie stared at both of them a moment, wagging her tail. Then she sat up on her haunches, her front paws dangling. She looked like a big golden bear, Audrey thought.

"I think that deserves something special." Audrey took a few bites of pancake from the skillet on the stove and dropped them in Millie's bowl. They barely hit the dish before being inhaled by the dog.

"Did you teach her that?" Rob asked.

"No, honestly. She comes up with this stuff all on her own. Here, watch this." Audrey held another bit of food in her hand and showed it to the dog. "Okay, Millie, dance."

Millie stood up on her hind legs and stumbled around a bit, practically turning in a full circle. Then she came down, trotted over to Audrey, and sat very tall and still, waiting for her reward.

Audrey dropped the pancake bit, and Millie caught it midair.

"Pretty good. I had no idea she knew all those tricks."

"Neither did I. They just sort of slowly revealed themselves."

Audrey took another cup of coffee and sat at the table again, her chair pushed back a bit. Millie trotted over. She stared at Audrey again, wagging her tail.

"She wants more food, I guess—" Rob said.

"No, she wants a hug," Audrey interpreted.

"A hug? You're crazy." Rob shook his head but was still watching.

"Watch this. Okay, you can come up," Audrey told Millie. She sat even farther back, making room. Then Millie jumped up on her so that the front half of her body was in Audrey's lap, her hind legs standing on the floor. She rested her head on Audrey's shoulder.

"Audrey, she's too big for that," Rob said.

"No, she's not. She just wants a hug," Audrey insisted.

Rob ran a hand through his hair. "Dogs don't just do things like that. Somebody taught her those tricks. I think someone misses this dog, don't you?"

"I do think of that," Audrey confessed. "But I've tried my best to find her owner. I just hope that whoever lost her would be comforted to know that she's found a good home and isn't in a shelter, sitting in some cold, damp dog cell, feeling lonely."

Rob rolled his eyes. "You make it sound worse than jail."

"It is worse than jail. At least in jail, you get a phone call. You should have seen this place."

Secretly, Audrey wondered if she was really still pulling out all the stops, searching for Millie's owner. She and Rob had put up signs on the island and in Cape Light village. She even ran an ad in the local newspaper. But that was costly, so they stopped after a week. She told everyone she knew about finding Millie. But there was still no sign of her owner.

She patted Millie another moment, then coaxed her down and brushed the dog hair off her bathrobe. "Maybe someone just gave her up and let her loose. Or they moved and left her," Audrey offered, partly to soothe her own conscience. "People do that, you know."

"Yes, they do. I'm surprised she didn't tell you by now what really happened." Rob's expression was perfectly serious, but Audrey knew he was teasing.

"She doesn't like to talk about it," Audrey said with a grin.

"Obviously. Well, whatever happened, it looks like she's ours now, like it or not."

"I like it," Audrey said quickly. "She's so sweet. You know me, I was always more of a cat person, but Millie is the perfect dog. I wouldn't want any other dog in the whole world."

Rob smiled. He rose from his seat, and quickly kissed her on the forehead. "Maybe you and Millie were meant to find each other."

"I think we were," Audrey agreed. She glanced down at the dog again, who seemed to know they were talking about her. "I really do."

Rob went outside, and Audrey started cleaning up the kitchen. It was hard not to think of her sister's news. She wished she could just be happy for Tara and Dave and not think of herself at all. *But I'm only human,* she reminded herself, *weak and flawed—sometimes more flawed than other times.*

After cleaning the kitchen, Audrey headed for the garden, hoping to burn off her unhappiness with some hard work. The pungent smell of the tomato plants mixed with the scents of herbs and other vegetables were familiar and comforting, yet she felt her eyes begin to tear as she raked out weeds from between the rows of tall, staked tomato plants. She loved all the plant scents and the sight of carrots and lettuce and beets pushing up through the earth. Was it even possible for her and Rob to give all this up? The thought hurt so much that she raked harder and faster. A bit of dirt flew up and got in her eye. She stopped and wiped her eye with a tissue. "Oh, blast . . ."

When she looked up again and blinked, she saw the blurry outline of a man walking across the meadow that stood between her buildings and the inn. He was looking down, watching where he walked, taking each step with care. She thought it might be Daniel for a moment, but Daniel didn't walk that way.

Then he looked up and waved at her and she realized who it was. She dropped the rake and screamed, holding her hand to her cheeks. "Rob! Where are you? Come out here right this minute!"

Her husband ran out of the barn, still holding a pitchfork, bits of hay clinging to his hair and clothes. "What is it? Are you okay? Did you hurt yourself?"

She shook her head and pointed. "Look! I can't believe it. It's Nick Dempsey! He's come to visit us! Just like he said he would. He's really here. He really came!"

Rob spun around and stared at the movie star, who was now a bit closer. When he smiled, Audrey could see how his brilliant white teeth sparkled almost as much as the mirrored lenses in his aviator sunglasses. He wore a billowy-sleeved white shirt with worn jeans and cowboy boots—a casual, down-home ensemble that probably cost thousands of dollars, she guessed. She had to laugh. The perfect outfit for visiting a farm.

Audrey spun around and gripped her husband by both arms. "I've got to go inside and change my clothes. I can't show him around looking like this. Talk to him a minute. I'll be right back."

"Me? What can I talk to him about?" Rob looked pale and alarmed.

"Talk to him about our cheese. He loves cheese. Really," she shouted over her shoulder. She dashed back to the house with Millie at her heels, barking her head off.

"Silly dog. Don't you bother Nick Dempsey. That would be the one unforgivable thing, Millie," she warned her beloved pet.

Audrey shed her dirty garden garb, washed her face, combed her hair, and pulled on a sundress in record time. As she ran out of the house again, she remembered to grab the digital camera that sat on the dining room table.

"And the batteries are charged! Thank you, God," she said aloud, totally serious.

She flew outside again and found Rob and Nick sitting at the little umbrella table, just outside the farm shop.

Nick jumped up as she approached, the perfect gentleman, stretching out his hand. "Audrey, how nice to see you again."

She thought she might faint when he not only took her hand but leaned over to give her an air kiss.

"Welcome, Mr. Dempsey," she managed breathlessly. "We're so happy you could find the time to drop over."

I really never thought you'd take me up on my invitation, she nearly said aloud but caught herself just in time.

"This is such a pretty place. I can see it from my window at the inn. The goats are so cute, prancing around," he said, glancing at the herd, which was now grazing in the meadow by the inn. "It's captured my curiosity. And that cheese you gave me was awesome. Got to get some more of that."

"There's plenty more where that came from," Rob promised.

Audrey stared at him. Why did her intelligent, erudite husband suddenly sound like Old MacDonald?

"It's such a hot day. Would you care for some lemonade?" she offered. "We make it ourselves."

"That sounds nice but water would be fine," he replied. "Please don't go to any trouble."

"It's no trouble. Come into the shop. I have sparkling or plain."

"Oh, sparkling, please," he said eagerly. She could tell he didn't expect to have a choice at this island outpost.

"Can I get you anything, honey?" she asked her husband.

He shook his head. "I think I'd better get back to the barn and finish spreading the hay. You show Mr. Dempsey around, Audrey. I'll catch up with you later."

Audrey couldn't believe her husband was giving up a chance to hang out with Nick Dempsey, but she just nodded. "Okay, honey. See you later."

Nick followed her into the shop and Audrey walked to the back of the store, where she took two water bottles from the refrigerator.

"Oh, isn't this pretty." Nick strolled around the small shop, looking at the displays. He had slipped off his sunglasses, and they hung from a little red rubber cord around his neck. "You sell lavender, too?"

"Yes, we make soaps and oil and other things. We sell them here and at other stores in the area. We'd like to get wider distribution. My husband is putting up a website. It takes a little time."

"Of course. But this stuff is popular now, aromatherapy and all that." Nick picked up a bar of soap and breathed in the scent. "My wife loves lavender, says it helps her de-stress and detox. I'll have to buy a few things for her."

"Don't be silly. We have gift baskets all made up and ready to go." Audrey plucked the largest from her display. "Just let me throw a bow on this and you can take it away."

"Oh, you can't do that. I have to pay you. You already gave me a king's ransom in cheese," he pointed out.

"That's our pleasure, Mr. Dempsey," she said as she wrapped the basket in cellophane, adding a purple satin ribbon and a Gilroy Farm business card. "We enjoy your films so much. I've seen all them at least twice. It's the least we can do for you."

"That's very gracious. Thank you so much," he said as Audrey handed over the basket. "I'll get a lot of points for this when I get home, believe me." He glanced outside. "Can I meet the goats?"

"Sure," Audrey said, still marveling over his interest in their farm.

He left the gift basket on the table in the shade. He seemed pleased with it, she noticed. It was truly a gift from the heart, a fan's gift. But you never knew. Maybe Nick and his wife would find the lavender and goat's milk lotion so wonderful, they would order vats of it, delivered by air to California, and tell all their friends and mention it in interviews. It only took one plug from a mega-star in a magazine to get flooded with orders.

She had to get Rob working on that website. She was going to tie him to the chair in front of the computer tonight.

Audrey led Nick along the thin path that wound around the meadow. Millie followed, running circles around them and barking at the goats from time to time.

"Is she herding them?" Nick asked curiously.

"Just trying to play with them—or tease them," Audrey said.

Just then one of the larger goats, Hermione, leaped in their direction, making a loud *baahing* sound.

Nick ducked and put his arm up to shield his head, as if they were under fire. "My goodness, do they all do that?"

"From time to time. They can jump pretty high. We had to raise the fences. A few can still get loose."

"That guy was really airborne." Nick watched the goat, looking a little nervous. Audrey thought this was funny, since she had recently seen him in a movie where he faced terrifying wild animals in Africa.

"What is it like to work with animals in a film? Is it difficult?" she asked.

"Not too bad. I like animals. They usually seem to like me, too," he said, still looking warily at the goats.

"But they do have professional handlers," he continued. "A lot of the dangerous or unpredictable ones are filmed separately, and it's all pulled together with computers."

"That makes sense." Seeing the way he reacted to the frisky goat, Audrey was sure now that he had not faced down that roaring, ferocious lion in his last film. Despite his rugged looks and the roles he'd played, Nick was not exactly Mr. Nature. Audrey decided this up-close-and-personal visit was very enlightening . . . and amusing.

She spotted her husband across the meadow, going into the cheese shed. "There's Rob. Would you like to see how cheese is made?"

"Absolutely. That's one of the main reasons I came. When I have my restaurant, I might want to make my own cheese. I want to serve real artisanal foods."

That was just a fancy way of saying homemade, Audrey knew. "Our cheese is very artisanal," she assured him.

Rob gave Nick the full tour, explaining each step of the process and how the equipment worked.

"It's quite an operation and spotlessly clean, too," Nick said, sounding impressed. He glanced at his watch, and Audrey could tell he was getting ready to go. She felt the camera in her pocket and realized they hadn't taken any photos of him yet. Who would ever believe this story without some actual evidence?

"I hate to ask you this," she said, feeling suddenly shy, "but would you take a few pictures with us? It's such an honor to have you here. I'd love to hang them in the shop."

Nick graced her with a megawatt smile. "I'd be delighted. Where should we do it—in here, with the cheese machine?"

"I was thinking more outside, with the goats."

"The goats?" he asked, his smile fading.

"In the background, I mean. I thought the meadow and barn would look nice."

"Right. That sounds perfect."

They all trooped outside, and Audrey took a few pictures of Nick leaning casually against the Gilroy Goat Farm sign. Then Rob took a few of Audrey standing next to Nick. Nick slung his arm around her shoulders, and Audrey smiled so widely her face hurt. She expected she looked sort of loony in the photos, but that was all right. No one would be looking at her.

Rob handed the camera back to Audrey. "Would you like a lift back to the inn, Mr. Dempsey? I can bring my truck around."

"Thanks, but I have a car coming. I'm heading into the village for a little more sightseeing. I'm due on the set again tonight."

"When will the film be done?" Audrey asked, curious to know how long he would be around.

"Not too much longer, I hope. We are running behind schedule, though. We could wrap up here early next week, and there will be a few more scenes to shoot at a studio in L.A."

Audrey nodded. "I can't wait to see the movie. I hope you finish quickly so it comes out soon."

"That makes two of us," he said in a mock-serious tone. "Acting looks like fun, I'm sure, but working on a film is like being in a pressure cooker."

Rob smiled. "The grass is always greener?"

"Exactly. You folks are lucky, living the simple life, close to the land, in one of the most beautiful places I've ever seen. No traffic, no noise. No one bossing you around: Action. Cut. Do it again. And again. Go to some publicity appearance and smile for the cameras. Smile, smile, smile . . ." He sighed dramatically. "You know what I mean. I envy you, I really do."

"Thanks, that's nice of you to say. We do feel blessed to have found this place," Rob replied.

They truly did have a special life, one even a movie star envied. Which made it even harder to consider giving it up, Audrey thought. Even for the prospect of starting a family.

"You wouldn't care to change places with us—just temporarily?" Rob joked with him.

"I would love that. But I'm booked with projects for the next three years. I'll have to get back to you on that offer."

"Sure thing. Call anytime," Rob said.

Audrey wondered if they would still be here then. Even three months suddenly seemed questionable.

Nick picked up his gift basket, and they walked him to the front of the house to wait for his car. Millie had disappeared somewhere but now trotted over to Audrey, wagging her tail.

"She really is a beautiful dog. She looks like she'd do a great job herding goats," Nick suggested.

Millie sat next to him, looking very calm and well-behaved. *What an actress!* Audrey thought.

Nick reached down and stroked her head. "What soft fur. What a pretty girl . . ."

"She is pretty. Wait, let me take just one more picture, with Millie." Audrey pulled out the camera and took a few steps back, focusing on her dog with the movie star.

"This is going to be so cute. I love posing with dogs," Nick said. He turned to the dog, giving her his full attention. Millie stared up at him a moment, looking calm and adoring. Then she jumped up and put her big paws on Nick's brilliant white shirt. He put his face next to hers and they both turned and smiled for the camera.

"Oh my gosh, that was perfect!" Audrey said. "It's so adorable! I think we've got our next Christmas card."

"Really? Can I see?" Nick walked toward her, eager to see the photo on the camera screen. Then he looked down at his shirt, his eyes widening with dismay. But he didn't say a word. He just looked away and managed to smile.

Audrey nearly had heart failure. Two large muddy paw prints stood out on his shirtfront, as if they'd been stenciled there.

"Oh, I'm so sorry!" She ran toward him, not knowing what to do. "Let me clean it for you, please. No, let us buy you a new one. What kind is it? I'll find it on the Internet. I'll order it right away. It could be here tomorrow," she promised.

He touched her arm and took a deep breath. "That's all right. The shirt is custom made in London, and I have stacks of them. Don't trouble yourself. I think the photo was worth it. Please send a copy to my website. I'll put it up there in my gallery."

He really was such a nice man. Audrey couldn't get over it. "That's very kind of you. I'm so sorry about Millie. I should have realized."

"That's all right. I'm used to women losing control around me."

Audrey laughed along with the joke, though it did sound a bit vain.

A long, sleek black car glided up the drive as soundlessly as a shark. A driver jumped out and opened the door for Nick, who put the gift basket in first, then turned to Audrey and Rob. "So long, folks, this was great."

"The pleasure was all ours, honestly."

Nick sent one more dazzling smile in their direction then shut the car door. The car drove off, disappearing down the road.

Rob put his arm around Audrey's shoulder. "So, what did you think of your hero, Nick Dempsey, up close and personal? Are you going to run off to Hollywood?"

"He is handsome, even better in person than in the movies,"

Audrey admitted. "But I don't think you have anything to worry about, honey."

"Whew, that's a relief. He did seem very interested in the cheese-making business. Think he might give up the glamour and glitter for a goat farm?"

"He might," Audrey said. "But he'll have to find another herd and another girl. I'm spoken for."

"That's right. You belong to me and the goats . . . and Millie."

"Yes, Millie, too." They turned to watch the dog chase a butterfly across the meadow, galloping after the beautiful creature that flew just out of reach.

"I felt bad when Millie ruined Nick's shirt. But honestly, what type of person wears a fancy white shirt like that, custom made in London no less, to visit a farm?" Audrey rolled her eyes.

Rob laughed. "A real movie star, that's who."

That's who had come to visit them. Audrey still couldn't quite believe it. Well, it had certainly taken her mind off her troubles for a while and given her a lift.

If only a movie star could drop by every day.

Chapter Ten

Liza and Claire had a little break on Saturday afternoon before they needed to start dinner. They sat on the porch together, enjoying the late-afternoon sunshine and the beautiful view. They had both been up at six that morning and had spent a full day cleaning and cooking. It would soon be time to get back into the kitchen.

"I'm glad that we have a small group tonight for dinner," Liza said. "Though I doubt anyone will get a better meal in Newburyport or Spoon Harbor than they will here," she quickly added.

Claire took the compliment with her usual equanimity. She stopped knitting for a moment and glanced up at Liza with a brief smile. "Well, you never know. Some of them might go into town and still come back hungry. I'll put some leftovers aside, just in case."

"Good idea. Look, they must be done filming for the day. Here comes someone back from the set," Liza said, staring out at the drive.

Claire looked up, too, and they both watched a shiny black car pull up to the inn. Liza knew by now that only the stars and the studio executives were granted this type of transportation, and she waited to see who got out. It was Charlotte. Liza smiled and waved in greeting, but the actress didn't seem to notice. Still wearing her stage makeup, elaborate hairdo, and costume, she swept out of the car and up the front steps.

"Hello, Charlotte," Claire greeted her evenly. "How was your day?"

Charlotte suddenly stopped at the front door and turned toward them. Liza realized she hadn't noticed them sitting there, she was so deep in thought—or so upset about something.

"It was long and hard, but we got a lot done." She smiled at them, but Liza could tell it was a struggle. Charlotte looked exhausted and overwhelmed.

Claire put her knitting aside, walked over to the young woman, and gently touched her arm. "Would you like to sit with us a minute? I can bring you some iced tea or lemonade."

Charlotte shook her head. Her long, dangling earrings sparkled in the late-afternoon light. "Thanks, Claire. I'm just dying for a nice long shower. I have to get out of these clothes before I melt." She pulled at her outfit, a creamy satin off-the-shoulder evening gown and long satin gloves.

There didn't seem to be enough fabric on the gown to make a person feel that warm, Liza thought as Charlotte gave them another wan smile and headed into the inn.

Meredith had also returned and had been talking to the driver, going over something in her black leather planner. Now she came up to the porch and greeted Liza and Claire quickly. "I'm going up to see if Charlotte needs anything. Then I'm going out to meet some people in the crew, so I won't be staying tonight for dinner."

"Thanks for letting us know," Liza said. "How about Charlotte—is she going out, too?"

"No. She's staying in. I feel a little guilty leaving her," Meredith admitted. "Could you please make sure she has everything she needs tonight? She's very tired. It's been hectic on the set with the filming winding up and everyone pressured to keep the schedule. I think it's wearing on her."

Liza nodded. "Don't worry. We'll make sure she's okay. She's definitely one of our favorite guests," she added with a smile. That was true, too. Not just because they'd expected Charlotte to be a diva and she was so down-to-earth. But because she was such a sweet person, despite all her fame and glamour.

"Don't worry, Meredith. You go out and have a nice evening. I'll check on her personally," Claire promised.

Meredith seemed satisfied with that. She thanked them and hurried into the inn, unable to resist checking on Charlotte one more time.

Claire carefully put her knitting away. "I guess we'd better head into the kitchen and finish dinner. The rest of the group will be back soon."

Liza had the same feeling. She gave the ocean and blue skies one last longing look. She had hoped for a quick walk on the beach today, but that was not to be. Hosting the movie crew had been demanding, a good distraction from thinking too much about Daniel. Whenever her thoughts wandered toward missing him, some new task would draw her attention. But the pace seemed slower tonight. It was Saturday, after all. As the sun dropped toward the horizon into the blue waves, she couldn't help wishing that Daniel were back on the island with her tonight. He had promised to call around ten. At least she had that to look forward to.

Oh, the life of running a B&B. It's not all fresh scones and bouquets of wildflowers. And not nearly as glamorous as people think, Liza thought with a secret smile.

ABOUT a half an hour—and nearly an entire bottle of organic pomegranate shower gel—later, Charlotte flopped onto her bed, wrapped in a plush terry robe. The beating hot water had helped to ease the aches and tension in her body, but she still felt sad and empty.

It was ironic, since she'd had a good workday. They all worked hard, but Brad had actually praised her performance after the final take of a major scene, and everyone in the crew had complimented her as she left the set. She felt satisfaction, of course, but her pleasure was quickly overshadowed by thoughts of Colin.

Since she had left him the night before, he was practically all she could think about. Her emotions were churned up like a tide pool at the ocean's edge.

She had made a big mistake, saying good-bye in such a final way. She had hurt him and never meant to. She had just been trying to do the right thing, what she thought was best for both of them. But she wasn't sure now. She wasn't sure of anything—except the gnawing ache in her heart, the longing to see him again.

She picked her phone up off the bedside table and checked her messages again. There was nothing from Colin. She had called him during breaks and sent text messages all day. He didn't respond at all.

That's because I drove him away, Charlotte realized. *No wonder he isn't calling.*

Should she try to find him and talk it out, face-to-face? Would he even talk to her again? Charlotte knew she had to take the risk.

She just didn't want to leave the island on these terms. She just didn't want him to end up hating her.

She picked up the phone and tapped out another text message.

Really need to see you. Just want to talk. I'm at the inn tonight. Please get in touch or just come by.—Charlotte

She read the message over, wondering if she should say more. Then added:

I'm so sorry. Please don't be mad.

She hit the Send button and set the phone down beside her on the flowery spread. *Just answer, Colin. Please?*

She lay back on the pillows and closed her eyes, amazed at her own behavior. What had come over her? She could not remember feeling or acting this way about a man since—high school. *Am I in love with him?* Charlotte felt a sudden jolt at the idea.

And then a thought came that hit her even harder. *What if Colin is the one? The one she was meant to love.*

All she knew for sure right now was that she just couldn't bear it if she didn't see Colin again. If she didn't get one more chance to watch his slow smile spread across his handsome face, to look into his blue eyes, deep as the sea. To feel his strong arms surround her, like the moment they first met when he pulled her out of the ice-cold water.

Her thoughts drifted, and Charlotte soon fell asleep. She wasn't sure how long she'd been lying there, but when she woke up the sky outside was dark and someone was knocking on the door.

Claire's voice called softly to her, "Charlotte? I'm sorry to wake you up if you're sleeping. We just want to know how you feel. May I come in?"

Charlotte sat up on the edge of the bed and fixed the belt on her robe. "It's all right. You can come in," she called back. The lamp on the bedside table was on, casting the room in a soft glow. She checked the small clock and was shocked to see that it was nearly nine. She had been sleeping for over three hours.

Claire came in, carrying a tray. "I knocked before, around seven. But you didn't answer and I didn't want to disturb you. Do you feel sick? We could call Audrey Gilroy or Dr. Harding in Cape Light."

Charlotte shook her head, then brushed damp tendrils off one shoulder. "I'm all right, just very tired."

"Are you hungry? I've brought you some soup and that ginger tea you like. Why don't you eat a bite while it's hot?"

Charlotte smiled at her. "All right. I didn't think I was hungry, but the soup smells good. What kind is it?"

"Good old chicken, with garden vegetables. It's the universal elixir, I find. It can cure so many ills."

Charlotte wasn't sure about that, but the fragrant aroma drew her as she sat at the table near the window where Claire had set up the meal. A small china plate held a large slice of lightly toasted fresh bread and another held dessert. "Mmmm, this looks good. I am hungry." She started on the soup then took a bite of bread. Her damp hair flopped over her shoulder and she pushed it back. "I forgot to comb my hair out. It's a total train wreck. I'll be in trouble tomorrow with makeup," she added with a sigh.

"Oh, don't worry. I'll help you get the tangles out. Just eat your soup while it's hot," Claire coaxed. She straightened the bed and fluffed up Charlotte's pillow. Then she sat in the antique ballroom chair near the window, her hands folded in her lap, as calm as the slice of toast on Charlotte's tray.

Charlotte felt a wave of unexpected envy for the older woman's peaceful demeanor. Were people just born that way—or was it something you could learn?

I could learn to be more like that if I lived here, Charlotte thought. *Something about this island just seeps down into your soul, like a soothing balm.*

"How do you feel? Any better?"

"Yes, thanks. This soup is magic," Charlotte told her. She picked up the saucer to see what was for dessert. It looked like peach pie with vanilla ice cream. She couldn't resist. She took a bite and sighed. "This is delicious. At least good food is always a comfort."

"Yes, it can be," Claire agreed. "We all need nourishment. For our bodies and our souls."

That was true, Charlotte thought. She loved acting and found great satisfaction in her work, especially when she stretched herself and gave a performance that pushed her beyond her previous limits. Still, her soul called for something more in life. Something beyond her work or even the satisfaction that came from helping her family. Something a relationship with a man like Colin might give her.

Charlotte picked up her tea and took a sip.

Claire stood up behind her. "Would you like me to see if I can smooth out your hair a bit? I know a few tricks about tangles."

Charlotte glanced at her over her shoulder. The makeup artists and hairstylist worked on her for hours each day. It seemed too much to ask of Claire, but something in Claire's expression made her feel it was all right. "If you really don't mind," Charlotte said.

"Not at all," Claire assured her.

"I think there's some conditioning spray or something in the bathroom."

"I'll go check," Claire offered. "Why don't you sit in that chair in front of the mirror, and I'll see what I can do." Charlotte went over to the antique dresser where a large oval mirror hung over the dressing table. Claire soon returned, carrying a tall glass that had been in the bathroom. It was filled with water, a wide-toothed comb sticking out of the top. "I didn't find your spray, but I've mixed something that might be better—a home remedy for tangles with lavender oil and warm water."

Claire quickly got to work, gently separating Charlotte's thick mane into sections. She worked slowly and carefully, dipping the comb into the lavender mixture. The scent was very pleasant and relaxing. So was Claire's gentle touch.

"Am I hurting you?" Claire asked after a small tug.

"Not a bit," Charlotte said. The comb was slowly but surely slipping through the knots. This was different from the stylist working on her hair, Charlotte thought, more personal somehow. It made her feel cared for.

"Meredith told us that the movie is almost done," Claire said. "How much longer will you be with us?"

"Only a few more days. Brad and Mike expect us to wrap up Tuesday or Wednesday."

"Will you be happy to finish the film?"

"I will," Charlotte said honestly. "Though I've learned a lot from working with Brad. He's a tough director but he's made me push myself and grow as an actress. And I won't like leaving the island," she confessed. "It's so beautiful. Unlike any place I've ever been."

And Colin is here, she added silently.

"It's a special place, there's no doubt," Claire agreed. "There's even a legend about the island, which is how it got its name. Some people believe there are angels here, helping those who are troubled at heart."

Charlotte glanced at her, careful not to move her head too fast and pull on her hair. "Somebody mentioned a legend about the island to me. When I first got here. Do you know the story? He didn't explain it much."

Claire met her glance in the mirror, and Charlotte wondered if the older woman guessed that she was talking about Colin. Claire swept the comb through a smooth section of hair and started on another.

"There are a few versions," Claire began, "but basically the story goes like this: Colonists settled in the village of Cape Light in the mid-1600s. During their second winter here, an awful pox ravaged the area. None of the usual cures, herbs, or bleeding, could cure it. Most who caught the disease did not survive. The village fathers decided to quarantine the sick ones. It was a harsh fate, but they reasoned the rest of the villagers would not survive otherwise. They were probably right. So the sick were carried to this island. Crude huts were built for their shelter, and they were left with some supplies, though not very much. There wasn't much to give, and most people believed they would soon die anyway."

"How awful." Charlotte didn't want to interrupt but couldn't stop herself. She thought this was going to be a pleasant story, not a page from a history book illustrating how life in former times was nasty, brutish, and short.

"It was awful for the sick ones," Claire agreed. "Few villagers were brave enough, or merciful enough, to come out and help the quarantined after they were left here. A wagon would deliver food and water and other necessities each week, but not much more. That winter was harsh with many storms and high snow," Claire continued.

"The land bridge was flooded, Cape Light harbor iced in, and no one could visit the island for weeks at a stretch. Few believed that the people left here could survive. Finally, a group from the town came out, bracing themselves for a grim sight. But the truth was even more shocking than they had imagined. The quarantined islanders had not only survived the brutal winter and scant supplies, but were restored to full health."

Charlotte met Claire's glance in the mirror. "Really? They were all right?"

"They were. Healthy and well cared for, with sturdier huts and stacks of firewood, provisions, and water to spare. They claimed a group of very able, gentle people had come to the island and nursed them. But no one could say exactly where these helping hands had come from.

"Of course, they wanted to thank their rescuers once they returned to the mainland. Some of the survivors spent years searching for the ones who had answered their prayers. But they could never find anyone who knew about the quarantine—or who would admit to having gone to the island that winter. Many concluded that they had been saved by the healing touch of angels, disguised in human form," Claire added. "Some believe that the angels' powers can still be felt on the island and will be, forever after. The believers even point to the interesting shape of the island's cliffs that jut out like wings. The place came to be known as Angel Island. The name just stuck. People around here still debate the story. But most natives enjoy telling it," Claire added.

"That is quite a story. Very mysterious," Charlotte agreed. The legend was far-fetched, but some part of her believed it. She even felt goose bumps on her skin. Maybe it was just the way Claire had told it.

"What do you think? Do you believe the legend?" Charlotte asked.

"I believe anything is possible," Claire said evenly, "with God's help."

"I'd like to believe that, too. But I'm not sure I do," Charlotte admitted.

Was it true? Was anything possible? She suddenly thought about the voice she'd heard when she was drowning. The voice that said, "Be strong, Charlotte. You are loved."

Had that been an angel calling to her, bolstering her spirits until she could be saved? She had the impulse to tell Claire about it but felt too self-conscious. She didn't want the older woman to think she was losing her grip on reality. And what if the story went beyond this room somehow? She could just see the tabloid headlines: *Charlotte Miller Hears Voices During Near Drowning!*

Charlotte believed she had heard a voice and had not imagined it. The story about this island had convinced her even more. But she hadn't told a soul and didn't think she ever would.

"There you are. Your hair is finished, tangle free," Claire announced. She smoothed out one last piece then set the comb on the dresser top.

Charlotte ran her fingers through the strands. She couldn't believe it. All the knots were gone, and a light scent of lavender oil lingered. "Thank you so much. This is perfect."

"Oh, it was nothing at all. I'm happy to help," Claire replied.

"I wouldn't call it nothing." Charlotte straightened the items on the dresser top, looking away from Claire. "If only the knots in the rest of my life could be smoothed out so easily."

Her cell phone buzzed, and she pulled it from her robe pocket and quickly checked the screen. It was just Meredith, checking to see how Charlotte felt. Charlotte felt her heart sink again. Colin wouldn't answer her messages. She had to give up hoping, she told herself.

Claire stood watching her. "The tangles in your life . . . Oh, that's not so different, dear. You still need the same ingredients: Go slowly. Have patience. Believe you can figure it out, bit by bit. Quiet your soul and listen," she added. "You may hear the answers to your questions. It might be easier than you think."

Charlotte reached out and gripped Claire's hand a moment, then let go. "Thank you, Claire. I have a few more days in this place. Maybe the angels will help me." She tried for a light tone, as if she were teasing. But she could tell from Claire's clear, steady gaze that Claire saw through that and knew Charlotte was perfectly serious.

"Perhaps they will. Sometimes we just have to open ourselves to God's love." Claire stood by the door and smiled. "Get a good night's sleep. That will help you as much as anything. I'll see you tomorrow," she added as she left the room.

Despite her long nap, Charlotte fell asleep quickly while studying her lines for the next day's scenes. She woke to the sound of the phone and grabbed it off the night table. It was still early, a few minutes before seven. She wondered who would be calling and saw her sister's name on the screen.

"Lily? What is it?" She sat bolt upright in bed, feeling alarmed. "Is everyone all right? Is Mom okay?"

"We're all fine, Charlotte. But something happened last night. I wanted to call you, but it got too late . . ."

Charlotte took a deep breath and braced herself. She didn't want to panic. That wouldn't do anyone any good. "Slow down, honey. Just tell me. Whatever it is, we'll figure it out."

"I was with Mom at the movies, the one at the mall. We were just coming out and walking to the car and these two guys stopped us. One pulled out a little video camera and the other started asking us a million questions. Asking Mom questions mostly, about our family."

Charlotte sighed and pressed her hand to her chest. "Is that all, Lily? You scared me. I thought you and Mom were robbed or something."

"It was almost as bad, Charlotte. It wasn't just the stuff about you that everyone knows. I think these people know about . . . about Wayne." Lily said the name of their stepfather as if it were some foul-tasting potion she wanted to spit out. "And they want Mom to tell them more, to confirm it so they don't get in trouble when they put it on the Web."

Charlotte took a deep, steadying breath. "Did she talk to them at all?"

"More than I wanted her to. There were two of them. They sort of overwhelmed her. I finally got her in the car and drove away . . . But I'm afraid," Lily admitted. "I'm afraid she said too much, and I'm afraid that they'll come back. Oh, Charlotte, I'm so sorry . . ."

Being the oldest at home now, Lily felt responsible. But it wasn't right. She shouldn't have this weighing on her shoulders. *It's enough that I have to drag around this burden,* Charlotte thought.

"Please don't cry, Lily. It isn't your fault, none of it. It's not Mom's either," she added quickly. "Did you get a name or a card? Did they say what magazine or show they were from?"

"Something called *Hollywood Buzz,* I think. It's a TV show," Lily added.

"I know that one," Charlotte replied. It was a show that special-ized in low-down, sensational stories like actors with addiction problems or troubled marriages.

Charlotte glanced at the clock again. "It's too early to call Renee," she said, naming her publicist. "But I'll send her an e-mail right away and ask her to call so we can figure this out. She'll know what to do and how to get rid of them, Lily. Don't worry. In the meantime, just stick close to the house and be very careful if you go outside. Keep Mom close, too," she added.

"I will, Charlotte. Is the movie going all right?"

"Better than I expected," Charlotte answered. The film was going well. It was just other parts of her life that were messed up. "We'll be done here in a few days and need a little time in L.A. After that, I'll come home and visit you," she promised. "I'm sorry you were fright-ened, honey."

"I'm all right," Lily replied, sounding her usual self again. "Take care of yourself, Charlie. We miss you."

"I miss you, too. I'll call you tonight after I speak to Renee," she added. "And don't worry."

Her sister said good-bye, and Charlotte ended the call. Then she sent an e-mail to her publicist, alerting her to the situation. Did these reporters really have information about her past? Or were they just digging around?

Sooner or later, it would happen, Charlotte knew. If not this time, then the next. Or the one after that. Somebody would find out that the lovely, greeting-card picture of her childhood and family life was a big fat lie. Her mother had pressed charges against her stepfather more than once. There were police reports and photographs of her mother's bruised and battered face and body. That was the real family photo album. All of it on public record.

Was this going to be her moment of truth, her moment of shame? For surely someone would ask her how—when her younger siblings and mother had been trapped, at the mercy of a man who ended every night with shouting and the sound of breaking glass—she managed to get out, to run away to California to save her own skin. How she'd managed to totally abandon them.

A sharp knock on the door snapped her to attention. "Who is it?"

"It's me, Meredith. I just wanted to make sure you were awake. We have to be at the set early today."

"Yes, I'm up. I'm going into the shower. I'll be down in fifteen minutes."

Back to business. The schedule was tight today and would only get tighter. That was the one thing that kept her going at times, Charlotte realized. She was carried along by the wave of her commitments, no matter what else was happening.

A short time later, Charlotte grabbed her big black tote that was stuffed with her script, iPad, knitting, and other necessities for the day, and started down the stairs.

She wasn't very hungry but wanted to grab a cup of coffee before her car arrived. She had just turned at the landing when she heard voices down in the foyer, near the front door. Liza was talking with a man. Charlotte thought at first that it was her driver. Then she realized it was a reporter, and Liza was doing her best to fend him off.

"Yes, you've already told me that. But Ms. Miller is not giving any interviews while she's staying here. You need to leave. Immediately," Liza said in a stern tone. "If you give me your card, I'll pass it on to her."

"But this is urgent. This is her chance to have her say, to confirm or deny our information. We're going to put it out there either way."

Charlotte stood stone-still on the landing. She felt her heart racing in her chest. She could barely breathe.

They had found her. Here. She took a few steps back so she couldn't be seen from the lower level.

"Well, either way, you have to go," Liza insisted in an even stronger tone. "I can call the police," she added. "This is private property . . ."

Charlotte didn't wait to hear more. She doubted there were any police officers out on the island, and by the time one came from the town . . .

She just had to get away from this place. She had to hide somewhere.

She ran back up to the second floor then all the way down the long hall, stopping only to stash her tote beneath a narrow table in the hall. She couldn't afford to be slowed down by anything now. She quickly found the back stairway that led down to the kitchen. The wooden steps were narrow and bare. She moved quietly, knowing the smallest sound could give her away.

When she reached the kitchen, she opened the door a crack and peeked inside. Tantalizing smells greeted her—coffee, bacon, a buttery, cinnamon smell, and citrus, all blended into one. Charlotte longed for some hot coffee and a bite to eat but didn't dare delay. The room was empty. She quickly walked to the back door, opened it quietly, and let herself out.

Charlotte wished she could sneak a bicycle out of the barn or even borrow a car. But that was too risky. She had been lucky to sneak out of the inn without being spotted.

A clever mouse has many holes. That had been a line in a little mystery drama she played in once. She had never forgotten it.

After slipping out the back door, she moved carefully around the building, avoiding windows where she could be spotted. She made her way across Liza's property to the gate in the fence that led to the goat farm. Then she crept across the meadow, never turning her head to look back.

She practically held her breath the whole way, sure she would be seen. But miraculously, no one came after her.

At the goat farm, she turned down toward the main road, then kept walking, looking straight ahead. When she heard a car or truck coming, she ran to the side and hid behind a tree or in the brush. There wasn't much traffic on the island since it was still early on Sunday morning.

Charlotte had no idea of where to go. Her first thought was to leave the island. But it was a very long walk into town, and she felt wary of that route. It was the only way on or off the island by car, and the reporters probably figured she would head for the mainland right away. It might be smarter to stay. She had only brought what was in her pockets: her phone, a wad of bills—she had no idea how much—and one credit card. Nothing else. Not even the picture ID that she would need to board a plane. She'd been in such a state, she barely knew what she was doing.

All she knew was that she had to hide right now. Hide and think this out: What was the right thing to do?

She loved being an actress. She loved making movies and felt so grateful for her success. But it was so hard to be a celebrity, to be followed every minute and hounded by reporters. She knew she should be used to it by now, but sometimes it got to her. Even if she didn't have anything to hide, it was still a difficult way to live. She wished she could be free, be her true self and not just the airbrushed picture the public loved so much.

Something had to give. Her life had to change. *She* had to

change. She had felt it from almost the first moment she set foot in this place. And she felt it still, an intangible, invisible force. But it was definitely there, like the steady wind blowing off the ocean, cooling her skin and lifting her hair as she quickly walked along.

Without realizing where she was headed, Charlotte found herself at the opening in the brush where a path from the road led down to the dock, where Colin sometimes kept his boat. The same place where she waited for him to meet her on Friday afternoon for their day alone together.

That seemed so long ago now, those dashed hopes still stinging. She heard a car coming on the road, and jumped into the brush, hiding herself. When the car passed, she decided to walk down to the dock. Colin might be there. Maybe he would put aside his hurt feelings and help her.

Or maybe she could pay someone to give her a ride to Cape Light harbor or even Newburyport. Maybe she could find a boat to borrow and sail away. The possibility cheered her.

The dock was empty, as it had been the night before. But this time, Charlotte saw Colin's boat moored out on the water. She stood at the end of the dock, her hand shielding her eyes, waiting to see if he was onboard.

The boat looked empty, the cabin and cockpit sealed up. It was the perfect place to hide, she realized, and it wouldn't be hard to get aboard.

She pulled a light dinghy from the rack on the beach, as she had seen him do, put two oars inside, then pushed out into the water and scrambled aboard. She wasn't used to the maneuver and nearly tipped the small craft over but soon got her balance. She took a seat at one end then started rowing. It was hard work but she was in good shape and reached Colin's boat in a few minutes.

She steered the dinghy alongside the fishing boat and slowly stood up. Then she grabbed on to the rope ladder and pulled herself over the edge of the boat, falling on the deck with a thud.

If there was anyone in the cabin, they surely would have heard her landing and come out, she thought. But no one did.

She had remembered to keep hold of the line from the rowboat and now tied it to the end of the large craft.

Now what, she wondered. She walked over to the cabin door and opened it easily. It wasn't locked. Colin didn't have anything of value onboard. She already knew that. She envied someone who lived this way, without a care or fear, without even locking doors.

She felt a pang of conscience, realizing that she was trespassing on private property and not a guest this time. But she just needed a place to hide out for a while and gather her thoughts. Colin wouldn't mind that, would he? She hoped not. Maybe he would never even find out.

Charlotte looked out at the blue water and the blue dome of the sky. What a beautiful day, she thought. It reminded her so much of the afternoon she spent with Colin.

That made her sad again. She glanced at her watch and realized that by now everyone would know that she had left the inn. She had cleverly silenced her cell phone before sneaking out, so that an incoming message wouldn't give her away. Now she looked at the list of missed calls and text messages. She felt bad about causing everyone worry and concern, but she just couldn't go back now. If one reporter had found her out on this island, Charlotte was sure there would soon be more.

She saw two figures on the dock and froze. Then she realized it was just a father and son, about to go fishing.

She hurried down into the cabin anyway, afraid to be spotted.

She sat on the bunk with her knees pulled to her chest and pushed open the little round porthole.

She wasn't sure what to do next. She could just call Judy and apologize for running out on them. She could say she was trying to duck a particularly annoying reporter, without giving any more details. Brad and Mike would be livid—another delay, more money wasted. Still, it was a short scene they were supposed to be shooting, and she was the only actor in it. She would find a way to make it up to them, pay them back if necessary. She pulled out her phone again. But she couldn't hit Judy's number.

It was so nice on the boat, so peaceful. The solitude and quiet were a balm to her soul.

This is what I really need right now. Just a few minutes of peace and quiet and complete solitude so I can figure this out.

Somehow, they'll have to understand.

Chapter Eleven

"CHARLOTTE? What are you doing here?"

Charlotte opened her eyes to find Colin standing over her, looking at her as if she'd dropped out of the sky. She'd gotten so comfortable curled up on the bench seat that she had fallen asleep, the gentle waves rocking the boat side to side, and the warm sunlight on her face. Was he angry? She didn't think so. More like shocked. Her mouth felt so dry, she could hardly speak.

"I'm sorry . . . I needed to get away from everyone. I didn't know where to go . . . There was a reporter at the inn. I didn't want to talk to him . . ." Her voice trailed off. She didn't want to tell him what the reporter was after, and hoped he wouldn't ask.

"A reporter? Aren't you used to that?"

"He's from a really awful show. All they do is dig up dirt on people. My sister called this morning and said two other reporters had been bothering my family last night. So they must be working on a story about me. Something dreadful, I'm sure."

He stood with his hands on his hips, staring at her. "I see," was all he said, and she wondered if he did.

Then something in his gaze softened as he watched her sit up and smooth her hair off her face, and it made her feel a spark of hope. She looked up at him. "Did you get my messages yesterday or last night?"

"I didn't have my phone with me yesterday. I forgot it at home. I saw the messages when I got back."

She wondered if he'd gone out last night and where—and with whom. But she didn't dare ask.

"Were you going to answer me?" she asked quietly.

"I didn't know if I should. I didn't know if it would make any difference."

"Oh." Charlotte didn't know what to say to that. Did he mean he didn't care about her anymore? She suddenly felt very awkward, as if she had totally misread him.

"Listen, I'm sorry I just barged in here. That wasn't right. I sort of lost my head. I can go now. It's all right—"

"You don't have to go. I didn't mean that." He still seemed wary of her, but at least he didn't want her to leave. He looked around, seeming self-conscious. "You want some tea? I could do with a cup."

"Okay, thanks," she said. She watched him walk over to the galley and fill the small pot, then set it on a burner.

He turned and faced her, his arms crossed over his chest. "Does anyone know you're here?"

Charlotte shook her head. "I went down the back staircase and snuck out of the inn. The reporter was at the front door, trying to get past Liza. I walked over the meadow at the farm next door and went out onto the road. Then I wandered down here . . . for some odd reason," she added, watching to see if he had any reaction to that.

The corner of his mouth turned up for a moment as if he were about to smile. Instead, he turned and found two white mugs and dropped tea bags into them.

"So you are really hiding out, huh? On the lam?"

"I guess you could say that. I sent a message to my publicist to see if she could do something, deal with these reporters, maybe talk to the producer of their show. But she's in California and it's still so early over there, so that's going to take a while."

Colin checked his watch. "Yup, it's only half past nine. You've accomplished quite a lot for one morning. Shaking off a rabid reporter. Escaping from an inn. Breaking into a boat. What else do you have planned?"

He was warming up a little and she felt relieved. She hugged her knees to her chest and stared at him. "I don't know. Do you have a disguise I could wear, or some invisibility potion? It would help me plan my next move."

The pot reached a boil, and Colin took it off the flame and poured the water into the mugs. "Here, drink some tea. It won't make you invisible, but you might feel better."

She looked up at him as she took the mug. "You think so?"

He shrugged, smiling a little. "My grandmother used to tell me that. It works sometimes."

The expression on his handsome face made her smile, too. He sat down near her. "They're probably going nuts right now up at the inn, looking for you."

"Yeah, I bet they are. Maybe they think I dove off that jetty again."

He laughed quietly. "I don't think so. Nobody would pull that stunt twice, Charlotte."

"Probably not. It was pretty dumb the first time."

She suddenly knew what he was thinking, what they were both thinking. "I was so lucky that day. You were there to help me."

"Yes, you were." He paused and met her glance. "I was lucky, too. How else would I ever have met the famous Charlotte Miller?"

She stared at him and sighed. His eyes were so blue they took her breath away. "I don't know. I think we would have met anyway, someday. I think it was just . . ." Meant to be, she nearly admitted. But she didn't say that. "Bound to happen."

"Maybe so. I was the right man at the right time, anyway. And now, here I am again."

"Does that mean you'll help me?"

He put his mug aside and shrugged. "If that's what you want. I'd hate to see you jump in that dinghy and try to row yourself to Boston Harbor."

They both laughed, though Charlotte had secretly wondered how far she could row herself, if it came to that.

"Do you think the reporter will come down to this dock and look for you? Does anyone know you might come here?"

"I'm not sure. I guess they'll search the island. I think they'll find out the movie crew is looking for me, too. If they're still at the inn, that won't be hard to figure out."

"The movie crew, right. I almost forgot about them. Won't they call the police if you're missing?"

"I don't think so. Not for a while. That becomes public record, and they wouldn't want bad publicity."

"I hadn't thought of that. Good point. That gives us some advantage. Did anyone see you row out here and climb aboard?"

Charlotte shook her head. "The beach and dock were empty, except for a man and boy who were fishing."

Colin stood up and looked out the porthole. "They're still there, but otherwise the dock is empty. Do you want me to take you to Cape Light or another village around here? You can hire a car to get into Boston. It would be harder for a reporter to find you there."

Charlotte thought a moment. She wasn't sure what she wanted to do. Right now, she just wanted to stay with him.

"I want to wait until I hear back from my publicist and find out if she can solve this for me. I just need to hide out and wait a few hours, I guess."

"All right. The smartest thing to do might be to just stay on the boat. We can take her out for a ride. I have enough fuel. Out of sight, out of mind. As long as your Hollywood friends don't call the Coast Guard. I don't want to get arrested for kidnapping you," he joked.

She laughed but didn't put that possibility past Mike or Judy, who would definitely be leading the charge. "You can tell them I hijacked your boat and forced you to drive it."

She wasn't sure how long he was willing to help her or how far he would go. But a few hours alone with Colin on the water was just what she needed right now to soothe her soul and help her sort things out.

"Okay then, we have our plan and a cover story if captured. Let's get under way." He rubbed his hands together, looking cheered by their plan. "You'd better stay below for now."

"I will. Let me know when the coast is clear," she said as he headed for the stairs. "And Colin?"

He turned and looked at her. "Yes?"

"Thank you. Thanks for coming to my rescue . . . again."

"No thanks necessary. I'm getting used to it." He sighed and smiled at her. His wariness and anger had finally melted, and she felt as though the sun had come out again from behind a bank of clouds.

She heard him up above, starting the boat's engine, and then felt the boat cruise away from the mooring, slowly at first, then picking up speed. She watched out the window as the dock and the boats tied up there grew more distant. On the steps leading down to the dock she saw two men descending. Even at a distance she recognized them as members of the movie crew. The lighting technicians, she thought. They walked out to the dock and one spoke to the man who was fishing with his son. She saw the man shake his head and shrug. The other crew member looked out at the water. He seemed to look directly at Colin's boat. Did he suspect she was onboard? She hoped not.

Charlotte sat back on the cushions. She and Colin had made their getaway in the nick of time. Just like in the movies, she thought.

THEY stayed out on the water all day and even did some fishing. Charlotte caught a large sea bass but decided to throw it back. She told Colin she felt bad for the fish once it was in their bucket. He laughed and said she must be identifying with it and helped her toss it back.

They headed back as the sun was starting to set. Charlotte grew tense as she saw the land come closer. She had a horrible feeling that no matter where Colin pulled the boat in, reporters who knew about her past would be there, waiting for her.

She had spoken to her publicist twice during the day. Renee was still trying to track down the person in charge of the show to find out exactly what they knew and didn't know. Charlotte wanted to call Mike and explain why she had run off, but she was too afraid that Mike would insist she come back before the coast was truly clear.

"Don't panic, Charlotte," Renee had said. "It could be something completely different from what you think. But keep your head down until I call you back, okay?"

Charlotte agreed that's what she would do. She had sent Meredith a short text, explaining that she was trying to duck a pernicious reporter and would be back as soon as she could. Meredith had texted her back right away. Charlotte hadn't opened the message.

The boat was coming closer to the land. Charlotte stepped up beside Colin as he steered the boat. "Are you going to pull in at the dock again?"

It had grown cool and he had given her a hooded sweatshirt to keep warm. It was much too big and she had to roll the sleeves but she loved wearing his clothes.

"I was thinking of going around to the other side of the island. I can tie up at a dock near my cottage, and we can walk to my house. I think you'll be safely hidden there. Reporters come by once in a while, looking for movie stars. But not that often."

His teasing tone made her smile and put the situation in perspective. Of course she was safe out here. No one would find her in a million years.

"Is it a long walk to your cottage?" she asked, wondering how long she would have to be out in the open. Maybe reporters didn't roam these streets, but one of his neighbors might recognize her.

"About half a mile. But we'll give you a disguise." He glanced at her. "The first thing we have to do is hide that hair. I have some hats in the cupboard under the bunk, and some old jeans and boots in a cubby somewhere. Go see if you can make yourself look like a fishing buddy, okay?"

"Good idea. I'll pretend I got a role, playing a guy," she said, heading below again.

Her answer made him laugh. "Highly unlikely, but give it a try."

A short time later, Charlotte came back on deck. They had reached the dock, and Colin was slowly and carefully bringing the boat alongside so he could tie up.

"How do I look?"

He glanced at her. "Not bad. I'll have to call you Charlie while you're in that getup."

"That's fine. My family calls me Charlie all the time." Hearing him say the nickname touched her.

"It suits you. Here, take the wheel a minute, Charlie. Just hold it steady. I'm going to jump on the dock with the line."

Charlotte quickly did as he said, then watched as he nimbly straddled the boat and dock and quickly tied the first line on to secure it. He extended his hand and helped her off the boat, then went back for the bucket of fish they had caught.

"Hold this net over your shoulder. It's a nice prop as we're walking along."

Charlotte took the net and they set off. She felt a little nervous at first and couldn't help looking around the dark dock and beachfront for any signs of people searching for her. But there were none.

They soon reached the cobblestone streets of the fishing village, and Colin led the way to his house. Some of the cottages were dark and empty looking, but many windows glowed with warm lights within. Charlotte couldn't help peering inside at the people who lived there: women cooking in their kitchens, children playing games, a man reading a newspaper. She envied their quiet, anonymous lives.

"So far so good," Colin said as they turned a corner.

He glanced around at the next street. She couldn't tell if he was teasing her, thinking she was paranoid, or if he, too, feared they would be spotted. "Not too much longer."

"Good. How am I doing?"

"Not bad. But you need to walk more like a guy, *Charlie*," he said, glancing quickly over her shoulder at her rearview. "No one would ever take you for a man with that wiggle."

"Oh, right. I forgot." She quickly adopted a lumbering, side-to-side male strut. "Better?"

"That's the idea. You look a little like a chimpanzee," he commented casually. "But it's definitely an improvement."

"Glad you approve. These clothes you loaned me smell like dead fish, by the way."

He gave her an appreciative grin. "I was wondering when you'd notice."

They reached his cottage, and Colin led her around to the back door and let them in. He turned on a few lights and closed the curtains. "In this neighborhood we pretty much look out for each other. But that does sometimes translate into my neighbors knowing more about my private life than I like them to."

"I guess I should stay away from the windows then." Charlotte pulled off the baseball cap, and her pinned-up hair tumbled out in all directions.

When she looked up, he was staring at her. "Uh . . . yeah. That would be a good idea."

He turned and headed for the kitchen. "I'll go fix us something to eat. I think fish is on the menu. I hear it's very fresh."

She smiled, knowing he meant the fish they had caught that day. "Sounds great."

So he could cook, too? This guy was too good to be true, Charlotte thought. She helped Colin in the kitchen as much as she could. It was a simple meal of broiled fish, boiled potatoes, and frozen beans, everything seasoned with butter, parsley, and salt.

While the food cooked, Colin showed her the bathroom and gave her some towels and extra clothes he thought might do if she wanted to freshen up. Charlotte appreciated his thoughtfulness. There was certainly some awkwardness and tension between them, being in such close quarters, but he was trying to make it as easy for her as possible.

When they sat down to dinner, Charlotte thought she had never tasted anything so good, not even in the fanciest five-star restaurants. They were both tired from the day and didn't talk much. Colin had put on some music, a light baroque melody. Charlotte didn't know much about classical music but she found the delicate harmonies very soothing, the perfect ending to a nearly perfect day.

As they sat in easy silence, Charlotte realized she felt a genuine sense of peace, even protection here. Once again, Colin had stepped in to help her and even take care of her, without any self-serving motives. He hadn't been hired as an assistant or security guard and wasn't part of the production staff. He was just . . . Colin. And she was here because he cared for her. She wasn't used to that. It rarely happened in her professional life—or her real life.

After dinner was cleared, they went into the living room.

"Should we check the news, to see if there's a manhunt on for you?" His tone was teasing, but she could tell he was partly serious.

"I sent Meredith a text that I was alive and well, just waiting out an aggressive reporter. So I don't think they have the bloodhounds looking for me."

"That's good. Because I don't own a TV. But we could look on the Internet," he added.

She couldn't help asking, "You don't miss having a TV?"

He shrugged. "I'm not the best-informed person you'll ever meet. But I figure your brain is like an attic; there's just so much useless junk you can dump up there. Pretty soon the useless stuff crowds out the important stuff. And I don't want to waste time I could be using more efficiently."

"For your writing, you mean?"

He nodded. "Like my writing. Exactly."

She respected that. He was willing to make so many sacrifices for his work, living a rustic life out here, all alone. Focusing totally on his dream.

"That's real dedication. I hope it pays off for you."

"I do, too," he admitted. "But everyone has to pay their dues. I'm sure you had a lot of little, invisible roles before you got leading parts."

"I did," she agreed. "I was lucky, though, that the right people saw my work and offered me better parts. I worked hard for years, without getting very far—then boom. It sort of all came at once. I still can't believe it. Sometimes, I feel as if I don't quite deserve it," she said honestly.

"I wouldn't say that. There's such a thing as natural talent. Some people can study writing or painting or acting all their lives and never be any good at it. And some people don't have to study at all. They've just . . . got it."

Charlotte had never thought of it that way. His words made her feel better.

He gave her a curious look. "Is that why you don't like talking to reporters? You feel as if you haven't worked hard enough for your success?"

Charlotte was surprised by his question, though it did hit a nerve. She did fear being found out. Not about her acting. She felt confident enough about her abilities there. But about her past, the fake happy childhood that had been cooked up to hide the dark truth of her family's dysfunction.

She didn't answer right away. She gazed into her mug of tea, as if she might find the right words there. She wanted to be truthful with him, but there were truths she could never tell anyone.

He reached over and touched her hand. "I'm sorry. I can be too blunt sometimes. You don't have to answer that. I just want to know you better. I want to understand you."

She looked up at him. "It's a fair question. But that's not what I'm afraid of. That's not what I think the reporters will find out about me either."

His blue eyes studied her as if they could see into her soul. He was still holding her hand, his touch warm and reassuring. "What is it, Charlotte? You look so . . . worried and scared."

Charlotte wondered if maybe she had been wrong. Maybe she *could* tell someone the truth she had been hiding for years. Still, she wondered if she could trust Colin with it. Would he think less of her for pretending all this time to be something she was not? Would he think she'd been selfish and cold to leave home and desert her younger siblings the way she had?

During her first few years in L.A., she had barely had contact with them. She didn't have any spare money to send home but would call every month or so, talking only to Lily. Even that limited contact was painful. Charlotte always hung up feeling terribly guilty and tugged back toward that toxic household. But Lily would remind her that the only way to really help the family was for Charlotte to follow her own path, and become strong enough and successful enough to someday help them all get away.

It had taken time, but Charlotte had started secretly sending money to her mother, begging her to take the kids and leave. About that time, her stepfather had died, and Charlotte was able to fully support them. She had been supporting them ever since. Still, so much damage had been done.

Charlotte glanced at Colin, who was still waiting for her answer. She had been lying and hiding this so long, it was hard to tell the truth to anyone.

As she sat there, trying to find a way out of her own secrets, her cell phone buzzed in her pocket. She pulled it out and saw that it was Renee calling. She quickly answered it, wondering what her publicist had found out.

"Well, it's all settled. You can come out of hiding," Renee announced cheerfully. "I finally tracked down the producer of *Hollywood Buzz* and got him to tell me what they have on you."

Charlotte braced herself. "What is it exactly?"

Renee knew the truth about her past. She had in fact been one of the authors of Charlotte's fake story. But she seemed to take these situations so casually at times, claiming any publicity was good publicity, a theory that had never made sense to Charlotte.

"It's not what you think, so don't worry. It's not even about you really. They want to know about your sister Lily. It seems someone's found out she might come out to the West Coast to go to school, and they're already wondering if she's going to be the next hot young actress. They want to interview the two of you together."

"A story about Lily? That's what they're after?" Charlotte didn't entirely believe it. It was definitely not the disaster she had imagined, but she also hated the idea of her little sister being pushed into the public eye. Lily had no desire to act, and Charlotte wasn't about to let anyone try to change her mind.

"Don't worry, they promised they would leave her alone. For now. But I had to promise you would give them an exclusive interview when you finish this film."

"All right. I guess that would be okay." Charlotte was reluctant to help the show at all, but knew she couldn't refuse. Better to give them a story that she wanted them to have than to let them dig up one of their own.

"So, back to work, kid," Renee said briskly. "The little escape is over. Do you want me to call Judy for you?"

"No, I'll call her. Thanks for your help, Renee."

"That's what I'm here for. I'll see you soon. We'll have lunch when you get back, okay?"

"Yes, of course." Charlotte said good-bye and ended the call.

She turned to Colin. He'd been listening. He couldn't help it, since he was sitting so close. "Good news?" he asked.

"In one way, I guess." Charlotte explained that the reporters were after a story about her sister and that her publicist had called them off by promising an exclusive interview for their show.

"I see. So you can come out of hiding?"

"That's right. I can shed my alter ego, Charlie, the fishing buddy." She tried for a light tone, but the moment felt bittersweet. Just when it seemed they were growing closer to each other, she had to go.

"Well, that's a plus at least. I could never quite see you as a guy, I must admit."

He smiled, but she saw a flash of disappointment in his eyes.

"I'll take that as a compliment," she said.

"You should," he agreed.

He stared at her a moment, then pulled her close and kissed her, softly at first, then more intensely. Charlotte melted against his strong body, feeling swept away. The same way she'd felt carried off by the ocean current . . . and just about as powerless to resist, too.

She wasn't sure how long they stood holding each other. Finally, she lifted her head and leaned back. She cupped his cheek with her hand. His stubble felt rough against her palm. He really was so wonderful and dear to her. She had to step away now, or she never would.

"What now? Do you need to go back to the inn?"

She definitely didn't want to. She wanted to stay here all night, sitting and talking with him. Asking him every question she could think of, hearing him talk and laugh.

But she could already feel the pull of responsibility drawing her back. People were depending on her. She had already wasted two days of filming. She had to go back right away.

"Yes, I do. I'd better call Judy and tell her where I am."

He looked very unhappy but not surprised. "I can take you. You don't have to call anyone."

"No, it's okay. You've helped me a lot today. I don't want to put you out," she said quickly. *It will be so much harder that way,* she nearly added aloud.

She picked up her cell phone and sent Judy a text, telling her she was in Thompson's Bend and gave her Colin's address. "They must think I'm really nuts for running off that way today," she said as she tapped out the message. "I guess I panicked. It was just a reporter, but the whole thing pushed my buttons. I've had so many bad experiences with the media."

"I understand that part, Charlotte . . . I just wonder if there's something you're not telling me," he said slowly.

"What do you mean?"

"Well, you seemed so afraid of that reporter and now, so relieved. As if you dodged some kind of bullet. Was there something you thought he knew about you? Something you need to conceal from everyone?"

Charlotte felt her pulse race. She tried to look him in the eye but couldn't. He knew she was hiding something. He was smart about people, highly observant. A born writer, she thought. Could she tell him? She would feel so relieved telling someone. But she was so afraid. Right now he thought she was wonderful. She could see it in his eyes. He might not ever look at her that way again. He might decide she was selfish and cold, out for herself and unfeeling about other people's pain—even her own family's.

"There is something," she said finally. "I wish I could tell you. But I can't."

Colin ran a hand through his hair and gave her a look that was both sympathetic and exasperated. "If you can't tell me, I can't help you. If you can't be honest with me, how can we really know each other?"

Charlotte stared at him, stunned. She knew what he was asking her and knew everything between them rested on this moment, on her answer.

"I want to tell you," she repeated. "But it's so . . . complicated. Please don't judge me, Colin. Please don't make everything between us come down to this. You don't know the story. You don't understand."

He didn't answer her for a long moment. "You're right. I don't understand you. I'm trying to, but you won't let me."

"Colin—"

"What I do understand," he went on, "is that it's important to be honest with each other if you want something real, something serious. I want something more than a fling with you, Charlotte. I guess you just don't trust me that much. I guess you don't see a real future for us, do you?"

She suddenly understood something about her life, a truth that had eluded her. All these years, she wondered why she could never find a good relationship with a man. She had never met anyone like Colin, that was true. No one had ever made her heart race the way he could with just a smile. But he had just summed up a deeper problem. As long as she walked around with this secret inside, never letting anyone close enough to see the real Charlotte Miller, she would always feel alone. She would always keep anyone who cared about her at arm's length. She would never be free to fully love or know happiness.

And if she told him the truth, what then? He would be stuck in the same trap, forced to keep the secret, too. Was that even fair to do to someone?

"Colin . . ." She reached out her hand to him, but he didn't respond. "This is so hard. It's not that I don't trust you. And it's not that I think that you're just a fling. That's not the way I feel about you at all."

He was the only one she could see in her future. The only one she really wanted beside her.

"It's all right. You don't have to say anything else. You don't have to explain it to me."

He stood up and touched her cheek with his hand, and she thought he might kiss her. Instead, he turned and walked to the back door. "All things considered, it's probably better if I'm not even here when they come to pick you up. Good luck, Charlotte," he said, pulling open the back door. "Good-bye," he said finally.

Charlotte was so stunned, she didn't know what to do. She couldn't believe he was just walking out on her this way. She ran to the door and followed him outside. "Colin? Please don't go like this. Come back. Can't we talk a little?"

Colin was walking down the gravel drive next to his cottage. He didn't turn around to look at her. There were only a few lights on the street, old-fashioned gas lamps that gave off a soft glow in the damp night air.

She watched him walk away and disappear into the darkness.

Then she covered her face with her hands and began to cry. She was shaking with sobs and couldn't stop herself. She had never imagined her time with Colin ending this way, on such a sad, bitter note.

But it had to end, one way or another, she reminded herself. *In time, I'll look back and know that it was all for the best. It's better this way. It would be much harder later—when I would be even more in love with him.*

She went back inside and waited by the front window. The long black car soon appeared and parked in front of the cottage. Charlotte ran out and jumped in the backseat. The door locked with an automatic click.

"Are you all right, Ms. Miller?" the driver asked.

"Yes, I'm fine," Charlotte replied, though she felt anything but. She leaned back in the plush seat and sighed. Back into her plush world, a movie star again.

The car pulled away and she looked back at Colin's cottage with longing. It was as if she were leaving another world, a perfect world she'd made up in her imagination. A place she could only return to now in her dreams.

Chapter Twelve

"I GUESS all that rain was good for something," Audrey said. "Check out these tomatoes, Rob. They're positively monstrous."

"It's the Attack of the Giant Tomatoes, all right." He stepped forward to help Audrey with the overflowing bushel she carried from the garden.

"I'm going to cook one of these big boys for dinner, instead of a roast chicken," she announced.

She was teasing, but not entirely. The bounty of their summer garden made it easy to go vegetarian. Audrey had collected a lot of recipes for savory pasta dishes and stews with all-vegetable ingredients.

"Where do you want the rest of these?" he asked her.

"Over by the spigot. I'll rinse them off and put them in the shop." Fridays through Mondays were usually the four busiest days in the shop during the summer, but they'd had a lot of customers today, too, though it was a Tuesday. It was just another sign of summer winding down, the final wave of summer visitors, the ones who left their vacations for the very last weeks of August. There would be a steady stream of visitors to the island—and to her shop—from now until September.

"I think we should put up the roadside stand, too. Until the end of the season," she said as they walked to the house. "We can make some money from that garden patch this year. It's going to be a huge harvest."

"Maybe those fences finally kept the deer and rabbits from eating half of it."

"Maybe," Audrey agreed as she rinsed the dirt off a pile of tomatoes and carrots. "Millie helped, too," she added.

The dog was nearby, as usual, and wagged her tail. Audrey flipped her a carrot and she happily crunched it down.

"She loves carrots," she told Rob as he placed the clean tomatoes in a wide-slatted wooden crate. "They're good for her, too. I looked it up on the Internet."

Rob smiled as he sorted out the tomatoes. "Sounds like you've been studying those dog sites pretty carefully, Audrey. You're becoming an expert."

"I just want to know how to take care of her and train her. Neither of us knows much about dogs," Audrey reminded him. But she did feel found out. The time she spent lately reading up on dog care was a pleasant distraction from her endless research of their fertility problem.

Audrey's cell phone sounded. She wiped her hands on her jeans and fished the phone from her back pocket. She was expecting a call from Liza. But she saw it was a Boston number, then quickly realized it was the fertility specialist. She glanced at her husband. "It's Dr. Barnes. Maybe he has the test results."

Rob dropped a tomato and came toward her. "Answer it, honey. Before he hangs up."

Audrey yanked off a garden glove and tried to pick up the call. Her fingers fumbled. Finally, she hit the right button. "Hello? Dr. Barnes?"

"Hello, Audrey. I'm just getting in touch about the tests you and your husband took last week. When can you come in to see me, so we can go over the results?"

Audrey glanced at Rob and nodded. "We're so glad you have the information, Doctor. We've been dying to hear how the tests turned out, but it's hard for us to get to Boston. This a really busy time at our farm," she added, exaggerating so much that Rob made a face. "And I really can't stand the suspense," she added honestly. "Can't you please just tell me what you found out?"

"I'm sorry, Audrey. I'm sure you're both anxious to know. But it's best if you come in. There's a lot of information here, and it's not just one issue—"

"Doctor Barnes, please? I'm a nurse. I get this stuff. What if we agree to come in, but you just answer one question: What's the bottom line? Can we have a baby, or not?"

Rob put his arm around Audrey's shoulder and she put the phone on speaker so he could hear everything. The doctor didn't answer for a long time, and Audrey worried that she had disconnected him by accident.

Then they heard the doctor sigh. "I suppose I can make an exception this once. Again, it's not that simple to answer unequivocally, but since you want me to boil it down, I'd have to say that you have a low probability for unassisted conception. However, you're also a candidate for quite a few treatment options, including in-vitro fertilization."

Audrey felt as if a stone had lodged in her chest, even though she had expected this news. She glanced at Rob. He stared straight ahead, his jaw tight.

"Thank you, Doctor," Audrey said finally. "I appreciate your honesty. We're outside now, working. I'll call your office tomorrow and make an appointment to talk to you in person about all this."

"I know this seems like the worst possible news," the doctor said, his voice softer. "But it really isn't. There are amazing medical interventions that have helped millions of couples like you and your husband have beautiful, healthy babies. Don't despair. We'll get there."

"Thank you, Dr. Barnes. We'll try to remember that," she promised, though she knew it would be very hard. She stuck the phone back in her pocket and turned to Rob. "Well, that's it. We've got our answer. In a way, it's a relief. I was going crazy waiting to hear, weren't you?"

Rob shook his head. "It's certainly not the news we were hoping for. But I suppose it's better to know than not know." He put his arm around her shoulders and hugged her close. "Don't worry, honey. We'll figure this out. We'll have a baby."

She glanced up at him and forced a smile. "I know we will. It's just that now that we have the answer, it's hard to face it."

To face that they had a long ordeal ahead of them—and might need to give up the farm. That's what it always seemed to come down to, she meant. But it was too soon after this big news to get into the conversation again. Rob seemed to feel the same way. "I'll finish this later. Let's just go in now and make dinner. It's getting late and we're both tired."

They started off toward the house, their arms around each other. Millie dashed out from behind the barn, barking and wagging her tail.

"We're all going inside now, Millie. We're right behind you."

Millie stood up on her hind legs and took a few steps backward in a little dog dance, looking at Audrey as if to say, "Hey, look at this. Pretty good, right?"

"I guess she's happy we're going in. She knows you'll feed her dinner," Rob said.

Audrey nodded. Secretly, she was sure the dog sensed their sadness and was trying to cheer them up . . . And she wanted her dinner, too, of course.

Millie ran over and trotted alongside, her fur rubbing on Audrey's bare leg. Audrey leaned over and patted her head, receiving an adoring look and a lick in answer.

Millie, what would I do without you? she wondered.

It was just after seven on Wednesday morning when a sharp, quick knock sounded on Charlotte's door. "Come in."

Meredith opened the door a crack and stuck her head in. "The car will be here any minute. Do you want me to take anything else down?"

"I'm just closing my carry-on. I can handle the rest, thanks," she added in a tone that suggested she wanted to be alone.

Meredith nodded and disappeared. Charlotte walked back to the bed and put the last-minute items into her bag and zipped it.

She would miss this place. There was definitely something magical about it. She'd been on the island exactly two weeks, but it felt much longer.

Luckily, the last few days had flown by. The crew had been working nonstop since Monday morning, making up for the time lost when she disappeared. Miraculously, they finished right on schedule, Tuesday night.

Charlotte had been nervous when she returned on Sunday night, not knowing what to expect. But she apologized and admitted she'd overreacted to the aggressive reporters. Renee had also smoothed the way. Mike and Judy seemed to understand and apologized for the failure of the film's security team. The reporter should have never gotten a foot on the inn's property, they agreed.

As so often happened in the film business—no matter what the execs really thought—Sunday's misadventure was quickly forgotten and forgiven for the sake of finishing up the film.

There were a few more minor scenes left to shoot in a studio in L.A., but the film was basically done. They were flying back to California today from Logan Airport in Boston and due back on the studio soundstage tomorrow afternoon.

Charlotte was glad it was over. Part of her was eager to get back to California and get this film done. Another part yearned to stay and be with Colin. She kept picturing an impossible future, the two of them walking along the shore together, fishing on the beach of that perfect little island . . .

She had sent him a text late last night, to tell him she was leaving and she hoped they could talk one more time, if only for a minute or so. She couldn't bear to think that his walking away from her was really the last contact they would ever have. She had kept the phone close to her ever since, but so far, he hadn't answered.

It was foolish to hope he would appear at the inn at the very last minute, like a happy ending in some romantic drama. Foolish to hope he would even answer her texts, though that didn't prevent her from checking her phone again. Still, no reply.

Despite her common sense and natural resistance to totally humiliating herself, Charlotte tapped out another text and sent it:

Leaving in a few minutes. Won't you at least say good-bye?

Then she tucked the phone in her pocket and walked over to the window for one last look at the view. It was still early, and a faint mist clung to the beachfront, as if it had been painted there by some unseen hand.

She had nearly lost her life in that deep blue ocean. But she had found something there, too. The terrifying experience had changed her inside. So had meeting Colin. She just needed to find the strength now to change on the outside, too.

Down the road, she saw a long black limo turn into the drive, heading for the inn. How she wished it were Colin's truck. She pulled out her phone and checked it again.

Come on, Colin . . . just answer me. Please?

She wasn't sure how long she stood staring at the phone, willing a message to appear. She heard another knock on the door and knew it was Meredith.

"Charlotte, the car is here. We don't want to miss the flight, right?"

"I'm coming. I'll be right there."

Charlotte sighed, shut off the phone, then stashed it in her purse. She was tired of looking at it. Tired of hoping.

If this was the way he wanted to end things between them, there was nothing she could do.

THE inn seemed strangely quiet and empty as Charlotte headed for the front door. But she was pleased to find Liza and Claire waiting on the porch to say good-bye. She and Meredith were the last of the film crew to go. While Meredith helped the driver load up their bags, Charlotte had a moment with the two women.

"Thank you for everything. This is such a wonderful place. I'm going to tell everyone I know to come here. You'll be overrun with movie stars," she promised Liza.

"What a hardship," Liza replied with a laugh. "I'll try to meet the challenge."

"I'd bet none will be as lovely or charming as you, dear," Claire said, "or so easy to please."

Charlotte hardly thought of herself as easy to please, but it was sweet of Claire to say so. She hugged Liza and then Claire, feeling as if she might cry. "I'll come back to visit, I promise. If I can help you publicize the inn some way, Liza, please let me know. Can you use a photo or something in an advertisement?"

"That would be terrific. I'd really appreciate it," Liza said sincerely. "I'll e-mail you about it. You just finish this movie first. Don't worry about anything else."

"Yes, finish your film, Charlotte. We can't wait to see it," Claire added.

"I'll try to send you some tickets for a preview." Charlotte wished there was something more she could do for Liza and Claire. She hadn't known them long, but she felt as if they were both truly friends. They had been so understanding of her ups and downs. She hugged them both quickly. "I'll be in touch. I hope you enjoy the rest of the summer."

"Take care of yourself, dear," Claire said. "Let us know how you're doing."

"I will," she promised, looking into Claire's pale blue eyes a moment. "If you're ever in California, please let me know. You can come visit me."

"Oh, that's a lovely invitation, but I rarely leave the island . . . and I never travel that far," Claire replied. "I do have a little going-away gift for you and Meredith." Claire produced two brown bags. "The airline food is awful. Even in first class, I hear. I made you some sandwiches and brownies for the flight."

"Thank you, Claire, how thoughtful," Charlotte said.

Meredith was already out by the car, gesturing to her to hurry. She said good-bye again, then ran down the porch steps and into the car. Then it really was time to leave Angel Island. Charlotte sat back in her seat and fastened the seat belt as the car pulled away.

Liza and Claire stood on the porch, waving and smiling. She waved back then remembered they couldn't see her through the tinted glass.

Just as well, she thought. They couldn't see the tears that gathered in the corners of her eyes. *I knew it would be hard to leave here. I just didn't realize how hard.*

Liza and Claire spent the rest of the day cleaning up the many rooms the movie crew had used and putting the inn in order for guests who would arrive on Friday for the weekend. Two days were usually enough time to prepare, but there was a lot to do and many more rooms to clean than usual.

When Liza met Claire in the kitchen for lunch, she found a package on the table, wrapped in tissue paper, tied up with a piece of yarn. "What's this?" she asked curiously.

"I found it in Charlotte's room. She left a note on it." Claire reached into her apron pocket and took out a slip of paper. "'Please see that Colin gets this package. Thank you—Charlotte,'" she read aloud.

"Oh, a gift for Colin. Interesting." Liza looked at the small, lumpy package, wondering what it could be. "I thought he might have come this morning, to say good-bye."

Claire stood at the counter fixing two salads made with fresh lettuce and vegetables from the Gilroy Farm alongside some cold chicken from last night's dinner. She didn't share her opinion on the subject, and Liza did not expect her to. It was not like Claire to speculate on anyone's love life.

Of course, that didn't stop Liza. "I know I might be jumping to conclusions," she said carefully, "but Charlotte seemed so unhappy when she got back Sunday night from that running-away episode—unhappy and subdued. I just had a feeling she wasn't roaming around the island that whole time, the way she said she was. I think Colin helped her hide."

"Perhaps. There's no way of knowing, of course." Claire set their salads on the table and then sat down across from Liza.

"No, no way of knowing," Liza agreed. "I guess I'll call Colin and let him know he has a package from Charlotte. What does a movie star give the man who saves her from drowning?"

"Good question," Claire admitted. "It doesn't have the look of a store-bought gift to me, more like something given from the heart. So maybe that tells us all we need to know. Or have the right to know," she added.

Liza had to agree. Leave it to Claire to sum up the situation so simply.

COLIN came to the inn that evening. He parked his pickup truck at the side of the building and strode up onto the porch, where Liza and Claire sat watching the stars come out over the ocean.

It was a fair night, the breeze off the water cool enough to require a light sweater. The first hint that summer was fading, making way for fall.

"Good evening, ladies." Colin walked toward them, his hands dug into the pockets of his denim jacket. "Quiet around here with all the movie people gone."

"Yes, they're all gone. The movie crew left last night, and Charlotte and Nick left this morning," Liza said. She thought she saw a flicker of reaction in his expression at Charlotte's name, but he quickly tried to hide it. He sat down on the top step of the porch, and she couldn't see his face.

"You two must feel relieved," he said. "That was a lot of work, and those Hollywood types must have been hard to please."

"Oh, it wasn't so bad," Liza said. "I think we managed to keep them happy."

"I'm going to miss Charlotte," Claire said. "She's a sweet girl. Nothing like you'd expect."

"No, she isn't," he agreed quietly. He turned and looked at Liza. "Did she really leave a package for me?"

"She did. I have it right here." The package sat nearby on a wicker table. She picked it up and gave it to him. "There wasn't any note for you, just the one for us. Maybe there's one inside."

He stared at the package so long, Liza wondered if he was going to just take it and open it in private. Then, much to Liza's relief, he tore off the paper.

She recognized the gift immediately: Charlotte's knitting project. She hadn't been making a hat and scarf for her brother, as she claimed. It was for Colin, and nicely done, too, in dark khaki-colored wool with thin yellow and navy blue bands of color

"Oh, the hat and scarf. She made that herself," Claire told him, "sitting right here with us. There's no finer gift than something made by hand. A person puts their special energy into a gift like that, a part of their heart."

Colin glanced at her, then looked back at his gift, touching it with his fingertips. He kept it neatly folded on his lap, just as Charlotte had wrapped it. After a moment, he noticed a note in the tissue paper and read it to himself. Liza could see that it wasn't very long, just a line or two. But she couldn't see what it said.

He took a deep breath and put the note in his shirt pocket. Then he stood up, the gift wrapped in the torn paper.

"Are you going already, Colin? I made a plum tart," Claire told him. "First of the season."

"That sounds delicious. But I have a lot to do tonight, packing for a trip up north."

"A fishing trip?" Liza asked. She knew that some fishermen headed up to cooler waters this time of year for a bigger catch. Sometimes they were gone for months. "When are you leaving?"

"Friday. I only have one more day to prepare."

"How long will you be gone?" Claire asked curiously.

"I don't know. That depends," he said vaguely. "I'll see how it goes. I don't have anything tying me down. I can just do as I please."

"That's true." Claire nodded. "Are you going up there alone, or with some other boats?"

"On my own. I'm used to it." He shrugged. "Guess I'll see some guys up there I know. But I rarely fish with anyone else."

"We'll miss you," Claire said. "Take care of yourself, Colin. Come back safely."

"Yes, have a safe trip," Liza added.

"Don't worry, I'll be all right. But thanks." He said good night and then headed for his truck, Charlotte's gift tucked under his arm.

"Well, what do you think now?" Liza asked her friend as Colin's taillights faded down the drive. "Still think I'm speculating wildly about them?"

"I never said you were speculating wildly," Claire corrected her. "I still think that private matters are best left private. I will say he seemed sad, not his normal self. I think he liked the gift. But it didn't bring him much pleasure, did it?"

"No," Liza agreed. "It seemed to make him even sadder."

Claire didn't answer, just picked up her knitting again and sighed. There didn't seem to be anything else to say.

WATCHING Rob at the dining room table with all their business papers, bills, and files spread out around him made Audrey nervous. He usually only got this way once a year, at tax time, and that was over pretty quickly.

He had been at it for a few days now. She knew this was just his way of coping with the bad news from the doctor, his way of avoiding the pain and trying to take some constructive steps forward. But Audrey wished he would just finish his calculations. She already knew what he was going to say.

"Any progress?" she asked. It was Sunday morning, and he had woken up before her and gone straight to his desk with a cup of coffee. She brought him a refill and set it in a safe place.

"I found an e-mail this morning from that man who said he might be interested in leasing the farm. He made me a ballpark offer. I just wanted to run the numbers and see how they came out," he said, staring at his computer screen.

"How did they come out?" She sat at the table, not really wanting to hear the answer.

He sighed and sat back. "It's tough, Audrey. If we can actually get this amount, it would cover most of the mortgage. But there are still taxes and general upkeep of the property to consider. And we won't have the income from the farm store and stand, or from the cheese distribution."

"But we'll both have jobs, in the city, presumably." Audrey knew she could make a good salary as a nurse. Nurses were always in demand.

"Audrey, be practical. What if you have a difficult pregnancy? During some of those treatments, I think it's hard to work at all. And you probably won't want a full-time job once we have a baby."

"I know," she said quietly. "I just . . . Well, I wish the math would work out for us, that's all."

"I know, hon. I'm the number cruncher here, and I'm trying to make the pieces fit. But I'm not sure we can swing it."

Audrey swallowed hard and said the impossible words. "If we have to leave the farm then . . . well, that's what we have to do. Having a family is more important than living here, as much as we love it," she added quietly.

"I agree," Rob said. "We can always come back here someday. We can visit with our beautiful children and show them this place and tell them about a time in our lives that was fun and different— but empty in a certain way without them."

That was it entirely. As much as they loved their life here, their dream to have a family was more important and starting to make the farm seem like some sort of consolation prize. "Why is this so hard for us?" she asked. "Other people aren't forced to make these choices, Rob. This farm was always your dream. If we give it up to have a baby, how are you going to feel? Five or ten years from now, maybe you'll resent it. Maybe you'll resent me," she said, voicing a real fear.

"What if we go through the treatments, and it ends up that we're never able to have a child? That could happen, too, you know," she added. That was her worst fear. "Will it have been worth it to you? To both of us?"

Rob took her hand. "I dreamt of having a farm like this for years before we actually bought it. I won't deny that. And I love waking up every morning and going out there and working in the garden or with the goats or making cheese. It never feels like work to me. But I've seen that dream come true and lived it. Most people can never say that. Our dreams change, Audrey, that's what I've learned. Now my dream is to hold our own little one in my arms, and raise a baby with you. If we have to leave here to do that, then that's what we'll do. There are no guarantees in life, honey, you know that. Everybody has got to hoe their own row. Saying it's not fair doesn't matter. This is our row. This is what we have to deal with. All we can do is try our best. In the end, it's all in God's hands, right?"

Audrey nodded, feeling tears well up in her eyes. She was so emotional lately. It was just an up-and-down time for them. "When you put it that way, it makes it a little clearer, a little easier to face."

She rested her hands on Rob's shoulders. "I propose that we table this discussion. It's almost the end of August, two more weeks to Labor Day. I think we should just work out the season and not try to figure it out right now."

"Dr. Barnes said we shouldn't wait. He wants us to get started on this right away."

"Oh, Rob, I'm not that old. A few weeks won't make a difference. This is a major decision in our marriage and in our lives. We're going to feel the effects of this for a long time. I want to feel as if, whatever we do, it's settled into my bones and I just know it's the right thing."

"Okay, that seems sensible to me," Rob agreed. "We shouldn't decide this in a rush. As long as we aren't procrastinating."

"It's not procrastination, I promise. I'm just a little confused," she told him.

He laughed at her explanation, then stood up and hugged her. "I am, too, but at least we're confused together."

The day had begun with light rain, too wet to work in the garden. The skies cleared and the sun came out around noontime, but they still decided that a ride into town would be a pleasant way to spend the afternoon. They both loved the farm but needed a break from time to time.

They finished their morning chores quickly. Audrey had showered and dressed and was waiting in the kitchen for Rob to come down when the phone rang. She picked it up and answered. "Gilroy Farm."

A man on the other end of the line introduced himself. "Is this Audrey?" he asked. He sounded elderly, and like a customer who wanted to order some cheese.

"Yes, it is. How can I help you?"

"I think you found my dog. My dog Sunny. I saw a flyer yesterday in the post office. I could hardly believe it."

Audrey felt the earth drop away from her feet. She felt as if there were no air in the room. Her immediate reaction was to slam down the phone—or tell the old man he had the wrong number. But she couldn't do that. For one thing, it just wasn't right.

Calm down. Millie might not even be this man's dog. He might be mistaken.

"Yes, we found a dog. Quite a few weeks ago now. When did you lose your dog, Mr.—? I'm sorry, I didn't catch your name."

"Broussard, Leonard Broussard. I lost her a few weeks ago,

too . . . I didn't actually lose her. I've been away. Broke my hip and had to go into one of those rehab places for six weeks."

"That's too bad, I'm sorry," Audrey said sympathetically.

She scolded herself for feeling mean-hearted. Poor old fellow. It sounded as though he was having a very rough time.

"I left Sunny with a neighbor. But they weren't careful enough with her. She got out of their yard and ran off. They were afraid to tell me she was gone. But of course, I found out when I came back to Cape Light."

Another sad turn in his story. Imagine going through all that and then finding out someone lost your dog. But there was another reason his Sunny and Millie couldn't be the same dog. Mr. Broussard lived in the village. Millie must have been lost by someone on the island, or someone visiting.

"Mr. Broussard, I found the dog out here, on the island. I don't think she could be yours. How would she have gotten across the bridge?" Audrey asked gently.

He was quiet a moment. "I don't know. Dogs are smart. Maybe she was looking for me."

Audrey had to smile at that theory.

"I can tell from the picture, that's her. That's my Sunny. I need to bring her home," he insisted. "I can come right now. It won't take long," he promised.

Audrey didn't know what to say. She doubted it was the man's dog, but she could tell he had to see her for himself and wouldn't take no for an answer. Having Millie around the last few weeks, she understood that. "Of course. Come on out. Do you know where we are?"

"Yes, I do. I'll be there in a jiffy. And I'll bring you some proof," he added.

They said good-bye, Audrey thinking that some proof of owner-ship would be a good thing. She wasn't normally so picky or formal. But Audrey needed some solid proof before she would hand over Millie to anyone.

Rob came downstairs a few moments later and Audrey explained the call to him. "I can't see how she could have made it all the way from the village out onto the island. But he was convinced, so I told him to come."

Rob's expression was serious. "You did the right thing. But that picture on our flyer was so blurry. Millie probably isn't his dog. He just misses his dog so much, he wishes it were her."

Audrey nodded. She hoped that was true. Millie had come inside and now sat under the table. Her fur tickled Audrey's bare legs. Audrey reached down and stroked her silky head.

She felt very nervous but didn't want to overreact. In all these weeks, there had not been one call about the dog. This was a total long shot. This old man would come, see the dog, and be disappointed. Which would be sad. But he wouldn't take Millie with him. Audrey couldn't even think of that.

A short time later, they heard a car drive up toward the house. Rob got up and walked toward the front door. Millie went with him. Though she wasn't much of a watchdog, she loved to greet vis-itors. Audrey followed.

Rob took a leash from a hook near the door, then clipped it onto Millie's collar. "You said he was old and just got out of the hospital. I don't want Millie to knock him down," Rob explained to Audrey.

"Oh, right. Good idea," she agreed.

Rob opened the door and held on to Millie's leash. The three of them looked out and watched Leonard Broussard slowly making his way up the walk toward the house. He used a cane and took each step very carefully. He was dressed a bit formally, Audrey thought, in dark pants and a white shirt with a bow tie, even though the day was very warm. His canvas hat with a large brim gave him a rakish, old-fashioned air.

Millie pulled at Rob's hold and started to whine. Mr. Broussard had come a little more than halfway up the path and now glanced up at them.

"Hello, Sunny girl. It's me. Do you recognize me? Surprised to see me after all this time?"

Millie gave a low whine, and her tail began beating happily against the porch. She tossed her head back and barked, then tried to run to Leonard Broussard. Rob kept her on a short lead, but it was hard to hold her back.

She always gets excited when she sees strangers and wants to greet them, Audrey reminded herself. But this was a different kind of excitement, a different tone in her bark, even. Audrey couldn't deny it.

"She remembers me," Mr. Broussard said happily. "She didn't forget me."

Millie tugged on the leash, trying to get down to Mr. Broussard, and Rob had no choice but to be pulled along behind her. He glanced back at Audrey a moment with a "What can I do?" expression. Audrey took a breath and followed. The old man stood still, balancing on his cane, beaming down at the dog.

Rob walked up to him, holding Millie down by her collar.

"That's okay, you can let her go. She won't hurt me," Mr. Broussard insisted.

He bent over so that Millie could see him better. She ran around in excited circles, stopping now and then to lick his face. Audrey watched Mr. Broussard close his eyes, chuckling to himself. The old man was half laughing and half crying as he reached out and took hold of Millie's large head, petting her fur and then kissing her on the forehead.

"Sunny, my sweetheart. How I missed you. I never thought I'd see this day. I was about to give up . . ." His words were choked with emotion, and Audrey wasn't sure if he was talking to them, or the dog. Probably a little of both.

She felt overwhelmed, too. Millie and Sunny were obviously one and the same.

Only Rob seemed to be keeping his head, though he had come to love Millie, too, Audrey knew. "Would you care to come inside and have a cold drink?" he asked. "We can talk more about the dog inside."

"I would like that very much," Mr. Broussard replied.

Millie was off her leash now. She followed the group up into the house. They walked back to the kitchen, and Audrey took a pitcher of tea from the refrigerator. When she reached into the cupboard for glasses, her hands shook so badly, she could hardly handle them.

Mr. Broussard sat in a chair at the table, and Millie sat right next to him, pressing her body against his leg and leaning her head back every few minutes, as if to make sure he was really there. Audrey felt her heart breaking. It was so hard to watch this. She felt the loss so keenly.

"Before we go any further, I told you I'd bring you folks some proof that Sunny is my dog. I have it right here." He reached into his jacket pocket and pulled out a small plastic bag, wrapped with a rubber band.

There were photos inside, Audrey saw, as he put the stack on the table. "These are some photographs of me and Sunny, from when she was a puppy," he explained. "Her spots are so distinctive; if you look closely, you'll recognize it's got to be her. And me," he added with a laugh.

Rob picked up the photos as Audrey came to the table. "So you've had her quite a few years."

"Yes, I have. I never wanted a dog," Mr. Broussard admitted. "But my neighbor's dog had puppies, and all of them had been given away, except one. They were moving and didn't know what to do with that leftover pup. My wife had just died and I was grieving," he added. "I still didn't want a dog, even though they'd asked me a million times to take her. One morning, I found her in a box at my front door with a note. It said, 'Keep her or bring her to the pound.'"

Mr. Broussard rested his hand on Millie's head. "I didn't like being tricked that way, but what could I do? They had moved away. I meant to bring her to the shelter. I just never got around to it," he added, laughing. "She was a great distraction when I was so lonely. I couldn't sink into myself anymore. I had something—someone—to take care of. She made me feel okay again. Like it was worth going on. Just watching her is entertainment. She seems so happy all the time, just to wake up in the morning and go outside, sniffing the smells in the air."

He looked up at Audrey as if wondering if she understood.

She did understand. She felt just the same about Millie. She was surprised—but not so surprised—at the way Millie had come into Mr. Broussard's life when he had most needed comfort and encouragement.

Millie had arrived in her life at the right moment, too. That seemed to be her talent. *But I still need Millie,* she thought desperately. *It's too soon to give her back. I didn't think I'd ever have to give her back at all.*

Audrey reached out and petted Millie's head. Millie came to her and rested her head on Audrey's knee.

"You've been good to her. I can see that," Mr. Broussard said. "She looks very well cared for. Thank you so much. I wish I could repay you for your trouble."

"Not necessary, not at all," Rob insisted. "We loved having Millie—er, Sunny—with us. Right, Audrey?"

Audrey nodded. "Yes, we love her. She's a wonderful dog." She looked up at Mr. Broussard. "Did you teach her all those tricks?"

"She was showing off for you, was she?" He laughed and shook his head. "I did teach her a few. She's a fast study. It didn't take much." He paused as the dog wandered back toward him and nudged his hand with her head, asking for another pet. "I'm so sorry, folks . . . I can see this is hard for you, too. I didn't even think of that when I found the flyer and called. I am sorry to cause you any pain."

He looked up at Audrey. She could see he was sincere. She wished with all her heart it wasn't so, but there was no way around it. Millie was obviously his dog, and he needed her as much as Audrey felt she did, if not more.

"Thank you for saying that," she quietly replied. "It is hard to give her back," she admitted. "We're going to miss her."

"You can come and see her anytime you like. I don't live far, right in Cape Light, off Main Street. Please come. I'm sure she'll miss you, too. Here, I'll write down my address and phone number for you."

He pulled out a small pad and a stubby pencil from his pocket and scribbled down the information.

Rob got up and began gathering Millie's things—an extra leash, a few dog toys, her tin dishes, and some dog food—and put them all in a paper bag. They wouldn't need them anymore, Audrey realized.

Audrey and Mr. Broussard rose, too. Millie was lying on the floor now between them.

"Come on, Sunny. Time to go," he called. The dog sat up and looked at him expectantly. Then she looked at Audrey, seeming confused.

"It's all right, Millie," she said, trying to sound calm, though she felt as if her heart were breaking. Rob slipped his arm around her shoulders as they walked Mr. Broussard and Millie down to his car, and Rob put the bag of Millie's things in the backseat.

Audrey leaned down and gave Millie one last hug. She was crying openly. She couldn't help it. Millie sat very still and licked the tears from her face. She looked sad, too, or at least subdued, Audrey thought. Very subdued, for Millie.

But when Mr. Broussard opened the passenger door and invited her to get in, Millie jumped right up in the car and settled herself on the front seat. Rob patted her head through the window and shook hands with Mr. Broussard.

"Good-bye now. Come and see us. I really mean that," the old man said happily.

"We will," Audrey replied, though she wondered if she would ever be able to keep that promise. She stood watching Mr. Broussard's car drive off the farm. Millie looked out the window, her face in the wind, her ears flat against her head.

Audrey wondered if the dog knew what was happening. Maybe she did. She seemed so intuitive.

Rob stood beside her, and she turned into his comforting embrace and buried her head on his shoulder. "I know, honey," he said. "I know it's hard to see her go. But what could we do? Millie is his dog. We were just keeping her safe for a little while."

Audrey couldn't answer at first. She was crying so hard. Sobs shook her body. It felt like everything had been taken away, all possible hope and comfort. She was already feeling so weighed down about not having a baby and probably having to give up the farm. But at least she'd had Millie, an eighty-pound bundle of love and happy energy. A sweet, blithe spirit. Did she have to lose her, too?

"I know it's his dog. But it doesn't seem right, Rob. We love her, too."

"I know," he soothed her, patting her back. "Let's try to remember how happy that old man was to see her again. He's had some sadness, too. It sounds like he's all alone and needs her just as much as we do, maybe even more."

Audrey nodded and took a deep, calming breath. Mr. Broussard did need Millie. He had lost his wife and didn't mention any children. At least she and Rob had each other. Still, it was going to be hard to get over this. Audrey knew she would miss that silly dog for a very long time.

Chapter Thirteen

"So when is Daniel getting back? This weekend, right?" Audrey smiled at Liza as she poured them each a glass of lemonade.

"He was supposed to get back this Friday, for the holiday weekend. But now he says there have been delays getting materials. And they have to wait for the property owner to walk through and sign off on the job. That means he'll probably be up there all of next week." It was the Monday before Labor Day. Daniel had only been gone a few weeks, but somehow it seemed much longer.

Audrey's expression was sympathetic. "That must be rough. I'm sure you miss him."

"I do," Liza said honestly. "We talk on the phone almost every night, but every time I get off the phone with him, I seem to miss him even more."

They sat in the shade at the umbrella-covered table next to the farm shop. This final blast of August heat would have felt unbearable if it hadn't come so close to Labor Day weekend, reminding everyone they ought to savor the last warm days of the season; they would be chilly soon enough.

Liza had just finished cleaning up the inn after the weekend wave of guests and had wandered over to the farm for a quick visit with her friend. She took a sip of the cold, tart drink and met Audrey's gaze. "I bet you miss Millie. It seems pretty quiet around here now."

Audrey sighed and tried to smile. "The cats are happy about it. But I think they're in the barnyard minority."

She had told Liza the whole story over the phone last week, soon after Millie's owner had taken her away. Liza knew that it had been very hard to give up the dog.

"It's only been a week, and one day," Audrey added. "I keep reminding myself that she was just a dog and worse things could happen, but it's hard. I still keep finding things that remind me of her—a chewed sock or a dog toy."

"I'm sorry." Liza patted Audrey's hand. "She wasn't just a dog. She was a wonderful companion. Dogs give such unconditional, unlimited love. They never criticize us or think that we've said something dumb. Or disapprove of our outfits—or turn up their noses at our cooking. Of course you miss her."

Liza didn't know what else to say. It seemed dumb to suggest that Audrey and Rob get a new dog, not when their living arrangements were up in the air.

Audrey gave another halfhearted smile. "Yes, I know. I'm just trying to keep things in perspective. We definitely have some bigger fish to fry right now."

"Have you made any decision about the farm?" Liza hated the idea that she might lose her good friends and neighbors, but she always tried to sound positive about their plans. She knew how much Audrey wanted a baby, even if they had to move off the island to make that happen. Liza couldn't imagine how hard that would be for them. She wanted to support them any way she could.

"Rob and I agreed to keep things status quo until the end of the summer, but it looks like that deadline is creeping up on us. I told Rob he could have a real estate agent come out and look at the place sometime next week. And I'll see the new fertility doctor in Boston, on the ninth. So things are moving along on that front, I guess."

"I would hate to see you guys leave here. I don't even want to think about it. But it doesn't have to be for good," Liza reminded her. "You could come back and get another place in a few years. And you can definitely stay at the inn anytime. I'll give you that big suite on the second floor and I have plenty of baby equipment—"

Audrey laughed. "You have it all planned out, don't you?"

"I do. I'll even babysit if you want to go into town for a movie."

"Babysitting, too? Watch out, we might take you up on that." Audrey finally smiled again. She sat back and fanned herself with a magazine. "Guess what? I got a special order for bath products from—hold on to your lemonade—Mrs. Nick Dempsey. It came by e-mail this morning."

"That's great! I hope she starts a trend on Rodeo Drive."

"That makes two of us. Let's face it, it's been pretty dull around here since the movie people left. Did you see this article about Charlotte?" Audrey reached for a magazine that she had stashed beside the table. "I never buy these magazines, but I saw Charlotte's photo on the cover and couldn't resist."

Liza picked it up and scanned the cover. The celebrity news magazines weren't her cup of tea either, but she was eager for any news about Charlotte.

"She finished filming the movie they were working on here, *A Wandering Heart*. She was due to start another right away, but the article says she's gone home to visit her family for a while, instead . . . Here, I'll read it to you," Audrey offered, flipping to the right page. "'A spokesperson for the actress has stated that Ms. Miller has returned to her hometown, Greenwood, Ohio, to visit her family. She has not told the press how long she plans to stay, but she has pushed back the start date for her next project by at least two months.'"

"I hope she's taking a break," Liza said. "From what I could see, she was really feeling the strain—of all the work, the crazy schedules, and the pressure of being famous. Like I said, I'd love the shopping sprees, but not necessarily the rest of it. Can I take this to show Claire?"

"Sure." Audrey was quiet for a moment. Ice cubes tinkled in her glass. She glanced at Liza. "I wonder if Colin is wearing his hat. It must be cold out on the water this time of year. Where did he go again?"

Liza had told Audrey about the gift Charlotte had left for the fisherman, swearing her to secrecy. Not that Colin had asked her to do such a thing, but it only seemed polite.

"Up to Maine. I think he sailed out of Bar Harbor."

Liza finished her drink and stood up. It was time to head back to the inn. "Thanks for the lemonade. Do you want to get together for dinner when Daniel gets back? We can do a big clambake on the beach. One last party before it gets too chilly?"

"That sounds great." Audrey smiled but Liza could see a shadow of sadness and worry in her eyes. She had so much on her mind now.

"Okay, we'll figure it out. But let me know what's going on with you guys. Call me after you see the doctor next week, okay? What day did you say it was?"

"It's a week from Friday, September ninth. They'll probably just poke and prod me a little more." Audrey shook her head. "Can you believe it's almost September?"

Audrey laughed but Liza knew the entire experience was grueling. "You're such a trouper, Audrey. God bless you." They shared a quick hug, and Liza headed across the meadow to the inn. She turned and waved to Audrey, then realized that she missed Millie, too. The dog would normally be lying at Audrey's feet during their visits and then escort Liza across the meadow.

But Millie was gone. Just like that, no warning. The summer had been full of rain and surprises, Liza decided. And it wasn't over yet.

When she got back to the inn, she found Claire sitting on the porch, shelling peas. They dropped into a metal bowl with a soft rhythmic sound.

Liza dropped a basket of vegetables on the top step then took a seat next to it. "Look what Audrey gave me. Her garden is overflowing."

"My, what a bounty," Claire said. "I could make a nice soup with all of that. What's that on top, a magazine?"

"There's an article about Charlotte in here. I brought it back to show you. It sounds as if she's taking a little time off from making movies. She's gone home to Ohio for a visit with her family."

Claire peered down through her glasses and read the short article. "I'm glad for her. I think that's just what she needs."

Liza agreed. "I'm going to e-mail her and see how she's doing. She may not answer, but I want her to know that we're thinking of her."

"And cheering her on from a distance," Claire added. She picked up the peas again and finished the last few.

"From a great distance," Liza said.

She was sure Charlotte had the best intentions, but truly doubted the movie star would ever return. Look at how hard it was for her to visit her own family. It had practically made headlines. But perhaps they would hear from her from time to time. She didn't think Charlotte would forget this place—or the people she'd met here—that easily.

Labor Day weekend had come and gone, with a last wave of summer guests passing through. On Thursday afternoon, Liza was upstairs adding hand towels and some of Audrey's goat's milk and lavender soaps to each room. She worked unhurriedly. There were no bookings at the inn for this weekend at all, which was fine with Liza.

She heard Claire call from the hallway. "Liza? There's someone here to see us."

Liza quickly left her task and ran to the head of the stairs. A certain note in Claire's voice made her suspect that the unexpected guest was Daniel, and he had come home early to surprise her. But the voice she heard mingled with Claire's in the foyer was distinctly female and Liza's heart sank.

She wandered down the steps, not caring much whom she might find. Then she nearly tripped down the last two when she saw who was standing there.

"Charlotte? What are you doing here?"

"I told you I'd come back to visit." Charlotte smiled warmly at her.

"Yes, but . . . I didn't expect you back this soon. It's so good to see you. You look wonderful," she said honestly.

Charlotte met Liza's gaze and leaned over to give her a hug. Liza noticed a calm expression in her brilliant blue eyes.

"I saw your e-mail the other day. I'm sorry I didn't answer. I was afraid that no matter what I said, I'd give away my surprise."

"We read that you were in Ohio," Claire said as she led them all into the front parlor.

"I went there right after the movie wrapped up. I needed to go home and sort out a few things with my family—things that have been on my mind a long time," she added. "Coming here really affected me. I didn't even understand how much at the time. But once I left, I felt very different. Changed, deep inside. I knew I had to change on the outside, too."

Claire nodded and smiled softly, as if she'd been expecting this revelation. "That night when you asked me to tell you Angel Island's legend, I had a feeling that you were beginning to see things differently."

"Yes, I was. But it all really started on the first day I came here, when I nearly drowned. And met Colin," she added.

"Getting to know him and just being in this place helped me face a problem I've been avoiding for a very long time. A problem that has really kept me from being truly happy," Charlotte confessed. She seemed lost in thought for a moment, then suddenly looked up at them. "I want to tell you more. But I really need to talk to Colin first. Have you seen him lately? I hope he comes in early from fishing today."

"Colin is away, dear," Claire said gently. "He's on a long fishing trip, up north. Off the coast of Maine, I think he said."

Charlotte looked shocked. "He is? When did he leave?"

"Almost three weeks ago. A few days after you did," Liza said. "I'm not sure when he's coming back. It sounded like he could be gone a month or more."

"I had no idea. I just assumed he would be here." Charlotte

looked down and shook her head, clearly thrown by the news. "I guess I can try his cell phone. Or I could drive up to Maine and meet him somewhere . . . if he'll see me."

"Oh, I think he'll see you," Liza said. She had a feeling Colin would swim to shore if he knew Charlotte was waiting for him. "But his cell phone might not get coverage that far out on the water. We can try to find someone with a ship-to-shore radio. Let me think—"

"Marion and Walter Doyle, at the General Store," Claire said. "They have that type of radio. I'm sure they'll be happy to get in touch with their nephew."

"That would be wonderful." Charlotte sounded relieved. "If I just leave a message on his cell, I'll have no idea of whether or not he ever got it."

A few minutes later, they were sitting in the convertible Charlotte had rented at the airport and headed for the village center. Charlotte drove a little faster than necessary, sending gravel and dust flying. Liza couldn't blame her. She had come all this way and was eager to hear Colin's voice at the very least, even if she couldn't get to see him.

Marion was behind the counter, reading a magazine. She looked up in surprise as the trio of women marched into the store. Then she did a complete double take when she realized who Liza and Claire's companion was. "Mother of pearl, are you really Charlotte Miller?" Marion pressed her hand to her chest.

Charlotte smiled and nodded. "Yes, I am."

"I was just reading about you." Marion held up the magazine; its cover showed a photo of Charlotte in a red evening gown. "I thought I was hallucinating or something. I thought all of you movie people left here weeks ago."

"Charlotte came back to visit us—and to visit Colin," Liza explained. "We know he's up in Maine somewhere fishing but don't know how to get in touch. Can you find him with your ship-to-shore radio?"

"We can try." Marion paused and stared at Charlotte again. "Did you really come all this way to see my nephew? I know he pulled you out of the water and all that. But—" She shook her head and waved her hand. "Never mind. It's none of my business, I'm sure. Wait till his mother hears about this. She's a big fan," Marion said. "Follow me. The radio is back in that little office. It's so small you can hardly swing a cat. Half a cat, maybe. Walter's the only one who knows how to use it. I'll go get him. You just wait."

The women waited by the doorway to the small office. They heard Marion in another part of the store calling for her husband, "Walter, come on out here. Liza needs you to work the radio, to call Colin's boat."

Liza guessed that Walter had been somewhere unpacking goods or straightening out shelves. He came toward them, carrying a can of baby peas in each hand. He blinked and squinted when he saw Charlotte, then put on a pair of glasses that hung around his neck from a string.

Marion was trotting right behind him. "Yes, that's Charlotte Miller, the movie star. You're not imagining things."

Walter glanced back at her. "I know who it is, Marion."

He coughed into his hand. "Marion said you want me to call Colin on his boat?"

Charlotte nodded. "I'd be very grateful if you could."

He looked curious but didn't ask any more questions. "I'll give it a try," he said. "But if Colin's up on deck fishing, he might not hear the radio. No way of knowing."

The black radio was on a narrow table under a window. The rest of the room was filled by a desk, old metal file cabinets, and a bulletin board covered with invoices, most of them yellow and stained. There was no room for the women in the office along with Walter. Liza and Claire remained in the narrow hall between the office and the store and let Charlotte stand in the doorway.

Walter sat down at the radio, put on a pair of headphones, and began working the controls. "We have a special number for Colin's boat now. It's a new system, almost like a telephone," he added, tapping numbers on a keyboard.

"Have you heard from him much since he left?" Claire asked.

Walter shrugged. "I had a little chat with him one night, about a week ago. Said the fishing was good, but there were a lot of boats up there now. He was thinking of heading back but was going to take his time. Didn't say much more though."

Heading back? That was good news, Liza thought. Maybe he wasn't that far away.

A harsh static sound came out of the speakers, and Walter spoke into his headset. "Calling *Sea Star*, 9054781. Hey, Colin, it's Uncle Walter. Can you read me?" There was no answer and Walter tried again, repeating the same message.

They waited. There was no answer. Just the crackling static sound. Liza had a funny feeling in the pit of her stomach, a worried feeling that she tried to brush aside.

Marion had gone out to the store to help a customer but now returned. "Hear anything yet? Did he answer?"

"Not yet," Walter said without turning to the women. "He must be fishing. Or working . . . or sleeping."

That about covers it, Liza thought. She glanced at Charlotte. She looked eager to hear any sound at all from Colin's boat, but didn't say anything.

"Let me try again. Maybe I dialed wrong." Walter hit the numbers on the keypad again. A sound suddenly came through the receiver. Not Colin's voice, just a sharp, repetitive signal.

Walter suddenly looked worried and fiddled with the radio dials. "What's wrong? Is his radio broken?" Charlotte asked.

"I hope so. That's a Mayday signal. If his radio is working, it means his boat is in trouble."

Walter quickly turned the receiver to another channel, then spoke over his shoulder. "Ladies, if you could please give me a moment and wait outside. I have to call the Coast Guard and tell them Colin may be in trouble. This may take a little while."

Liza heard Charlotte gasp as she covered her mouth with her hand. Claire was closer to her and put her arm around her shoulder. "Let's step outside, Charlotte, and let Walter concentrate." Charlotte nodded and followed Claire and Liza from the office.

Marion waited near the register. She, too, looked upset. "I was just talking to a fellow out here, another fisherman. I told him we're trying to call Colin, and he said there's some heavy weather up in Maine right now. He heard a few boats from Cape Light are caught in a bad storm."

Liza felt a moment of panic, then took a breath. She couldn't get too alarmed and upset Charlotte. The poor girl looked worried enough.

"What should we do?" Charlotte looked around at the other women. "Is there someone else we can call? Maybe I could find someone up in Maine who can sail out and look for him—someone with a bigger boat? Or take a helicopter?"

Charlotte could surely afford to pay anybody any sum to look for Colin's boat. But there was really no way they could arrange that sort of search and rescue operation from Angel Island. It was hard to tell her that, though.

Liza took hold of her hands, which were ice-cold. "The Coast Guard are trained for exactly this type of situation, Charlotte. Colin activated his emergency signal and probably has a GPS on his boat, too. If Walter heard the call over the radio just now, the Coast Guard and other boats in the area have surely heard it."

"People are already out there, looking for him, dear," Claire said quietly.

Charlotte nodded, her chin trembling. Then she covered her face with her hands. "I just feel so helpless. I wish there was something I could do—anything. I shouldn't have waited like this to talk to him. What if something happens? What if—"

"Now, now, dear. Please don't do this to yourself." Claire put a comforting arm around Charlotte's shoulder again. "This is just one of those times in life when there's nothing to do but sit and wait. And say a prayer or two, and trust in God's mercy."

She caught Charlotte's gaze, her words falling like a soothing balm. Charlotte nodded again and took a deep breath. Then she closed her eyes, and Liza realized she was probably sending up a silent prayer for Colin's safety.

Walter came out of the office, his expression grim. "I just spoke to the Coast Guard. There are a few boats up there in trouble. A storm hit early this morning, much stronger and wilder than they expected. They've picked up two boats so far and are doing their best to get all the men in."

"At least there's help in the area," Liza said. "That's encouraging."

"How will we know when they find Colin?" Charlotte asked quickly.

"I gave them the name of the boat. The Guard said they would call me when they found it."

"Will you call us at the inn when they do? There's no sense waiting here. It might take a while." Liza looked at Charlotte. Would she insist on staying? She looked like she was tempted.

Finally, she nodded her head. "Yes, we should wait at the inn. The Doyles still have a store to run."

Marion followed the women outside the store. "We'll call you as soon as we hear something, I promise. And Walter needs to get in touch with his brother. I think they've gone on vacation someplace," she added, referring to Colin's parents. "I bet Colin's folks don't even know he went up north."

That was going to be a hard call to make, Liza thought. She waved good-bye from the car. "Thanks for your help, Marion. We'll be waiting."

As soon as they'd returned to the inn, Charlotte found the weather channel on TV and sat glued in front of it. The channel was giving the storm in Maine lots of coverage.

Liza wasn't so sure watching the minute-by-minute news reports was a good thing. The weathercasters tended to be dramatic and exaggerate bad weather conditions. This storm needed little exaggeration, however. When they interviewed a fisherman who had been rescued, his wide, fearful stare and thankful expression told the entire story.

"It was bad out there. The weather turned on us, and we were looking at high winds and swells of twenty feet or more. We were lucky the Coast Guard found us and towed us in . . ."

There was more to the interview, but Liza didn't hear it. Charlotte turned to her, looking even more worried, if that was possible. She'd had enough of waiting; Liza could see it in her eyes.

"I think we should call Mr. Doyle. Just to see if he's heard anything. Anything at all," she added, checking her watch. Not quite an hour had passed but Liza was impatient, too, to hear some word about Colin.

Walter answered on the first ring. "General Store."

"It's Liza, Walter. Have you heard anything about Colin? We've been watching the weather channel, and the reports have been troubling," she confided.

Walter didn't answer right away, though Liza could tell he was still there. His hesitancy made her heartbeat quicken. "I didn't want to call until I had all the information," he began. "They found the boat, not far from Portland. But . . . there was no one onboard." His voice dipped down on a sad, frightened note. "They're looking for him out in the water now," Walter continued. "It hasn't been that long, and they tell me the weather is letting up. I'm sure he has his life jacket on. He's a strong boy. Brave, too," he said, his voice choked with emotion.

Liza felt stunned. This was not the worst possible news . . . but almost. She turned to see Charlotte staring at her, desperate for information.

"I've been talking to a Coast Guard station in Portland," Walter went on quietly. "That's where they brought the boat and where they'll bring him in, too, most likely."

If they find him, Liza could almost hear him say.

It couldn't be. Colin had to survive. He had to see Charlotte and see how much she loved him. Liza was sure now that was the reason she had returned. Could Colin possibly save Charlotte from drowning and then lose his own life to the sea?

"I'll call you with any news," Walter said.

Liza thanked him and said good-bye, then turned to face Charlotte. Liza wasn't sure how to tell her what had happened.

Charlotte seemed to know. "Something bad has happened. I can see it in your face, Liza." Charlotte got up from her chair. "Did Colin . . . Is he . . ." Her voice trailed off. She couldn't say the words out loud.

"They found Colin's boat but it was empty," Liza spoke as calmly as she could. "They assume he was washed overboard, and they're searching for him. There's a good chance they'll find him, Charlotte. The weather is clearing and there are several boats looking."

The ocean was vast and a single person, floating alone in the water, most likely without a flare or any means of attracting attention . . . Oh, the odds were not good. Not good at all, Liza knew. But she had to sound positive for Charlotte. They all had to keep a positive frame of mind.

Charlotte's expression trembled. She sank down onto the love seat, covered her face with her hands, and began to sob. "I can't lose him, not now. Not this way . . . Please don't let this happen. Please save him," she cried out loud. Liza realized she was talking to God, begging Him to spare Colin.

Claire sat next to her and held her as she wept. "I know it's hard and frightening," she murmured. "But we mustn't lose faith."

Charlotte lifted her head and took a steadying breath. "What can I do? Can't I wait up there to hear what's happening? Can't I be closer to him?"

Dead or alive, she meant. Liza felt her own eyes fill with tears.

"We can go to Portland. Walter said that's where they brought his boat. It's the Coast Guard station that's closest to the search area. It's only about two hours by car. I'll drive you," Liza offered.

"I'll drive," someone else said.

Liza turned to see Daniel standing in the foyer. She gave a little cry of amazement and ran into his arms. "You're back," she said, holding him as if she'd never let him go. "I can't believe you're back."

Amusement flickered in his dark eyes. "You thought I was going to stay in Canada?"

"No," she sputtered, nearly crying tears of relief. "It's just your timing. Colin's gone and—"

"I know," he said. "I was just at the Doyles' store. I heard about Colin's boat. Walter told me you were all waiting here for news so I came right over." He looked over at Charlotte. "You want a ride up to Portland?"

"I think it's an excellent idea to have Daniel drive," Claire said. "We're all so . . . overwrought. If you take Liza and Charlotte, that will be a blessing. I'll stay here, in case the Doyles need help."

In case the news was so dire that their neighbors needed emotional support from Claire and possibly, their minister, Reverend Ben, in Cape Light. Claire would know how to take care of them and whom to call, Liza realized.

A few minutes later, Liza, Charlotte, and Daniel were on the road to Portland, sitting side by side in Daniel's truck. They had the name and number of the Coast Guard officer who was coordinating the search-and-rescue efforts for Colin.

They drove in tense silence, listening to the news station on the radio. The rescue of the fishing boats and the search for Colin were mentioned in the news, but not much was known and no information given beyond what they already knew. When they reached Portland, they found the Coast Guard station at the waterfront and went inside.

Daniel spoke to a Guardsman working at a reception and security desk. "I'm sorry, there's no further information about your friend," the man told Daniel. "I'll tell the officer in charge that you're here. We'll let you know if there's any more news."

Liza glanced at Charlotte. She was wearing a hooded sweater

and had the hood pulled up, hiding her famous hair. Her face was bare of makeup, her eyes puffy from crying, and she looked nothing like a movie star. Which was just as well, Liza realized, because being recognized was probably the last distraction Charlotte wanted right now.

"More waiting I guess," Daniel told them.

They sat on cushioned benches in the small waiting area between the front door and the security desk.

"How long can a person survive, floating in the water?" Charlotte asked.

"Oh, hours. A very long time," Liza answered quickly, though she really wasn't sure. "People have been known to survive for days, right, Daniel?"

Daniel nodded. She had a feeling he didn't know either, but didn't want to say anything negative right now.

"Colin is an experienced sailor," Liza went on. "He knows what to do. He's young and fit. He has the very best chance to pull through this, Charlotte. He really does."

Charlotte nodded, but her eyes looked blank. "I'm going to get a cup of coffee from the machine," she said, standing up. "Does anyone want anything?"

Liza and Daniel both said no. Daniel was sitting beside Liza. He took her hand and twined his fingers through hers.

"You're worried about Colin," she said quietly.

"Yeah. More than I want to tell Charlotte."

"I am, too," she admitted. "Thanks for taking us up here."

He glanced at her. "I wouldn't want to be anywhere else right now, Liza. I wouldn't want you to be up here alone if I could help you. Something like this, it makes you count your blessings. You're one of mine."

"You're at the top of my list, too." Liza turned her head and smiled softly at him. He smiled back and started to lean closer, to kiss her cheek.

They both sat back suddenly as a man in uniform walked toward them. "Are you friends of Colin Doyle?" he asked.

"We are." Daniel stood up and Liza did, too. "Any news?" Daniel asked quickly. "Wait . . . there's Charlotte. Let's wait for her to join us before you say anything."

Charlotte, who was walking toward them, doubled her pace when she noticed the officer. "Did you find Colin?" she asked.

Liza reached out and took her hand. Charlotte squeezed back, very tight.

"We do have news—good news. He was picked up a short while ago by another fishing boat, not too far from here. They're on their way and should arrive in"—the officer checked his watch—"about twenty minutes. He's suffering from exposure, but otherwise, seems in good condition."

Charlotte had taken a deep breath and now nearly collapsed with relief. "Thank you . . . Thank you so much . . . He's alive! I can't believe it . . ."

Liza was so happy, she was hugging Daniel tight, as if it were New Year's Eve and the Boston Red Sox were winning the World Series, all wrapped up in one.

"Can we meet the boat? Where should we go?" Daniel asked the officer.

"They'll be coming into this dock. We've already got an ambulance on the way. Your friend will have to go to the hospital to be checked out."

"Of course," Daniel said. "He's probably dehydrated. He'll need to be watched, at least overnight."

Charlotte was already heading toward the dock. "I'm going to watch for the boat," she said.

"I'll come with you," Liza called.

"I'll call the Doyles and Claire," Daniel said. "If they haven't heard the news yet, they'll still be worrying."

And praying for Colin's safety, Liza thought. Now there would be prayers of thanks for God's mercy. As boundless as the deep blue sea. "Thank you," she said quietly. "Thank you. Thank you. Thank you . . ."

Down on the dock, Liza stood with Daniel. Charlotte couldn't help herself; she ran up ahead, as far as the Guardsmen would allow her. An ambulance was already there. The EMTs stood waiting with a stretcher ready.

She hoped Colin was conscious, and she would get to see him. She just wanted him to know she was there. Later, there would be time to talk, time to tell him everything she needed to say. There would be time for them now, thank God.

Finally the boat pulled up, a battered fishing boat with a noisy engine, just a little larger than Colin's.

The EMTs ran onto the deck. Soon, Colin was carried out on a stretcher. Charlotte ran to his side and grabbed his hand. He was already wrapped head to toe in blankets. His eyes were closed and his face so pale, she felt terrified by the sight. "Colin . . . can you hear me?"

His eyes opened slowly. "Charlotte? Is that really you?"

She felt herself laughing and crying at the same time. "Yes, it's me. Who else would it be?"

"A dream?" he asked with a small smile.

Charlotte couldn't answer. She bent over and quickly kissed him.

"Ahh . . . now I *know* I'm dreaming." His reply made even the EMTs laugh.

"Can I ride in the ambulance with him?" she asked.

"Sure thing. We'll get him secure, then you can hop in," one of the men handling the stretcher told her.

Liza and Daniel were standing nearby. Daniel took Colin's hand. "You made it. You're too stubborn to drown," Daniel teased his friend in typical male fashion.

"You got that right, pal," Colin joked back in a croaky voice.

"We'll meet you two at the hospital," Liza said as Charlotte climbed into the ambulance beside Colin.

The ride to the hospital did not take long. Colin rode with his eyes closed, an IV in his arm. He gripped Charlotte's hand steadily, though he didn't say a word. The siren's sound made it impossible to talk anyway.

Once they arrived at the hospital, Colin was whisked away by the EMTs. Charlotte waited with Liza and Daniel again, this time in the hospital waiting area. She was so exhausted, she fell asleep in the hard plastic chair. When she woke up, Liza was standing over her, smiling.

"Colin is in a room. The doctor said you can go in and visit."

Charlotte got to her feet. "I can? Where do I go?"

Liza gave her the room number and pointed her in the right direction.

Charlotte ran off, tugging the hood off her hair. She guessed that she looked a mess, but for once in her life, she honestly didn't care.

SHE found the room easily and pushed open the door. There was only a low light over the bed. Colin was sitting up against the pillows, his eyes closed. She wasn't sure if he was asleep and didn't want to wake him. She crept to the edge of the bed and took his hand.

His blue eyes flew open. He stared at her and smiled. Then, moving gingerly, so as not to dislodge the IV, he opened his arms wide. She practically threw herself at him, hugging him close, her face pressed against his chest as he buried his face in her hair.

"I love you, Charlotte. I love you so much. That's all that matters. The whole time I was in the water, I kept picturing your face. I didn't want to die without telling you. You're the only reason I survived. Whether we can be together or not, I need you to know that I love you and always will."

Colin's words filled her heart with joy. Charlotte could hardly speak to answer him. "I love you, Colin. I should have told you before I left the island. That night, at your cottage—"

"I was such a total jerk that night. I don't even want to talk about it." His voice was hoarse, and he nearly started coughing.

Charlotte stroked his face with her hand. "It was all my fault. You were right. I wasn't being honest with you, and things between us can't work that way. There's something I have to tell you, something I came a very long way to say . . . besides that I love you."

Charlotte took a deep breath and stared down at her hands. She had imagined this moment so many times, but it was still hard to say the words.

"The reason I was so worried about the reporter who came looking for an interview is because I do have a secret I'm hiding. From the public, from my friends, from everyone except my family. They're part of the lie.

"All the time I was growing up, after my father died and my mother married Wayne, her second husband, our family life was . . . a living nightmare. Wayne drank day and night. He could barely hold a job while my mother worked two. He was horribly angry at the world and at himself and took it out on all of us. There were rules on top of rules around the house and if we broke one, off came his belt . . . Or we got his fists."

Colin took her hands. "Charlotte, please. You don't have to go through all this. No one should—"

"I have to tell you everything," she insisted. "I started and I have to finish. My mother never wanted anyone to know she made such a huge mistake marrying Wayne. When we were out in public, we all had to act like a happy family. Or we'd pay when we got home, believe me. She didn't even let her own parents or relatives know, much less a teacher or someone who might have helped us. Before she realized that he was a monster, she let him legally adopt us. And he used that. He threatened to take us away from her if they divorced. He probably couldn't have won in court, but she was too afraid to risk it—or risk what he would do if she tried to leave him.

"My official bio says that once I graduated high school, I 'left Ohio to follow my dream of becoming an actress,' but really, I ran away from home. I left my sisters and brother, and my mother. I left them with that monster. It felt as if I'd just escaped a burning building and left all the little ones inside to fend for themselves . . . So you see, I'm not that wonderful, perfect, all-American girl you've read about or seen in the movies. I'm not even a nice person, Colin. I'm a coward. I ran out on them. That's what I've been so afraid to tell you, so afraid it would be found out." She couldn't even look at him to gauge his reaction. He was so quiet, just letting her talk.

Finally she felt his hand lifting her chin. He stared into her eyes with a very serious expression. "Charlotte, listen to me. It's all right. You were only eighteen, and you weren't a coward, not then, not now. You did what you had to do to survive. That took incredible bravery. I feel horrible for your sisters and brother and your mother. But you're not to blame. Your stepfather is the one. He's to blame for all this pain and tragedy. How can you blame yourself for even a moment?"

Charlotte swallowed back her tears and nodded. "I try to tell myself that, but it's going to take a long time to believe it. Ever since I've had any money at all, I've helped them. But my mom, she's still traumatized. All those horrific years, she still doesn't want anyone to know. That's part of the reason my agent and publicist cooked up my fake happy childhood story. But I went home after the film wrapped up and talked to my family. We all agreed it was time to be honest now, with the public and most of all, with ourselves. I'm going to get her into a good program for battered women. I just want her to be happy now and stop blaming herself for what happened."

Charlotte paused and took a deep breath. She could hardly believe it. She had finally laid down this huge burden. She had been carrying it so long, she felt as if she were about to float away with relief. Of all the people she could have chosen to tell, Colin was the right one. The one worth waiting for, she suddenly realized. All the strange coincidences that had brought them together, that had brought them to this moment . . .

It all suddenly made perfect sense.

"It's going to be hard when it hits the press," she added quietly. "But I think I can do it. If you're there with me."

"I'll be there, Charlotte. Don't ever doubt it. I understand now why you kept yourself at a distance, why I always felt there was some wall between us. I thought it was because you were famous and I was . . . an ordinary guy. But I see now that you were just fighting to hold it all together." He brushed a tear from the corner of her eye. "You can stop fighting now," he said gently. "You don't have to feel guilty or unworthy—or unlovable. If you let me, I'm happy to show you every day of your life that's just not so."

Those were the only words Charlotte needed to hear. When he reached for her, she melted into his warm embrace and there was no need for any more talking for a very long time.

Chapter Fourteen

A UDREY raced up the drive and braked so quickly, she jerked against her seat belt. She was usually such a slow, cautious driver, Rob called her Mrs. Magoo.

But she had made it back from Boston in record time, not stopping once at a store or even a gas station, though the fuel gauge was hovering over E. She noticed a strange car parked close to the house. Rob stood there, talking to a woman. She wore a smart business suit and stood with a black binder tucked under her arm. Audrey guessed it was the Realtor who had come to look at their property. She had forgotten all about that. But not even that sight could dampen her spirits right now.

She hopped out of her car and walked toward them "Hi, honey. I'm back," she called out, beaming at her husband.

"That was quick. How did the appointment go?"

"Great." Audrey planted a big kiss on his cheek and squeezed his arm.

Rob seemed surprised by her happy mood. And confused. "That's good. Can't wait to hear about it. This is Linda Babcock, from Bowman Realty. She's going to work out a quote for the farm." His tone was even and businesslike, but Audrey could tell how it pained him to say the words aloud.

Before Audrey could respond, Linda reached out to shake her hand. "Nice to meet you, Audrey. You have a beautiful place here. Great location."

"Yes, it is," Audrey agreed. "We love it. Don't we, Rob?"

He nodded, looking at her curiously again.

"I need to go back to my office and look at comparable sales on the island," Linda told them. "But I'll get back to you soon with a number."

"Thanks," Rob said. "I'll be interested to hear what you think we should ask."

"Thanks, Linda," Audrey chimed in as the Realtor got in her car. "No rush . . . We'll be in touch," she added.

The Realtor pulled out and drove away. Rob stood staring at his wife. "Are you all right? What happened at the doctor's?" His brow furrowed as he stared at her with concern.

"Rob, I have some news." Audrey reached up and put her hands on his shoulders. "The doctor examined me and asked me a few questions. Then he gave me a routine sort of test that they start off with and—you'll never believe it—I'm pregnant!" Audrey practically shouted the last part, jumping up and down as she waited for her husband's reaction.

Rob looked dumbstruck. He grabbed her by the waist. "Are you sure? Totally positive?"

Audrey nodded wildly, her head bobbing up and down. "Yes, yes, I took the test twice, and he also took a blood test, though he's

288

sure it will come back positive. You know how irregular I am. I missed last month and didn't think anything of it. I thought it was just stress from everything we're going through. But I was wrong! We're having a baby, honey! Finally! Can you believe it?" She jumped into his arms without waiting for an answer.

Rob hugged her tight and spun her around, pressing his face into the crook between her head and shoulder. She felt his body shaking. He was crying, she realized. Tears of joy and gratitude. Their prayers had finally been answered.

"Thank God," he said quietly. "Thank you, God . . . so much. I don't know what else to say."

"Me either," she agreed. He set her down and they stared into each other's eyes. "I don't know what to say or feel or do. I'm just so happy. By this time next year, we'll have a baby. Right here. We don't have to leave this place."

Rob brushed the tears from his eyes. "We're so lucky, honey. We have it all now, don't we?"

Audrey nodded, too happy to even speak.

They walked toward the house in the late-afternoon light, side by side, their arms around each other. Audrey's heart felt ready to burst with joy. She wondered whom she should call first to share the news. What she really wanted, she realized, was to just sit with it awhile and savor the blessing, just her and Rob.

Still, as they strolled along, she couldn't help but think that if Millie were here right now, she would be doing her happy dance, prancing along beside them. Not knowing why the humans were so ecstatic but thrilled to share the joy.

Oh, Millie. If only we still had you here. I was hoping you would walk with me and the baby someday. I never got to thank you for bringing me comfort and so much love, in my darkest days.

* * *

As soon as Liza heard Audrey's voice on the phone, she knew something was up. She didn't even have to ask how the doctor's appointment had gone yesterday. Audrey told her right away. "Guess what? I'm pregnant!"

Liza was so shocked, she dropped an egg on the floor. It fell and broke with a soft plop. She glanced at it then jumped up and down with happiness for her friend, careful not to make an even bigger mess.

"That is the very best news, Audrey! I'm so happy for you." Her friends wouldn't have to leave the island now. That made it even better. Liza would have missed them so much.

Audrey told her all the details of the doctor's visit and finding out she was pregnant and then described how Rob had taken the news.

"He's getting used to the idea a little more today. But he's kind of in a daze. I just saw him walk into a wall and not even notice."

Liza wasn't sure if she was kidding or not, but laughed anyway.

"So, what's going on with you? I bet you can't top that one," Audrey challenged her.

"Well, actually, I do have a story for you," Liza began. "Charlotte Miller came back to visit. She was really looking for Colin Doyle," she added. "But he was out at sea, on a fishing trip. And when we tried to get in touch with him . . ."

She quickly told Audrey the story about Colin's near drowning and dramatic rescue and how the two had finally worked out their relationship.

"He's coming out of the hospital tomorrow, and Charlotte is going to drive him back here and stay with him a few days, at his cottage. Now I really need to have a party! There's so much to celebrate. I want you and Rob to come over tomorrow night. We'll have a big clambake on the beach."

"Great idea! I'll bring some salad and stuff . . . and some cheese, of course." Audrey went on for a few more minutes, listing her contributions.

Liza nearly laughed out loud. "All right. Bring what you like, but you're not allowed to do any work. You have to take it easy now. We just want to see you. And celebrate."

"I'm trying to get the concept, but it's going to take a while," Audrey admitted. "See you soon. This is going to be fun."

"Yes it is. I can't wait."

Liza quickly made plans with Daniel and Claire. The clambake was an inspiration. The inn had been so busy, she hadn't relaxed in weeks, or entertained her friends. Summer didn't officially end until September twenty-first, Liza reminded herself. This was the best weather of the season, still warm during the day but not super hot, with crystal-clear skies and pleasantly cool nights. And they all had so much to celebrate. So much to be thankful for.

On Sunday afternoon, Audrey called. "Can I bring a guest? We have a surprise visitor and I hate to leave her alone." Audrey was whispering, and Liza imagined the person she was talking about was in earshot.

"Of course you can bring a friend. We have enough food for an army, as usual."

DUSK turned the sky a pale lavender. Liza was out on the porch, packing the cooler and totes of food and paper plates to bring down to the beach, when she spotted Audrey walking through the meadow toward the fence between their property. She was coming over a little early and without Rob. But that was just fine. They would have some time to talk privately.

Liza wondered what had happened to Audrey's friend. Then she suddenly noticed that Audrey was not alone.

A big dog ran circles around her, barking playfully at the goats then returning to Audrey's side.

Not just any dog either. It was Millie.

Was this Audrey's mystery guest? The friend who had dropped over unexpectedly? Liza could hardy believe her eyes, and ran down the porch steps to meet them.

"Audrey, where did Millie come from? Did she walk all the way back to the farm from town?"

"Not exactly. But she did come back to us." Before Audrey could say more, the dog recognized Liza and ran over to give her a trademark greeting, putting her paws on Liza's shoulders and slathering her face with licks.

"Down, Millie! Liza loves you, don't worry." Audrey pulled the dog down and smiled. "She's still the same. We have to work more on training. She can't be this rowdy around the baby."

"Around the baby . . . Does that mean you have her back permanently?"

"Yes, she's come back to us—two miracles in one week. I can't even believe it myself. Mr. Broussard called last night. He told us that he's been planning to move into an assisted living community, and they suddenly had an opening so he had to move quickly. Since he broke his hip, it's been too hard for him to live alone. He couldn't take Millie and thought of us right away. Of course, we wanted her back. He was relieved; he didn't know what to do with her otherwise. We promised to bring her to visit him once a week. He likes that idea very much. And so will Millie, I think."

"Oh, Audrey, that is the greatest news." Liza leaned over and gave her friend a hug. "Not as great as you being pregnant," Liza quickly added. "But it's right up there."

"Yes, it's right up there," Audrey agreed.

Liza took the big basket Audrey was carrying, full of vegetables, cheese, and other tasty contributions for their celebration.

"This is a wonderful way to end the summer. What a great idea," Audrey said. "Good food, good friends, and so much to be grateful for."

Liza could not agree more. "We certainly had our challenges this summer," she said, thinking of Audrey and Rob, in such despair and now happily expecting. And of Charlotte and Colin—how this special place had brought them together, and their impossible, against-all-odds romance somehow worked out. How right now, they were planning a beautiful future together.

"Some things are just meant to be," Liza said finally.

Or maybe, the way heaven wants them to be? Surely, someone above had heard all of their prayers this long rainy summer.

Now the season had come to give thanks . . . and count their blessings.

Here is one of Claire North's favorite recipes, often prepared at the Inn at Angel Island in August, during blueberry season. Wild blueberries are plentiful on the island. Provided there's time enough to go berry picking, Claire and Liza rarely buy them at a store. When berries are scarce, Claire uses cranberries, raisins, or even dried cherries instead. Whatever you choose, these flaky, fragrant scones, served warm from the oven with butter, jam, or whipped cream, are an irresistible addition to any breakfast, brunch, or afternoon tea.

Claire North's Blueberry Scones

(MAKES APPROXIMATELY 16)

4 cups all-purpose flour

2 tablespoons baking powder

3 tablespoons sugar

¼ teaspoon nutmeg

¾ pound butter, cold

4 eggs

1 cup heavy cream

1 teaspoon vanilla

1 cup fresh blueberries, rinsed and thoroughly air-dried (or use dried fruit, as noted above)

one egg yolk mixed with 2 tablespoons water (optional)*

1. Preheat oven to 400 degrees and prepare a baking sheet by covering with parchment paper.

2. Combine flour, baking powder, sugar, and nutmeg with an electric mixer.

3. Dice butter into small pieces (1/2 inch by 1/2 inch) and blend at lowest speed, using paddle attachment and scraping beaters from time to time. Mix until butter is in pea-size bits, not entirely blended.

4. Beat 4 eggs in a separate bowl. Beat in heavy cream and vanilla until just mixed.

5. Add egg and cream mixture to the flour mixture. Blend until just mixed. Do not over blend or scones will come out heavy and dense.

6. Sprinkle a little flour, about a tablespoon, over blueberries to coat. Add to mixing bowl and quickly blend in. Mixture will have formed dough.

7. Place dough on a clean, flat, cool surface that is lightly dusted with flour, such as a board, pastry rolling sheet, or marble pastry slab. Lightly dust a rolling pin with flour and roll out dough to rectangle shape, about 3/4-inch thick and the size of average cookie sheet. Using a sharp, thin knife or a cutting wheel, cut the dough into 8 equal squares. Then cut each square diagonally, into a triangle shape. Place triangles on cookie sheet covered with parchment paper.

8. *For a shiny scone, brush the top of each with a wash mix of one egg yolk combined with 2 tablespoons of water.

9. Sprinkle tops lightly with sugar.

10. Bake for 20 to 25 minutes. Scones should be crisp on the outside and flaky and moist within, but cooked through.